Praise for the n
USA TODAY bestselling auth

"London's characters leap off the page… it's a delightful start to a series that promises to be good fun."

—*Publishers Weekly* on *The Dachshund Wears Prada*

"Funny and sweet, with great characters and a diva dog who completely stole my heart. I devoured this book in one sitting!"

—*New York Times* bestselling author Jennifer Probst on *The Dachshund Wears Prada*

"Don't sleep on this heartfelt romance."

—*Kirkus Reviews* on *The Dachshund Wears Prada*

"This is the romcom Carrie Bradshaw would have written if she were a dog person, and I'm obsessed!"

—Teri Wilson, *USA TODAY* bestselling author of *A Spot of Trouble*, on *The Dachshund Wears Prada*

"One of the year's most delightful rom-coms. Ms. London pens a sparkling confection of all the feels and I devoured it."

—*New York Times* bestselling author Julia London on *The Dachshund Wears Prada*

"Heartwarming, charming, and adorably sexy, *The Dachshund Wears Prada* made my dog-loving heart smile."

—*USA TODAY* bestselling author Tawna Fenske

"At turns both witty and tender, *The Dachshund Wears Prada* is a delightful treat of a novel, guaranteed to give you the warm fuzzies."

—*USA TODAY* bestselling author Melonie Johnson

"London pairs…satisfying romance with a deep dive into dysfunctional family dynamics, the corrosive power of secrets, and the importance of communication. This is sure to win hearts."

—*Publishers Weekly* on *Pets of Park Avenue*

"London's likable characters resonate with hidden depths as she mines their hearts to deliver a fun, revealing story that will have readers rooting wholeheartedly for love—and dogs—to conquer all."

—*Shelf Awareness* on *Pets of Park Avenue*

Also by Stefanie London

Paws in the City

The Dachshund Wears Prada
Pets of Park Avenue

For additional books by Stefanie London, visit her website, stefanie-london.com.

Confessions *of a* Canine Drama Queen

STEFANIE LONDON

ISBN-13: 978-1-335-49821-2

Confessions of a Canine Drama Queen

For questions and comments about the quality of this book, please contact us at CustomerService@Harlequin.com.

Canary Street Press
22 Adelaide St. West, 41st Floor
Toronto, Ontario M5H 4E3, Canada
CanaryStPress.com

Printed in U.S.A.

To my parents, for always fostering my love of books.

1

Was it too much to ask for a decent, normal guy who wanted the same happy, successful three-point-two puppy life as you?

August Merriweather certainly didn't think so. But, if her dating history was anything to go on, apparently it *was* too much to ask. Her last few dates had ranged from less appealing than a smelly tennis shoe to "engage fake emergency phone call" status. The guys ran the gamut from dull to infuriating, and every single time she went home alone wondering what the heck was wrong with her.

In her mind, the dating jungle was more like the dating fight pit.

Don't be negative. You never know, this guy could be the one!

That had been her cautiously optimistic mantra as she'd walked into the restaurant where she was meeting her latest swipe right. And while August wasn't the kind of woman who needed a man to be happy, she *wanted* a relationship. A partnership. A person with whom she could share in life's joys and challenges. Someone who made her heart flutter.

Spoiler alert: Carter Edward Driscoll III did not make her heart flutter.

You should have known better than to accept a date from a guy with a number in his name.

"So that's when I told her, *babe*, I simply cannot marry someone who wants to own a tiny home. Like, where would I put my shoe collection?" The man sitting across from August shuddered. He was classically handsome, but in a way that looked a little…sterile. Had he Botoxed his face? His eyebrows didn't move that much.

August caught herself staring and brought her eyes down to the plate in front of her. She'd barely touched the croquettes they'd ordered to start, her appetite waning the second her date decided to talk about all the women he'd refused to marry.

All six of them.

Frankly, the fact that the guy had found even *one* woman interested in marrying him said more about his bank account than it did about his personality.

"I mean, can you believe it? A tiny home? Like, what am I? A minimalist?" he scoffed. "I should have known she'd be into that hippie shit the first time she used natural deodorant. That was a red flag."

Oh boy. Was it too soon to pull the emergency phone call thing again? Or was this date bad karma for doing it last time?

"So anyway, that was potential wife number five scratched off the list. Number six…she was a doozy."

August watched his eyebrows again, trying to see if they moved when he talked. Hmm. It was hard to tell. Carter droned on about the next poor, deluded woman who'd thought she could snag a diamond from him.

"I have to think about these things, you know." This time he paused and took a breath, waiting as though he expected her to respond.

Shit. What had he just said? She'd totally zoned out.

"Uh..."

"I can't exactly curse my future children with those issues, now, can I?" He snorted and nothing above his nose moved. He'd definitely had *something* done. "I need to pick someone whose genes are at least as good as my own."

August blinked. "Wait, you're saying you're going to choose a wife based on what genes she's likely to pass on to your children?"

"Exactly." Carter tossed his hands in the air. "Finally, someone gets it."

"Are you looking for a wife or a mare?" Her lip curled in disgust.

"Mayor? I don't really want someone who's involved in politics."

"Not mayor. *Mare.* Like a female breeding horse." Ugh, why was she even bothering to argue with him? "And not all women want children, you know."

He made a snorting sound. "Sure, they *say* that. But then biology happens...tick tock."

She ground her back teeth together. August *hated* the idea of the biological clock. People made it sound like the second she turned thirty some kind of internal switch would flip and suddenly she'd be desperate to have a child.

So far, nothing.

It wasn't as though she didn't *like* kids. She looked forward to being the cool "aunt" to her friends' Mini-Mes. But she didn't have the urge to have one of her own. Who knew, maybe it *would* change in the future.

But then again, maybe it wouldn't.

She suspected it would be the latter and she wholeheartedly resented the idea that either A, she was in denial, or B, something was wrong with her.

"Let's get a second opinion," Carter said, and before August could protest, he'd flagged down a young waitress. "What do you think? Would she and I make attractive children?"

He pointed to August. The waitress looked like a deer in headlights, and August wanted to sink into the earth. The people at the tables around them were *definitely* watching. God, knowing her luck there was probably someone live tweeting it!

Or worse, filming it for TikTok.

"Stop it," she hissed at Carter, but he waved her away as if she were a fly.

"Come on, you can be honest." He laughed, as though he wasn't making everyone around him cringe. "I mean, she's a little solid, but she has a pretty face, right?"

August's mouth popped open. The guy was lucky there was a table between them and that she wasn't the type to throw a drink in someone's face, because right now she was *very* tempted.

You do not *need to put up with this.*

August happened to like the fact that she was "solid." She was strong! Her muscles helped her in her job grooming animals, and it was very physical work, especially with the bigger clients. And yes, she shopped in the plus-size section and her thighs rubbed together when she walked and she jiggled in places. So what? Was a little chub rub the end of the world? Hell, no.

And it certainly didn't give anyone the right to make her feel lesser.

August pushed her chair back and stood up. "Congratulations, Carter. You are, without a doubt, the worst jerk I've ever swiped right on. Gold star for you."

He looked at her pityingly. "Is this because I called you solid? I didn't mean it as a bad thing. I happen to like—"

"I don't care what you like, and I'm perfectly comfortable in my body. But *you* are arrogant beyond belief. I pity any woman who's fooled long enough to marry you." She grabbed her purse and fished out enough money to cover the food they'd ordered. Carter looked at her incredulously as the bills fluttered onto the table. "I hope you remain single for a long, *long* time. Like, forever."

Slinging her purse over one shoulder, she stalked toward the front of the restaurant, aware several phones were raised in her direction. One woman yelled, "You go, girl," at her as she walked past. What a disaster! But August had more self-esteem than to let someone treat her like that. Fury bubbled in her veins.

At the last minute, fueled by frustration, she turned around to face the people sitting at the artfully decorated tables and along the opulent bar.

"That's Carter Edward Driscoll III, ladies. Make sure you swipe left!"

Turning on her heel, she walked past the head server, whose hand was clamped over her mouth, and out of the restaurant, the sound of applause and cheering fading as the door swung shut behind her.

It was official. Despite being a badass business owner, respected animal wrangler, and—she liked to think—decent human being, it was clear that August Merriweather could not tell the good guys from the dickwads.

Maybe she was going about this all wrong. Maybe looking for love on dating apps and in crowded bars was like trying to find quality in a discount store bargain bin. Hell, maybe looking for love full stop was putting her focus on a fantasy.

Perhaps what she needed was a more measured and practical approach: someone who had the same goals as her, where love might grow over time. A partnership, rather than a romance.

It was time to engage professional help.

Keaton Sax stared out of the expansive window of his office—a large space, though not yet the corner office he coveted—and admired the view. Facing east, Manhattan's Financial District and Brooklyn sat glittering and pretty on the other side of the East River. It was nearing 10:00 p.m. and the sky was inky dark, yet the brightened windows of the towers around him showed plenty of worker bees busily tapping away at their computers or talking into their cell phones. Such was life on Wall Street.

Sleep was for the unmotivated.

A knock at his office door startled him and he swung his chair around to see who'd dared to interrupt his thinking time. Keaton's boss, Thomas Fairchild, stood in the doorway, his lean marathon runner frame encased in a dark suit and his shirt without a single crease even though the man had almost certainly arrived in the office before 5:00 a.m.

"Thomas. What can I do for you?" Keaton asked, gesturing for the older man to come in.

Thomas had bright blue eyes and thick silver hair—which had led to someone at their old firm nicknaming him the "White Walker" a few years ago behind his back. His reputation for ruthlessness and rigid adherence to his plans certainly fit the *Game of Thrones*–inspired moniker.

Bankers came in two forms, Keaton had discovered. There was the gluttonous type, who thrived on the glitzy dinners and wore diamond-adorned Rolexes and whose attitude of "more, more, more" permeated all areas of their work and personal life. These were the guys who inevitably ended up divorced because they got caught with a drug habit or a gambling addiction or a mistress or four on the side.

And then there was the fiercely ambitious win-at-all-costs high-achiever type, who didn't have an off switch. They were lean and hungry, and in their eyes you were only as good as your last deal. Whereas the first group were whales, these guys were sharks. Faster and way more dangerous.

Thomas was, without a doubt, king of the sharks.

"What's the update on the Waterline Press acquisition?" Thomas asked.

"The CEO refused our initial offer, which isn't totally surprising since we tried to lowball him." Keaton pushed up out of his chair and walked around to the other side of his desk.

"Next steps?"

"My research associate is digging through the financials to see if there's anything we can leverage. I suspect they have some bad debt that we could offer to relieve if they play ball on the sale price."

He anticipated the disappointment on his boss's face before it came. And come it did, swift in the tightening of his lips and the deepening groove between his brows.

"I honestly thought you would have dropped the Robin Hood act by now, Keaton." His boss made a tutting sound. "Relieving their debt? Why should we be responsible for their poor decisions?"

"We're not," Keaton replied. "But approaching them with a good faith deal will mean a smoother transition for the sale. We can negotiate a low offer while avoiding bad press."

"Who cares about bad press?"

"But what about our client's reputation?" He raised an eyebrow. "The last M&A was so aggressive, people petitioned for an investigation."

"You mean some basement-dwelling trolls on Reddit posted about it. Please." Thomas rolled his eyes. "Our job isn't to worry what people think, Keaton. Besides, the way the internet is these days you only need to wait a day or two before people are outraged about something else. Hell, if you're smart, you'll find something for them to worry about and point them in that direction."

Keaton sighed. To say that he and Thomas did not see eye to eye would be putting it lightly, and he knew this latest acquisition was going to be a challenge. His client, a fast-growing digital media group, was in the process of gobbling up several small companies who'd started making noise about fair use. For the big fish, it was easier to simply buy the company in question than deal with negotiations and potential court proceedings. Only, the big fish was perfectly fine using underhanded tactics to get what they wanted and Keaton was expected to toe the company line.

He'd been hoping to get out of this acquisition without blood on his hands, metaphorically speaking. But that was starting to seem more difficult than he'd first thought.

"Tell me your bleeding heart isn't going to get in the way of this one," Thomas said, looking at him pointedly. "Because there have been discussions about making you a named partner and I would hate for you to develop a reputation for being weak."

Keaton leveled a stare at his boss. "We both know what my numbers are like. You're better off with me working for you, even with the so-called bleeding heart, than working for a competitor."

For a moment, Thomas didn't move. It was hard to tell what the older man was thinking. This was a trait that had won him many negotiations over the years and had struck fear into the hearts of all the fresh-faced newbies that populated the bullpen back in Keaton's first job at a big investment firm on Wall Street. They'd scattered like pigeons every time he'd entered the room.

But not Keaton. He didn't scatter for anyone.

It was this reason—along with his talented nose for important details—that had seen the older man take him under his wing. Then when Thomas left that firm to strike out on his own, he'd written a check with more zeros than Keaton had ever thought possible. A life-changing sum.

And when Keaton's life had fallen apart in a way he'd never seen coming, Thomas had been there for him. Over the years, he became like the father Keaton had never had. He couldn't exactly say it was a "loving" father and son–type relationship, but Thomas had championed him in the industry, pushed him to be his best and had given him opportunities when many others were happy and willing to write him off.

Keaton owed Thomas a hell of a lot.

"Get it done," Thomas said eventually. "You know I want to see your name on the front door of this place. But you need to convince Hill. He's the holdout."

He walked out and closed the door behind him. Keaton let out a breath and went back to his office chair, digging his fingers into the tight muscles in the back of his neck. Fairchild & Hill could become Fairchild, Hill & Sax.

The thought of it—seeing his name in those gleaming gold letters—set off something inside Keaton. If only all the people who'd doubted him could see him now. His old teachers who told him he wouldn't amount to anything. The officers who dragged him off to juvie at seventeen and saw him as little more than a statistic. The other juniors at his first job who thought Keaton was a no-good criminal.

His name could be on the door to one of the most prestigious boutique consulting companies in all of New York City.

He could finally be at the top of the food chain. The crème de la crème of Wall Street. It was the goal he and his wife used to talk about while they lay in the ridiculously small IKEA bed that somehow still felt too large for their tiny bedroom. Named partners. They'd already planned how they would celebrate that milestone—with Dom Pérignon and a room at the St. Regis. She was convinced she would make it there first.

At the time, he'd believed her. Because Ellery could do anything she set her mind to. The sky was the limit.

Until it wasn't.

2

"Yes, darling. You're a tiger. You're the queen of the jungle! Roar for me, baby."

The photographer clicked the shutter release and August Merriweather tried not to roll her eyes. Good thing she was behind the scenes and not in front of the camera, because there was no way she would have struck a pose with someone shouting such ridiculous things at her.

Luckily, the alpaca in front of the lens didn't have that problem.

"I think Mr. OTT missed the biology class where they told us that alpacas were not part of the large cat family," August muttered as she packed up her grooming tools and supplies.

Scout, the pregnant woman standing next to her, snorted. "You should have seen what he was saying to the iguana last week. I was starting to think he had a lizard fetish."

"Don't laugh," August replied, her tone dead serious. "Dinosaur erotica is a real thing."

"No!"

"I'm serious. In fact, monster erotica is a whole genre. There are books about Bigfoot and aliens and Minotaur and everything." She grinned. "If you can think of it, someone has written a smutty book about it."

She liked to think of the genre as the more palatable version of Rule 34.

"Now tell me," Scout said, leaning against the table where August's grooming kit sat. "How do you know so much about niche erotica?"

"Dirty book club," she replied with a grin. "I'm part of an online group that reads all kinds of romance novels and we get on Zoom to talk about them. Our motto is: to smut and beyond."

August had been part of the book club for almost a year now and looked forward to their meetings each month. They had members all over the world, *and* it was easier to fit a Zoom session into her busy work schedule than it was to do anything in person.

Plus, she very much enjoyed the steamy books. They were a hell of a lot more interesting than her own love life; that was for damn sure.

She cringed every time she thought about her bad date last night. Thank goodness she'd had a jam-packed day to keep her mind off what a disaster it had been. But as an extra precaution, she'd turned her phone off because she didn't even want to *look* at the dating apps on there right now.

"Dirty book club sounds fun!" Scout clapped her hands together. "I need to load up my Kindle."

"I'll email you some recommendations."

"That would be great. Lane will get the shock of his life," she said with a chuckle. "We've got a shared account for our e-readers."

"Who knows, maybe he'll become a fan." August waggled her brows and Scout blushed.

Scout's husband, Lane, was a great guy. They'd been married for quite a while… Well, married but estranged. Then properly married, and now they had a baby on the way. They were the only people she knew who could legitimately have used the "it's complicated" relationship status on Facebook. Now they were back together and happy as could be, and August had to admit there was a part of her that was just a teensy bit jealous of how perfect they were together.

If she were being honest, even though growing her animal grooming business was hugely fulfilling, she wanted to have a shared e-reader account with someone. She wanted a hunky guy to come home to. She wanted a man who loved all her lumps and bumps and quirks. And she wanted someone to appreciate in return.

Too bad August had a knack for picking the worst kind of men—the commitment-phobes and the serial players and the "say whatever to get you into bed" types. For all the romance novels she'd read, one would think she'd be a little better at spotting a potential hero. Some days, however, it felt like she was a dud magnet.

And there were *plenty* of duds in New York.

That's why dating agencies exist. Because an expert is required to wade through all the trash.

The thought swirled in her mind. Perhaps hiring a professional wasn't such a bad idea.

"Some steamy books might spice up our sex life," Scout joked, cradling her protruding stomach and snapping August back to the present moment. "Lord knows we need to get in as much of that as we can before the baby comes. Seriously though, I'd be happy for something to help me unwind. Between the doctors' appointments and getting the nursery ready and work being super busy..."

She huffed and blew a strand of gleaming blond hair out of her face.

Scout was gorgeous—tall and willowy, with long blond hair and huge hazel eyes. At a little over six months pregnant, she was as radiant and stylish as ever and could literally wear one of those maternity potato sacks and make it look good. August, on the other hand, had inherited her mother's five-foot-two stature, large boobs and full backside, along with her father's curly red hair, pale skin and freckles.

And while she wasn't usually hung up on looks—a person had *way* more to offer the world than their appearance—there were times when she wondered if she'd be luckier in love if she didn't look like an extra from The Shire.

I could start cosplaying. Perhaps there's some guy out there who'd love to get in bed with a hobbit!

"It's a lot," Scout finished. "Plus, we're getting ready to start shooting the documentary, and with the talent competition and..."

"You got this, Scout." August placed a hand on Scout's arm and squeezed. "Just take it one day at a time."

"My whole life I never understood how people let work take up so much of their existence, and now that I have a job I love, I feel like I'm constantly being pulled in all directions." She laughed and shook her head. "It's a good problem to have—too many great things going on at once."

Scout worked for Paws in the City, a social media and talent agency focused on animals. The company had been started by her best friend, Isla, and Scout had been promoted to the role of client manager after Isla expanded the team. But they were still a small outfit in the grand scheme of things. Whenever they needed a groomer, August was the first person they called, and the three women had become great friends in the last year and a half. It made her proud to have kick-ass friends who supported one another.

"Trust me, it's a blessing and a curse." August packed away the last of her tools now that the shoot was wrapping up. "But I would take it over working a soul-sucking desk job any day of the week."

"One hundred percent agree!" Scout nodded emphatically. "And really, getting to work with all these adorable creatures is the best reward one could ask for."

"Now *that* is an accurate statement."

August had always been an animal person, ever since she was a little kid. She'd made friends with all her neighbors' dogs and cats and nursed injured birds back to full health and volunteered at animal shelters. She'd even wanted to be a vet…much to the disgust of her surgeon father.

Becoming a vet is like becoming a dentist, he'd told her snootily. *People will assume you weren't smart enough to become a real doctor.*

Cringing at the memory of her father's insulting—not to mention untrue!—statement, she closed the lid on her grooming kit and snapped the latch closed. Her parents were still disappointed with her choice of career, even though August had a constant waiting list for clients and had even groomed pets for actual legit celebrities *and* worked on movie sets.

Merriweather Grooming was the most sought-after pet grooming business in Manhattan and it was profitable enough that August had bought an apartment in Midtown all by herself.

Not to mention doing all that without *crippling student debt.*

Maybe that made her success worse in her parents' eyes, because they thought she'd been "lucky" instead of smart. But August didn't believe college was required for success and, for her, the proof was in her regularly jam-packed Google calendar and her healthy bank account.

"I'm going to skip out now," August said, sliding her bag over one shoulder as the photographer's assistant announced that the shoot was over. "I need to wash the smell of farm animals off me."

"Got a hot date?" Scout winked, having no idea just how painful that question was right now.

"The date was last night and it was less of the 'hot' variety and more of the 'I'm starting to think something is wrong with me' variety."

"Oh no." Scout shook her head. "There is *nothing* wrong with you. You're a total catch."

"Or maybe there's nothing but scum on dating apps." August sighed. She knew she shouldn't feel weird about using them—practically everyone did. But her parents had once said that "those apps" were only for people without social skills and, being a little awkward herself, the comment had stung. "I'm starting to wonder if I need a professional intervention. The DIY method just isn't working for me."

"It's always good to try something different," Scout said, encouragingly. "If you think it will help get you what you want, then I say go for it."

"You don't think it's archaic to use a matchmaker?"

"I married a guy I met in Vegas," Scout pointed out, laughing. "We all find love in different ways."

August nodded, feeling buoyed by her friend's open-mindedness.

"And if it goes well, you could share some of your monster

erotica with your date," Scout said with a wink. "Then you can both get a bit hot under the collar."

Fat chance. August hadn't gotten hot under the collar in so long that if it wasn't for the saucy books steaming up her e-reader, she might have actually forgotten how to have sex. Authors were helping her keep the dream alive, at least in her head.

But maybe that wasn't the only option available.

There was one thing Keaton *always* dreaded when he went to visit his little sister, Leah, and that was seeing her best friend, Molly.

Fact was, Molly was a pain in the ass.

She was one of those "beautiful and knew it" types, with ice-blue eyes and a load of thick, shiny hair and a tendency for drama that grated on Keaton's nerves. Not to mention she had her resting bitch face down pat. She might stop people on the streets of Brooklyn with her Instagram-worthy good looks, but she whined about everything. Oh, and she left her stuff all over the house *and* she hogged the couch. Seriously, do you think Molly would budge if someone else wanted to sit down and watch some TV?

Nuh-uh. Molly thought she owned the place and everything in it.

Damn dramatic husky.

Keaton walked along the street toward his childhood home, where Leah and Molly lived now. Bushwick had changed a lot since he'd lived there. Back then, it had been rough. Gritty. A bit like Keaton himself—especially in his younger years.

Not that anyone would look at him now and think he embodied either of those things. He'd long ago shed his baggy jeans and skater shoes and nicotine-stained fingertips, swapping it all for custom Italian suits and Amedeo Testoni monk straps. And the cigarettes were a distant memory, because career success was his new drug of choice.

He pushed through the small gate at the front of the house and jogged to the front door. Inside, the house glowed golden, and Keaton knocked loudly. As he waited for his sister to answer—knowing that she would take a while to get to the front door—he shrugged off his suit jacket and admired the view through the front window. Back when they were teenagers, this town house had been home to three separate families.

Despite Keaton having plenty of money to spare and a desire to give his family everything, Leah had refused his offer of a Manhattan apartment. He'd tried several times to move her closer to him, even dragging her along to a private viewing of a penthouse with floor-to-ceiling windows that made the Hudson look like a piece of art.

But stubborn Leah had dug her heels in, refusing to move from the family home.

So he'd waited patiently for the other families in the building to move on, buying up the two other units when they became available and eventually renovating the whole thing to Leah's exact needs—adding an elevator that would help her get to the top floor when she couldn't manage the stairs, redoing all the flooring and installing grab bars in the bathrooms, among other things.

Oh, and buying her a custom pink velvet sofa because it was impossible to say no when she turned her puppy-dog eyes on him.

"I'm coming!" Leah yelled from inside, and Keaton immediately smiled. His sister's voice would never not have that effect on him.

No matter how stressful his workday, no matter how difficult a client was being, no matter how much he *hated* pretending to be like all the other Wall Street wankers… Leah's voice could make it all disappear.

The door swung open and he drew her into his arms. She smelled like strawberries and powdered sugar, no doubt a preview of the dessert that would be in his belly before too long. Keaton hugged her tight, letting the day's irritations melt away.

When he pulled back, he saw Molly sitting in the hallway, glaring at him with her front paws crossed and her snout sticking slightly up as if she'd smelled something bad.

"Your dog hates me," he said, glaring back.

"Stop it." Leah frowned. "You know it's a house rule that you two have to get along."

Fat chance. The husky was about as agreeable as a toddler who was six hours overdue for a nap. Even the black-and-white markings on her face made it look like she was constantly judging everyone around her.

That thing about her resting bitch face? Not an exaggeration.

"Tell that to her." Keaton hung his suit jacket on the vintage iron rack by the front door and took off his shoes. The house smelled like heaven. "She's the one who's looking at me like she wants to go all *Friday the 13th* the second I turn my back."

"Maybe because she senses that *you* don't like *her*." Leah shot him a look. She was dressed in a pair of pink sweatpants and a matching hoodie, but her makeup looked ready for a night on the town. Her eyes were covered in some sparkly stuff that shifted purple and blue, and she had those big fringe things on her eyelashes that made her look like a Barbie doll.

"Nice makeup," he said. "Were you filming a tutorial?"

"I was." Leah beamed. "I got a new eyeshadow palette in the mail today."

One of the things Keaton had done for his sister was set up a room where she could film YouTube videos without having to move equipment around. She had permanent lighting and a sleek series of drawers for her makeup. The look on her face when he'd done the grand reveal had made his heart burst. Considering that back when they were kids he'd scrimped and saved for six months to buy her a single brush from MAC for her birthday, it felt like quite the turnaround.

"A palette that a *brand* sent me." She pressed a hand to her chest. "I'm getting PR from actual brands now, can you believe it?"

"That's awesome. I'm so proud of you."

Leah ran a burgeoning YouTube channel that was mostly beauty and fashion content, but which also touched on her life as a young woman with multiple sclerosis. There had been a time where persistent flare-ups had made it challenging for her to hold a traditional job traveling to makeup gigs like weddings and photo shoots, and so she'd turned to virtual work. The YouTube channel had started out as a creative outlet on the side, but she hoped to grow her social following and turn it into a career.

Keaton had zero doubt that she could achieve that goal.

"It's so exciting." She grabbed the silver cane leaning against the wall. "I'm starting to get traction now, you know. The algorithm can be so fickle sometimes, but I've had a few videos do really well recently."

"You're working hard. Of course the success is coming."

"Not as fast as you, Wall Street Whiz Kid," she teased. "But I'm getting there."

"Hey, you're the one living in trendy Brooklyn now. These

days you can't turn a corner without walking into a dude with a man bun sipping on a $7 latte."

"Yeah, because the coffee in Manhattan is *so* much cheaper." Leah rolled her eyes as she walked slowly but steadily with her cane, the soft sound of the rubber stopper tapping against the hardwood punctuating each step. "Besides, I still go to that little Italian place where it's two dollars for an espresso and the grandma behind the counter tries to fatten me up with sfogliatelle."

"Good. I'd hate to think you were giving money to the man bun brigade."

Brooklyn and Manhattan had both fallen prey to hipsters. Everything was small-batch this and farm-fresh that and the most confusing word of all: artisanal. What the hell qualified someone to be an artisan, anyway? Because he'd seen that word used on everything from chocolate to pottery to candles with awful Instagram catchphrases.

Live, love, laugh his ass.

"Keaton!" His mother, Jackie, walked out of the main room and into the hallway, arms outstretched. "Don't you look handsome as ever."

"Thanks, Mom." He wrapped her up in a big hug, noticing how tiny she felt in his arms. "Are you shrinking?"

"Oh my goodness, stop it." She pulled back and shook her head. Her dark hair was peppered with tinsel-like silver strands and her green eyes—the eyes she'd gifted both her children—glowed with mischief. "It's not nice to tease the vertically challenged."

"Ugh, tall people. Am I right?" Leah giggled. "The worst."

"You two always gang up on me." Keaton slung an arm around his mother's neck, and they all headed toward the kitchen and dining area. "Where's Harv?"

"Working." His mother sighed. "He really wanted to come but they were short tonight."

Harvey was his mother's second husband—after a failed engagement to Keaton's father and a disastrous first marriage to a bad man when Keaton was a teen. They'd only been married a year, but Keaton liked him a lot. He'd been a great influence on Jackie, helping her to find more confidence in herself and even encouraging her to go to art school. The woman his mother was now—someone who always smiled and was present—was worlds away from the emotionally withdrawn anger-fueled shadow of his youth. As far as Keaton was concerned, Harv was a great addition to the family.

And above anything else in the world—above sales targets and M&As and bonus checks and all—family was what drove Keaton.

The group walked into the open-plan kitchen and dining area, where the island was covered in Leah's favorite meal. The make-it-yourself pizza. There were premade bases with red sauce and herbs, and all the ingredients laid out in separate bowls. Leah and their mom had prepped all manner of things—greens, peppers, three different types of meat, eggplant, mozzarella, apples, walnuts and pineapple. She'd even infused her own oil with chili for drizzling over the top.

Molly walked in behind them, her toenails clicking on the floorboards. She threw Keaton a derisive look before pushing past him—leaving a fine dusting of hairs on his suit pants—and taking a slurp from her water bowl.

"Did Leah tell you the good news?" his mother asked as she started loading her pizza base up with spinach and thin slices of prosciutto.

"Good news?" Keaton looked at his sister.

"I'm putting Molly into a talent quest!"

Keaton burst out laughing, which made the dog look up from her bowl. Oh man, if looks could *kill.* "Sorry, I just… what talents does she have? Turning grown men to stone? Overreacting whenever you tell her to stop doing something? Pretending that a bath is a death sentence?"

He knew *exactly* how much Molly hated having a bath, since he'd attempted to bathe the dog a few times. Twice he'd ended up soaking himself more than the dog, and the third time she'd knocked him over so hard that he'd sprained his wrist when he fell back on the tiled floor.

After that, Keaton suggested it might be best if they have a professional take care of it. Thankfully, Leah's best friend was a dog groomer and had a knack for subduing even the most misbehaving pooch.

"I've trained her to do a bunch of things. Look." Leah held out a hand to Molly. "Shake."

The dog obediently placed one paw right into her owner's hand, her eyes never leaving Keaton.

"Drop." Leah pointed to the floor and the dog dropped down onto her belly. "Oh no, Molly! It's a full moon!"

The dog leaped back to her feet and howled at the top of her lungs like a wolf. Okay, so that was pretty funny.

"A talent quest, huh? Is there a big prize up for grabs?" Keaton grabbed a pizza base and started placing pepperoni slices on top, arranging them methodically so that every part of the pizza was equally covered.

"The winning animal will be signed with a pet social media agency called Paws in the City." Leah patted Molly on the head and cooed about what a good girl she was. The dog basked in the praise. Show off. "They're based in Manhattan, too."

"I've heard of them."

He'd read something in the *New York Times* about how the woman who owned the company had built it from scratch after being fired from her old job. He liked stories like that—where the little guy triumphed in a world designed to favor those who already had a head start.

"I think Molly could be a star," Leah said. "She's so beautiful and smart."

"She's *something*," Keaton muttered, and his mother elbowed him in the ribs. "Well, I know you'll kick butt at whatever you do. And if anyone can turn that devil hound into a well-behaved Instapooch, it's you."

Molly made a snorting sound to show exactly what she thought of being an "Instapooch." But Keaton's sister smiled, and it made the whole world seem brighter. Frankly, he would never understand what she saw in that dog, but he also knew that Molly had helped his sister out of a very dark place while she'd struggled with her MS diagnosis.

And for that, he was grateful. But he would never *ever* be a dog person himself.

Who are you kidding, you'll never be a relationship of any kind *person.*

Because being married once had almost broken him, and Keaton would never put himself through that kind of pain ever again.

3

Are dating apps ruining our chances of finding love?
(by Peta McKinnis,
Spill The Tea society and culture reporter)

There was a time where dating in New York meant stressing over what shoes to wear with what dress, and figuring out which cocktail bars had the best lighting. But now, with more dating apps than our phones have room for, has dating been reduced to numbers and algorithms? How is true love meant to survive when a potential match is assessing us against the checklist of their ideal mate, like we're a product being researched on Amazon?

There was a brief moment in the New York dating scene where women were protected by the ill-fated Bad Bachelor app. But now, with nothing more to go on than a photo that's likely been retouched and a bio shorter than a tweet, how do we know what we're getting ourselves into on a date?

One New York woman found herself in an uncomfortable situation where her match asked a waitress whether they would make attractive babies. She has since been identified as dog groomer August Merriweather, who owns a successful luxury animal grooming business and has been called "Manhattan's Dog Whisperer" by her celebrity clients. The viral video, which might be history's most cringeworthy date, has been viewed more than one million times...

"*Everybody* has seen it." August threw her phone across the couch, where it bounced and dropped onto the rug. It felt like everyone she knew had texted her a link to the article, and her phone hadn't stopped buzzing all day. She flung an arm over her eyes. "Literally everybody."

"Well, given there are over seven billion people in the world, that seems like a stretch," Leah said with a laugh. "And there's over eight million in New York alone."

"Great, so one in eight people here have seen it. Much better," she replied miserably, reaching for her coffee and taking a sip. "And now they know who I am. Why couldn't I leave without saying anything? Why did I have to open my big mouth?"

Carter Edward Driscoll III had well and truly gotten under her skin. Maybe she *had* been a little defensive when he'd called her solid, because it wasn't the first time some asshole had commented on her weight.

Or maybe it was his whole "women are nothing but baby-making machines" attitude that pissed her off.

Whatever the reason, by lecturing him in front of the room she'd guaranteed the video would get attention. The first time someone tagged her on social media, she'd made the mistake of reading the comments.

She should think herself lucky someone considers her attractive.

Solid? He was being kind. She's just fat.

Not all women want to have babies? Uh, don't you know the point of the human race is to reproduce?

Of course, there were plenty of people speaking in support of her, too. But the negative comments were the ones that stuck in her head most. They were like burrs, grabbing at her tender spots and hanging on for dear life.

"Augie?" Leah placed a hand on her knee. "It's a wonderful thing that you stood up for yourself. I've always envied that about you."

"What?"

"You don't let people steamroll you. Even when we were in high school and everyone treated us like lepers, you never allowed anyone to make you feel second best."

"Ugh, high school. That's *exactly* what this feels like." She shook her head. "Thank God TikTok wasn't around back then."

"Amen to that."

Being shipped off to a private school that her parents had scrimped and saved for in an attempt to break into better social circles had been a nightmare. Her peers had all come from old money, and she'd found them to be elitist and materialistic. Except for Leah Sax and her older brother, Keaton.

They were like her—people from modest upbringings who'd somehow found themselves impostors in the world of the one percent. Being outsiders, they'd stuck together.

"Even if I wanted to keep using dating apps, I don't think I could." August sighed. "Now I'm *that* girl from the video. People are interested in me more out of notoriety than anything else."

She'd already been receiving DMs galore across all her social media accounts *and* on the dating apps she used. Most people were probably looking for fifteen minutes of fame and hoping to hang on to the coattails she never even wanted.

The whole thing was very overwhelming. Plus, it was making it even harder to sort the genuine guys from the creeps.

"So, you're giving up on dating?" Leah frowned, her dark brows crinkling above her pert nose as she sipped her coffee.

"No, but I *am* going to change my tactics. I know what I want for my life, and one mouthy asshole isn't going to take it from me." She let out a sigh. "But I need professional help."

"Therapy?"

"Matchmaking," August corrected, cradling her mug. "I spent the afternoon researching executive dating services. It costs a pretty penny, *but* that means it automatically weeds out the people who aren't serious."

"Makes sense." Leah nodded. "Anyone can download an app and put whatever crap they want in their bio and you have no idea if any of it is true."

"Exactly. But with these services, the matchmaker fully vets everyone they add to their database and you know the people they connect you with are genuinely looking for a relationship, because who would pay that much just for sex?"

Leah snorted. "I'm sure some guys *would* pay that much for sex."

"Yeah, but there are other services specifically for that. They don't need a matchmaker if they want to get laid. So it gives me a bit more confidence about the whole thing and, frankly, I'm sick of getting my hopes up every time I meet a guy only to find out that they're either A, a jerk who thinks my only purpose in life is to pop out kids or B, just looking for a fuck buddy."

She let out a long breath, trying to shake off the frustration coiling in her body. The whole "life partner" thing had become a bit of a bee in her bonnet of late. Maybe it was because her dog grooming business was going so well—August had achieved all the major goals she'd set for herself in her first five years of business—that she was hungry for something else to tick off her perfect life checklist.

August was the kind of person who found it impossible to sit still. For her, the worst thing in the world was a vacation where you were expected to relax all the time, like those terrible ones at the beach where there was nothing to do. It made her skin crawl even thinking about it. Being a perpetual busy bee, she always had to be working toward something.

Did this have something to do with the fact that her parents had always made her feel like she wasn't good enough, and she was determined to prove them wrong? Maybe. Probably.

Definitely.

But she used it as fuel to work hard and improve her situation every chance she got. When life gave you lemons, you squeezed those suckers and made a Long Island Iced Tea and then you got on with achieving your goals.

"I'm curious to hear all about it," Leah said. "Do you have to meet with them?"

"Yeah. I've got an appointment next week." Her palms were already sweaty and she'd mentally changed her outfit ten times. "Am I being ridiculous? Is it old-fashioned to want to find a partner so badly?"

"No." Leah shot her a look and shook her head. "Why do

you think dating services even exist? Wanting to share your life with someone isn't old-fashioned."

"And even though I complained about the guys who just want sex and nothing else…it *would* be nice to have someone rattle my headboard." She sighed. "It's been so long."

Leah giggled. "Smutty monster books not cutting it any-more?"

"There's only so far the imagination can take a person." August grinned. "Speaking of which, did you read that one I sent you the link to?"

"The one with the blue aliens with the horns? I read the damn thing in one sitting." Leah covered her face with both hands, to hide her blushing. "Good lord, it was so wrong it was right! I couldn't put it down."

August cackled. Leah usually stuck to sweeter books where the characters didn't jump into bed right away, if at all. It baffled August. Who the hell wanted to wait a hundred and fifty pages for things to heat up? Her impatient ass wanted to get to the good bits as soon as possible!

"I'll convert you into a steamy romance reader yet."

"So long as you don't give me any books where the guy calls her 'kitten.' Ugh, what's with these awful pet names? I can't stand it." Leah wrinkled her nose.

"Ha! *Pet* name, get it." August made a *boom tish* motion with her hands and Leah shook her head.

"If Will called me kitten, I would lock him out of the house," Leah said, referring to her new boyfriend. "A woman should not be named after an animal."

"Frankly, a guy can call me whatever pet name he wants so long as he knows how to take me to Pleasuretown and won't bail as soon as it's over," August said, standing and reaching for the empty mugs sitting on the coffee table. "He can call me Puss in Boots for all I care."

"Make sure you tell the matchmaker that," Leah quipped. "Must be tall, dark and handsome…and knows the way to Pleasuretown."

August chuckled to herself as she carried the empty cups into the kitchen. Despite feeling rattled by the whole "going viral" thing, coming here to hang out with her best friend had certainly helped take her emotions down a notch. It would be easy to whine and feel sorry for herself, but August preferred to take matters into her own hands.

Next week, she would meet with the matchmaker, lay all her desires on the table and give up swiping right for good.

"Puss in Boots, huh? I have to admit, I've never used that one before."

The masculine voice made August jump and she almost lost the mugs in her hands. Whirling around in the kitchen, she saw Leah's older brother, Keaton, leaning against the wall.

He was wearing black suit pants and a crisp white shirt that fitted to his shoulders and chest like a dream. A gleaming black-and-yellow tie hung around his neck, and a heavy silver watch adorned one wrist where his sleeve was rolled back. The understated yet undeniably tailored outfit screamed money. And not just money like her parents tried so hard to exude with their secondhand BMW and consignment designer goods and snooty attitudes, but fancy office on Wall Street money. First-class-tickets-to-anywhere-in-the-world money.

Do-whatever-it-takes-to-win money.

"Why are you eavesdropping on girl talk, anyway?" she asked, pulling the dishwasher open and placing the mugs inside. "Hoping to find some tips?"

The truth of the matter was that Keaton Sax did not need tips about *anything*, especially not on how to attract a woman. With broad shoulders, hair the color of a perfect cup of espresso and vivid green eyes, the man was a certified lady magnet. This only served to make his perpetually single—and *not* looking to mingle—status all the more perplexing. Well, it was perplexing to some people, but August had known Keaton for years.

And she knew the real reason he was permanently off the market.

He smirked. "I'm not sure calling a woman Puss in Boots is much of a tip. Something tells me that might specifically be a *you* thing."

"Maybe it is," she replied loftily.

"Although, what did you say? He can call you whatever he likes so long as he takes you to Pleasuretown?" Amusement crinkled the edges of his eyes in the sexiest and yet most irritating way. "But no bailing in the morning."

"What's wrong with that?" She folded her arms across her chest. "Can't a woman express her desire for sexual satisfaction *and* commitment in this day and age?"

"Hey, fly your freak flag free, Puss in Boots."

"What are you doing here, anyway?" she asked, deciding to ignore the gibes. That was Keaton's MO. Whenever he was around her for more than a second, he took great pleasure in winding her up like she was one of those Christmas nutcracker soldiers.

"Leah said she was having issues with her internet and she wanted me to take a look at it."

August forced herself not to smile. For all the bad things she could say about Keaton, it was impossible to deny how much he loved his sister. Enough to make the trek over the bridge whenever she asked, no matter the size of the request, even when he could easily afford to send someone over to do whatever was needed.

He always came himself.

"Have you ever noticed how Leah randomly invites me over whenever you're here?" he asked suddenly, narrowing his eyes like it had only just dawned on him.

"I *have* noticed that, actually." August pulled on the hem of her top. She was pretty sure she had a mixture of animal fur dusted all over her from work, and she knew for a fact that her red hair had left curly behind three hours ago and straight up entered Frizzville. "Why do you think that might be?"

He lifted one shoulder into a sexy shrug. "Maybe she's trying to set us up."

That confirmed her suspicions. The last three times that August had visited, Keaton happened to show up. Leah always made some flippant comment about getting her days mixed up or her mind being a little scrambled, but then she would find an excuse to disappear and leave August and Keaton alone.

Which was hilarious. Because the thought of August and Keaton being together was like…

Well, it was so preposterous that she couldn't think of an example ridiculous enough to represent it. Orange juice and toothpaste? Peanut butter and anthrax?

At one point we might have worked…but not now.

She could practically feel the chill on her skin, the way the snowflakes had drifted down and caught in their hair, and smell the champagne on his breath and cologne on his skin. The flip of her stomach as his green eyes blackened and turned hungry. The feeling of his lips coming down to hers… before she chickened out.

Before he fell head over heels for someone else. Before August wondered if she'd made the biggest mistake of her life.

"I can't imagine that being the case," August replied primly, doing her best to shake the old-but-annoyingly-not-forgotten memory from her head. "And even if it was, Leah is barking up the wrong tree."

"I'm not your type, huh?" He walked over and leaned a hand on the kitchen counter, crowding August against the cabinets.

She tipped her face up to his and looked him right in the eye. "Not if you were the last man on earth, Keaton Sax."

"Oof, right in the ego." Keaton pressed a hand to his chest, but it was all for show.

He knew without a doubt that August's answer was one hundred percent bullshit. If not that, then at the very least, it was ninety-nine percent bullshit and one percent blissful ignorance. Because he still remembered August mooning over him as a teenager.

"Good thing you have plenty of ego to go around," she replied with a saccharine smile.

"Oh come on," he said, pulling his lips up into a smirk that he knew would drive her bananas. "I once remember a young ginger-haired girl staring at me through the kitchen window as I mowed the lawn with my shirt off. You didn't seem to mind me then."

Her cheeks grew pink and it seemed to make her hair look even more red. "That was a long time ago."

"And yet you remember it like it was yesterday."

"I do not."

"Do too."

"Do..." She snapped her mouth shut, realizing that she was

falling right into his trap. "How is it that I revert to being thirteen years old around you?"

"It's one of my many talents." He shrugged jovially.

"I'm not sure I would be proud of that," she muttered.

Keaton liked August. Always had. She was plucky and hardworking and she had a big heart. But the two-year age difference between them had felt like a chasm when he was a teenager. Back then he'd seen her as a kid—freckle-faced, with a halo of frizzy red hair, braces and a penchant for boy bands. It wasn't until he came home for the holidays during college one year and he'd seen her standing by the tree—hair like ruby silk ribbons and her short, curvy body poured into a little black dress—that he'd done a double take so hard he'd almost given himself whiplash.

After that he couldn't get her out of his head. So he'd decided to do something about it the year he graduated. That night had changed his world. He'd almost kissed August on the doorstep of his family home, only to be rebuffed, and then Leah had brought home another friend from school.

Ellery.

His heart clenched hard in his chest every time he thought about his wife. Their marriage had been so brief, but he'd loved her with a wholeness he hadn't even known possible. Yet by the following Christmas his whole life had fallen apart, and he'd gone from being a man with the world at his feet to a lost soul with a storm cloud where his heart used to be.

Why did you have to die?

Keaton shoved the question to one side. As much as he liked August as a person, every time he saw her it was like being reminded of all he'd lost. He couldn't disentangle her from that memory, no matter how hard he tried.

So, he kept his distance. Winding her up was an easy shield.

And making her think he was simply a teasing jerk who got his kicks making her blush was the best way to make sure neither one of them ever had the thought to revisit that night. Because she was stubborn like that—the harder he teased, the more she pretended to hate him.

Really, the dance was as much for her benefit as it was for his. August deserved someone who matched her positivity and zest for life. Someone who would give her everything instead of holding her at a distance like he would. Had he thought about them being together? Hell yeah. There was something about her slightly uptight, stubborn-as-a-bull attitude toward him that got him hot under the collar. Not to mention that he was a sucker for a woman with a sharp tongue. Yes, please.

But any time he thought about his attraction to August, his mind became a symphony of warning sirens. Love, he'd discovered, was not for the faint of heart.

And Keaton's had been permanently put into retirement.

"You'd do well to act like a teenager again, Augie," he said, using the nickname from when they were kids. He could practically see her back teeth grinding together. "Live a little! You work too hard."

"Not all of us get to wine and dine clients for a living," she replied.

If only. Keaton had spent so many hours at his desk the past week, he was starting to wonder if he was giving himself a vitamin D deficiency. But that was his little secret. Let people think he was some high-flying party boy who drank Dom like it was water.

"But you like that because entertaining clients makes it easy to look like you have a life, doesn't it?" She cocked her head, suddenly serious as if she'd seen past his bright, reflective disguise for a moment. He hated it when she did that. "You're not fooling me."

Keaton the Wall Street Whiz Kid. Keaton the Baller. Keaton the I-Don't-Care-What-It-Costs-Make-It-Happen Wheeler and Dealer.

It was all a persona. A way for him to protect the broken and bruised young man who lived inside him, hiding in a fort made of memories and grief.

Keaton the Widower. That's who he really was.

"You think I don't have a life?" he scoffed. "Please. One of the firm's clients is taking me to his private island in September."

"A work trip." She raised an eyebrow.

"A work trip with a private jet, a 24-7 private chef and a villa all to myself."

Truth be told, Keaton was dreading the trip. The client was a pompous asshole who'd recently tried to screw the firm out of part of their commission, and his wife often got drunk and made a pass at him. But August's comment about him not having a life had struck a little too close to home.

"Still a work trip," she said smugly. "When was the last time you had a *real* vacation, huh? Like time off where you weren't attached to your laptop."

"When was the last time *you* had a vacation, huh?" he fired back. "You're just as bad."

"Yeah, but I don't pretend not to be a workaholic, unlike you."

The conversation was interrupted when Molly entered the kitchen, her ice-blue eyes narrowed in Keaton's direction. She walked over to her food bowl and looked at it pointedly. When neither August nor Keaton immediately moved to fill it, she stamped her paws.

"Someone's hungry," August said in a sweet voice. Molly came over, tail wagging, and she pressed her head into August's hand. "Good girl."

"Good girl?" Keaton made a scoffing sound. "That dog is good so long as you do everything she wants the second she wants it. She's a spoiled brat."

"Now, why is Keaton such a meanie face?" August cooed, ruffling Molly's fur. "Sit."

The dog immediately plopped her furry ass onto the ground.

"See, she's such a good girl." August reached into her pocket and produced a dog treat. Seriously, the woman was—at all times—prepared for an animal interaction. He'd even seen her feeding the squirrels outside, which was basically a crime.

They were nothing but rats with good PR.

"Shake."

Molly lifted her paw into August's hand, eyes laser-locked on the treat. The dog was a canine garbage disposal unit, motivated by any and all kinds of food.

"Smile."

The dog pulled her lips back in what Keaton assumed was an attempt to follow the command. "Don't have her do that in front of any small children. She'll give them nightmares."

The dog glared at Keaton as if to say, *You're no oil painting yourself, dude.*

"Stand." August ignored him and snapped her fingers, making the dog lift her front paws while balancing on her hind legs. "Excellent work, Molly. Such a smart girl."

She held out her hand and Molly gobbled the snack from her palm, tail wagging. Keaton rolled his eyes. "You would think she's performing brain surgery the way you and Leah act."

"You're just jealous that she doesn't do anything for you."

"That's because I have no desire to waste my time on teaching an animal to do pointless things, like begging for food." He shook his head. August's and Leah's utter devotion to the husky was beyond him, and he refused to be one more person wrapped around her paw. "What's the point?"

"Fun, Keaton. You must not be familiar with it." She turned her face up to his, mouth pulled into a smirk. "Say it slowly with me, *fuuuuuun*. It's an activity that offers enjoyment and satisfaction."

"Like taking you to Pleasuretown?" he fired back, and her cheeks turned scorching red. "Huh, Puss in Boots?"

Out of the corner of his eye, Keaton saw that Leah had moved to the entrance of the kitchen and was not-so-subtly listening in to their banter. He really needed to have a word with her about this whole "trying to get him and August in a room alone" thing.

It was getting ridiculous.

Keaton would *never* get into another relationship as long as he lived. Love, no matter how good it felt at the time, was not even close to being worth the scars it would leave on his heart. Especially when the ones he already had refused to heal.

4

August's stomach fluttered with nerves. She was headed to a restaurant located on the thirty-third floor of a skyscraper, and from what she'd read online, it was one of those swanky places with white tablecloths and a wine menu as thick as the *Lord of the Rings* trilogy.

In other words, *not* her usual kind of dinner venue.

She preferred small hole-in-the-wall places with incredible food and minimal fanfare. But tonight was the first date the matchmaker had set up for her, and she was sure the fancy restaurant was meant to leave a good impression. It had taken a little over a week between August's first appointment with the matchmaker and this date, which somehow felt both too fast and too slow.

There's no point being nervous. Consider it a test run. A practice.

She'd dug out her go-to little black dress (the one that covered everything from funerals to weddings to New Year's Eve parties) from the depths of her closet, splurged on a new pair of heels, blow-dried her hair and attempted some winged liner while watching one of Leah's tutorials on YouTube.

It wasn't perfect, by any means, but as Leah always said: *Wings are meant to be sisters, not twins!*

In truth, August's wings were a little more like second cousins twice removed. But she liked the way the black liner made her eyes pop, and it made her feel a little bit like a '50s silver screen starlet.

As she walked through the gold-trimmed turnstile into the marble-floored foyer of the fancy tower, she pressed a hand to her stomach. But it didn't stop the nerves. Tonight felt like a very big deal. Her first chance to see if matchmaking might work for her. The head of the matchmaking company, a vivacious older woman named Maxine Diamond, had told her that the first date was about gathering information and not to be disheartened if it wasn't true love on the first attempt.

This was just a simple meet and greet. No pressure. No expectations.

"I'd be happy to get through the night without someone commenting on my reproductive abilities," she muttered to herself as she walked toward the bay of elevators.

After freaking out slightly about the fancy venue, she'd taken the time to get in the mood by having a glass of wine while she got ready, and she'd put on some relaxing music.

"You can do this," she said to herself as she entered the elevator and pressed the button for the thirty-third floor. "You're an intelligent, successful, kind woman and this is just a date. You have survived far bigger things."

The elevator moved silently upward, and August clutched her small evening bag to her stomach. All she knew about her date was that his name was Asher Benson, he was thirty-three and worked in finance, and he'd never been married nor did he have any children.

Oh, and apparently Maxine was confident their personalities would be well suited.

The elevator pinged and August walked out. The restaurant was dimly lit but had a view of the city that almost snatched her breath away. Tables were sprinkled around the room and along the window, with several velvet-lined booths running across the back wall. Trails of lights draped from the roof and everything was accented in gold, which enhanced the flickering candles inside and the world glittering outside. A woman with a chic bob and a black satin shirt greeted August with a smile.

"I've got a reservation under Asher Benson," August said, her voice breathy with nerves. Her stomach was about to explode from all the butterflies rammed in there. "For 7:00 p.m."

"Your dining partner is already here," the woman said. "Your server will see you through."

Punctual. That's a good sign.

Another woman, also dressed in black, motioned for August to follow her. She scanned the room as they walked, looking for the face from the profile on Asher that Maxine had sent through. Blond hair, light eyes, a slight dimple in the chin. When the server stopped at a table and a man stood up, August was taken aback.

He was even more handsome in person than in his photo.

"August, so nice to meet you." He stuck his hand out and then retracted it, laughing. "Sorry, that was awkward. I feel like I'm still in work mode. Can I give you a kiss on the cheek instead?"

Wow. What a gentleman.

"Sure." August laughed nervously as he leaned down to

brush his cheek against hers. She waited for some sparks or a tingle or…something. But nothing came.

That's okay. It's early days. Besides, you're not here for spark, you're here for a good, practical match.

He came around to pull out her chair and August sat, slinging her evening bag over the back. There was already sparkling water on the table and she reached for a glass, taking a sip to give herself something to do.

Asher sat down and waited for the server to take their drink order before asking, "Is this, uh…do you have much experience with the whole matchmaking thing?"

His voice was smooth and rich, with a nice warmth to it.

"It's actually my first time."

He looked visibly relieved. "Me too."

For some reason, the fact that he seemed a little nervous about the whole thing put her at ease. Already this experience felt a world away from her viral disaster. Why hadn't she thought to do this sooner?

Smiling and feeling her confidence coming back, August said, "I'm glad we're getting to do this together as first-timers, then."

Asher's eyes connected with hers across the candle gently wavering back and forth in the middle of the table. "Me too."

Keaton knocked back the remainder of his scotch as the man in front of him droned on and on about all the best golf courses he'd been to around the world. This was Keaton's dirty little secret—the so-called glitz and glamour of rubbing elbows with Manhattan's elite?

Boring. As. Bat. Shit.

Seriously, the conversations he was forced to grit his teeth through should be bottled and sold as a cure for insomnia.

Golfing, boating, tennis, watches. Superficial shit that immediately set Keaton's relevancy engine to "unimportant, disregard," which was a problem. In his line of work it paid to remember these things—like which brand of watch a client liked to wear so he could send some branded matching cuff links at Christmas. *Gag.*

It was the part of the job Keaton hated most of all. He was much happier burying himself in the data and numbers and chasing the thrill of finding the next big opportunity. Unfortunately for him, cutting out the people component of his job was not an option.

"You should come along one weekend, Keaton." The older man, who was dressed in a suit that definitely cost more than Keaton's college education, leaned back in his chair. His silver hair was thick and full, and his eyes were skating around the room as if he'd already lost interest in the conversation.

I know how you feel, buddy.

"You know the firm only lets us out on very rare occasions," Keaton quipped. "It's not often we get the shackles loosened."

"That's what I like to hear." The man chuckled. "Most people these days don't know the meaning of hard work."

Keaton had to bite back a salty response. "Hard work" to these guys included a leg up the likes of which only a select few would ever experience—family with old money, Ivy League education, a daddy with all the right contacts. Most of them went on to run companies that exploited the little guy, paying minimum wage to their workers while padding their own pockets with excess.

And that's different from you trying to strong-arm a small company into an M&A, how?

It *was* different. Because the intention behind it was different. Keaton didn't work to make himself wealthy—it was to protect his family, to build them a solid future. To give them stability. He wanted to know that his mom and Leah would be taken care of for the rest of their lives, regardless of what happened to him. Beyond the wardrobe required to keep up appearances and his apartment close to the office, there were no expensive golf club or country-club memberships. No fancy collection of cars. No home in the Hamptons. No private jet.

"It's good to see there are still young people willing to work and not constantly crowing about how difficult life is. Most people your age seem to think everything should be handed to them on a silver platter. But you're different." The man nodded smugly, as if pleased with himself for passing on a compliment.

Not that Keaton took it as one, mind you. None of these fools would know what *real* hard work looked like—and he didn't mean long hours at a cushy desk job. He meant the kind of work his mom did for years, working two to three jobs cleaning other people's toilets and existing on little more than four hours' sleep a night just to keep the lights on and put food on the table.

"Excuse me a moment," he said, pushing back on his chair and standing. "I need to visit the restroom."

He headed deeper into the restaurant toward the sign pointing toward the restrooms, but the second he was around the corner, he sagged back against the wall. The longer he did this job, the harder it became to keep his patience for all the bullshit small talk and elitist attitudes.

But what else is there?

It was a question that had been looming over him the past month or so. If he was growing so tired of certain aspects of his job, then what was next?

For the first time in his life he didn't have an answer. After he got out of juvenile detention, his life had been a steady endurance race from one goal to the next. Get into college, graduate with top marks, get a job on Wall Street, get promoted, make a million dollars.

Tick, tick, tick.

"You have a goal," he muttered under his breath. "Make named partner."

It was the final item left on the career bucket list that he and Ellery had created together, their ambition fueling one another to aim higher and reach harder. But what would happen when he got his name on the firm's letterhead? What then?

What if there was nothing else beyond that?

He swallowed against the lump in his throat. It didn't matter if there was no other rung to climb, because he could always make more money for his family. He could always give them more security. If Leah ever decided to have a child, he could make a nice, fat college fund for his niece or nephew. He could send his mom on all the vacations she never got to have as a young, single mother. He could make sure they were debt-free for the rest of their lives. He could give them everything they'd ever wanted.

But what then?

It was terrifying to investigate the future and see nothing but a deep, dark hole. To see the vast and endless emptiness of a life lacking in potential.

"Keaton?" A feminine voice snapped him out of the dark, spiraling thoughts.

August stood in front of him, looking like she'd stepped right out of his dirty dreams and into reality. Her red hair was smooth and hung down to her waist, her full figure was showcased to perfection in a simple black dress, and a pair of stiletto heels gave her some extra height. He caught a whiff of perfume in the air around her—something delicious, like a caramel-vanilla dessert. It was a "come closer" perfume and it sent a jolt of attraction right through him.

"What the heck are *you* doing here?" he asked, the question tumbling out of him, raw and harsh. He shook his head. "It doesn't seem like your scene, I mean."

She blinked, as if unsure whether to be insulted by his brash tone. "Actually, if you must know, I'm on a date."

She *definitely* didn't pick this place, then. August was all about finding the quirky places off the beaten path or the family-run restaurants that felt like you were dining in someone's home. Not places like this, with tiny portions on oversize plates and tweezer-handled garnishes.

"Your date has expensive taste," he said. "And clearly doesn't know what you like."

Her mouth tightened. "It's a first date. So no, he doesn't know what I like yet."

Yet.

She had hopes for this one.

"Point him out," he said, poking his head around the corner. For some reason, Keaton needed to see who she was with. A strange and unfamiliar tangle of protectiveness and jealousy swelled in his stomach.

"Why?" August crossed her arms, which only served to enhance her cleavage, pressing it against the delicate vee created by the wrapped portion of her dress. A small purse with a glittering gold chain hung over one shoulder. "It's not like you care who I date."

"Indulge me. I come here a lot, so I might know the guy." He shoved down his prickly reaction and winked at her.

"Wouldn't you want some potential inside information on the guy if it's only the first date?"

August chewed on her lower lip for a second. Then, seeming to agree with his logic, she pointed. "Third table across, near the cocktail bar."

Keaton followed the line of her finger to a table a few spots back from where he'd been sitting a moment ago. That explained why he hadn't seen her—his chair was facing the other direction, away from the entrance.

Keaton squinted. There was something kind of familiar...

"Asher Benson," he spluttered, recognition flooding him. "Are you pulling my leg?"

Shock registered on August's face. "You know him?"

"Yeah." He raked a hand through his hair, trying to keep control of the need to grab her wrist and haul her straight out of the restaurant.

You have no right to tell her what to do.

But he sure as shit could warn her.

"We were in the bullpen together at my first firm." His lip curled into a sneer.

Asher Benson was *everything* he hated about Wall Street wrapped into one smarmy snakelike package. It was Asher who'd found out about Keaton's "colorful" past and shared it with the rest of the juniors at the firm, shredding any chances that Keaton could pretend he was one of them. Asher was the one who'd nicknamed him Checkbox, claiming that the firm had only hired him because of a program for underprivileged youth, which was categorically not true. And Asher was the one who'd planted an item he'd stolen from the boss's office in Keaton's desk, attempting to get him fired when Keaton kicked his ass at an internal competition.

It was only Thomas Fairchild's belief in Keaton that saved his job.

Did Asher ever see any punishment for pulling such a move? Hell, no. His daddy was a big-time criminal defense lawyer and all those assholes knew they'd need someone like him in the future. In fact, Keaton was pretty sure it only proved to some of the higher-ups that Asher had the kind of ruthlessness required to make it on Wall Street.

"I take it you're not a fan," August said, her mouth twisted. "Why am I not surprised?"

They were back around the corner now, out of sight of their dinner guests.

"What's that supposed to mean?" he asked.

"You don't like *anyone*." She rolled her eyes.

"That's not true. I like...you." Hmm, maybe she had a point. Keaton tended to view the possibility of new friendships as something to be avoided. As far as he was concerned, a small circle of friends and family was preferable, but a tiny circle was even better.

After all, the less you let people into your life, the less of a chance you'd get hurt.

"You tolerate me," she replied with a smirk. "*Big* difference."

Keaton frowned. Hmm, maybe his teasing might have gone too far lately. "False. I don't tolerate anyone. You're either in the circle or you're not. There's no in-between."

The corner of August's lip twitched. "In any case, this date is going really well and I don't want your 'you shall not pass' vibes to ruin my night, okay?"

"How did you even meet him, anyway?" Keaton asked, ignoring her question. When he tried to poke his head around the corner to have another look, August grabbed him by the shirt and pulled him back.

The action brought them close together, and another wave

of her intoxicating perfume hit him. Up close, he could see that she'd coated her lashes with mascara and lined her eyes in a sexy way he'd never seen her do before. Her round face was perfectly framed by all that luscious red hair and she looked…

Stunning.

Clearing her throat, August let him go and stepped back as if she'd touched something very hot. "Keaton, can you just… not. *Please.* I don't need a big brother, okay?"

God, the way he was looking at her now…there was *nothing* brotherly about it. He swallowed as he dragged his eyes away from the sexy curve of her neck. "I'm curious, that's all. Because I know Asher lives on the Upper East Side and only eats at places with hundred-dollar appetizers, so I'm *really* curious about how you two crossed paths."

"Are you saying I'm not good enough for him?" Her cheeks reddened.

"What? No!" He shook his head. "Far from it. I just…"

Wait. Why wasn't she answering his question? If she really *did* have fears about not being good enough for the guy, then she sure as shit wouldn't let Keaton know about it. Usually, she'd laugh and tell him to shove it if he tried to get under her skin. So no, he didn't think this was a confidence issue.

Maybe there was another reason…

"Why won't you tell me how you met?"

"Because it's none of your business, Keaton. Jeez." She fiddled with the strap of her purse and avoided eye contact. "You're so pushy."

Oh, there was a story here. He was *sure* of it.

He could smell it on her—the way she avoided eye contact, the blush, fiddling with her purse…

"You're acting like you went to a goddamn matchmaker or something," he said with a laugh. But when her face turned from flushed to crimson, Keaton gasped. "You're kidding me. Asher fucking Benson going to a matchmaker? Oh, that is gold!"

"Stop it," she hissed, taking a step forward and jabbing him in the chest. "You will not breathe a word of this to anyone, okay? If you do, I will *never* forgive you. I'm not ashamed, but it's confidential."

He wasn't sure he bought her reasoning. It was unlikely she'd signed an NDA, unless the matchmaking company had some *majorly* famous clients on their list. Frankly, modern dating boggled his mind. What happened to meeting people the old-fashioned way?

Or in your case, not at all.

Hmm. He didn't have a leg to stand on as far as that argument was concerned. Maybe the dating scene had changed in the last ten years even more than he realized. Still, single men should be climbing over themselves to date someone like August. She had the kind of smile that could patch up the holes in a person.

Not you. Even she's not strong enough to fix you.

"Keaton, please." She grabbed his arm. "Don't…don't ruin this for me. I'm having a good time."

The words struck him hard in the chest, as did the desperate, pleading look in her eyes. What the heck was she doing shopping for a boyfriend at a matchmaker?

None. Of. Your. Business.

"Just be careful, okay?" He frowned. "Asher is…"

She sighed, shaking her head and looking away momentarily as if disappointed in him. "What? What is he?"

"He's very good at playing the affable *aww shucks* guy when he thinks it will get him what he wants, that's all. Don't fall for it. He's a liar and cheat."

"You know what, I don't want to hear it." She held up a hand.

"I'm not saying this to give you a hard time or ruin your night. I mean it." He sighed. "Just…don't take everything he says at face value."

"Stop, Keaton."

He touched August's shoulder briefly, wanting to say so much more—wanting to drag her out of the restaurant and away from a guy he knew was beneath her—but he held himself in check. She was a grown-ass woman and she could make her own decisions, and she deserved to have him listen when she told him to knock it off.

He just had to hope that Asher showed his true colors sooner rather than later, so August didn't get too invested.

"Get home safe. If you need a ride, call me and I'll send a driver over." He leaned forward and brushed his lips against her cheek, sucking in the sweet vanilla-caramel perfume and cursing himself for the personal torture it would provide well into the night.

But he did the right thing and left her standing there, befuddled.

Whatever urges he felt for August—whether brotherly or not—he had to squash them. Because he wasn't sure what he'd do if that adoring look came back into her eyes, like she'd had all those years ago. Something told him, he'd be powerless to resist.

And that would be a huge mistake for them both. Whatever August hoped to achieve with seeing a matchmaker, it was something he could never provide her.

5

Two weeks later...

Keaton jogged up to his sister's front door, a bag of groceries over one arm and a tray of lasagna from the Italian deli she liked in his hand. It was mid–Saturday afternoon and the sun was shining, making puddles from the earlier showers glisten like mirrors on the sidewalk. He'd spent the morning in the office and had planned to be there all day, until Leah rang.

The exhaustion in her voice had hit him like a freight train—she was mid-flare-up. The medication she'd switched to a few years ago had been working wonders for her, and the flare-ups were less frequent, but it didn't stave them off altogether, unfortunately.

Leah was a tough cookie. All she'd asked for was moral support because her mood was low, as it often tended to be in those instances—but Keaton had promised her the day she got diagnosed that whenever she needed him, he would be there. Didn't matter if he had to walk out of a client presentation or drop the ball on his work in some other way. Didn't matter who he had to blow off or piss off or push to the side.

Family was number one—no ifs, buts or maybes.

So he'd hoofed it across the bridge to Brooklyn, headed to the grocery store near her house to grab some essentials, and then he'd picked up something to heat up for dinner. Keaton was talented in a great many things, but cooking was not one of them. Not even close. And Leah was feeling crappy enough as it was, without having to suffer through his terrible cooking.

From the outside of her house, it looked like nobody was home. The curtains were drawn and it was quiet as he reached the front door. He juggled the food items and fished the key she'd given him out of his jacket pocket, then let himself inside. The light was dim, despite it being sunny outside. Leah was probably napping.

He closed the door behind him quietly and tiptoed through the house, toward the kitchen, knowing exactly where to step to avoid the squeaky floorboard that had gotten him in trouble for sneaking out. After stashing the lasagna in the fridge and putting the groceries away, he noticed there were a few cups in the sink. During a flare-up, Leah suffered with extreme fatigue and even something as simple as loading the dishwasher could be too much.

He made his way quietly around the ground floor of the house, finding a few more discarded and half-drunk mugs of herbal tea, and he loaded them all into the dishwasher. As he wiped the sink and countertops down, Keaton sensed movement behind him and felt the air shift. Nails clicked along the floorboards in a way that made him sigh.

"Molly," he said, turning around.

The husky sat in the entrance of the kitchen and narrowed her icy blue eyes at him. She let out a snort, followed by a disgusted shake of her head. Typical.

"Sorry, Your Majesty. Am I invading your personal space?" He did a mock bow toward the dog. "Please forgive me."

Molly tilted her snout up at him as if to say, *That's right, peasant. Remember who's in charge here.*

The dog walked toward her bowl, her voluminous tail swishing back and forth. She really *was* a stunning dog. Too bad she was fully aware of it. Stopping right next to her food bowl, she looked up at Keaton as if to say, *And why haven't you prepared my dinner yet?*

"I'm not here to feed you," he muttered. "Besides, I know you eat in the morning and late evening only. Nice try, though."

The dog made a sound of annoyance—the kind of almost-human whine that only a dramatic husky could make—and looked pointedly at her bowl. When Keaton didn't scramble to accommodate the request, she stared daggers at him and stamped her paw.

Literally stamped her paw.

"Are you going to throw a tantrum?" he asked. "See if I care. I'm not going to be manipulated into giving you an extra meal."

This husky would do literally anything for food. She'd beg, borrow and steal her way into whatever edible items she could get. Molly continued to look at him, the intense blue eye contact a little unnerving. Then, letting out a great big sigh like she hated herself for a moment, she lifted one paw into the shake position.

Smart dog. She knew tricks equaled treats.

But Keaton wasn't here to be at Molly's beck and call—he was here to take care of his sister.

"I don't care if you show me how to do the freaking can-can, dog. Not going to happen."

She put the paw down and glared at him. Why did he get the feeling she was trying to see if she could pop his head like a grape with her husky mind powers? Rolling his eyes, Keaton went back to the dishes. Molly, unimpressed with the fact that a human had refused to bow to her desires, flounced off in a huff, taking a moment to knock over a potted plant on her way out of the kitchen.

"Goddamn dog," Keaton muttered as he went to clean up the mess, scooping the dirt back into the pot as best he could.

He was sweeping up the remaining dirt and dead leaves when he heard footsteps and the soft thump of a rubber-stopped cane. "Kea?"

"In the kitchen." He used the dustpan to transport the mess to the trash. There, the kitchen was good as new.

"I heard a crash." She ground her fist into one eye, her other hand leaning heavily on her cane.

"Sorry." Even though it wasn't his fault, he felt a streak of guilt for waking her. She needed her rest. "Molly knocked over your plant. I think it was retaliation."

"For what?" A smile lifted the corner of her lips, but it only lasted a second before tiredness drew it back down.

"Refusing to feed her. I know her schedule, but she tried to trick me into giving extra." He reached a hand out to his sister's arm and squeezed. "You should get back to bed."

"I'm up now." She shook her head. "I might make some tea. Want some?"

"Sit. I'll make it." He went right to the cabinet where Leah's impressive collection of teas was stored.

Their grandmother was British and the love of tea had been passed down through the family. For Leah, it had become a passion, and Keaton took great pride in finding new blends for her to try whenever he traveled. He'd brought her some from Harrods in London, TWG from a trip to Singapore, and some David's Tea one time when he went up to Montreal. She loved every kind of tea—black, green, herbal, matcha.

"What do you feel like?" He rifled through the cupboard.

"Anything. I just want something warm and soothing."

Keaton grabbed for a caffeine-free blend containing chamomile, lavender and a few other aromatics. Better not to have anything that might disrupt her sleep when she got back to bed. He filled the kettle and set it to boil and put the tea bags into two mugs.

"Thanks for coming over. I know you're busy with work." Leah eased into a chair at the dining table. A second later, Molly came back into the kitchen and went straight to her, sniffing around with her ears flicking this way and that. The dog fussed over her, worried.

As much as he hated Molly's dramatics, it was clear she really cared about Leah and was a very good companion to her. For that, he appreciated the dog.

"I am always free to come help when you need it," he said, leaning back against the countertop.

"Well, that's a good thing." She nodded. "Because I'm going to ask for a favor."

"Okay. Whatever you need," he replied without hesitation.

"You'll want to hear me out before you commit." She

worried her bottom lip between her teeth. "And this is a request, *not* an obligation. You can absolutely say no. In fact, I fully expect it."

"Just spit it out, Leah." He was worried now. His sister, like him, was stubborn to the core, and this often manifested in her wanting to do everything herself, even when help was offered. The fact that she was asking for something meant it was important.

"So, remember how I told you that I'd entered Molly into that talent competition?" she began.

Oh no. Anything but that.

Molly lifted her head, her ears flicking at the sound of her name. Leah reached down to give her a scratch, and the big dog plopped her head on Leah's thigh.

"Well, it's next weekend."

Shit.

"In Upstate New York."

Keaton scrubbed a hand over his face. There was no way Leah would have enough energy to drive herself up to wherever the heck this talent competition thing was taking place, let alone be able to wrangle Molly into behaving herself for the judges.

Now he understood why she'd told him to hear her out before he agreed to anything. "Leah..."

"It's fine, Keaton." She held up her hand. "It's last minute and a *huge* inconvenience. You're incredibly busy with work. I totally understand. I'll contact the people running the competition and let them know I won't be there. It's not a big deal."

But it was a big deal. Because his sister didn't ask him for a favor unless it meant something. Yeah, she got all gaga over the pink couch knowing he would buy it for her, but Leah was very careful not to ask for too much. Too careful, in his mind.

"It's not so much the time. It's more that..." He glanced at the dog. "Molly hates me."

"Are you really worried about spending the weekend with a dog because she's a little fussy?"

"A little fussy?" he spluttered. "That dog has it in for me. I'm not convinced she won't try to kill me in my sleep."

Leah shot him a look. Her hair looked a little greasy, like she hadn't showered for a day or three. He bit back the urge to offer to get someone in to help, because Leah had already told him once she didn't want a stranger in her private space and he respected her boundaries.

"And you think *she's* the drama queen," she said, rolling her eyes.

"And she doesn't listen to me. Ever."

"Have you tried, Keaton? Ask her to do something."

He thought about refusing, but perhaps if he showed his sister just *how* terrible he was with Molly, then maybe he wouldn't even need to decline her request. His lack of talent would do it for him.

"Molly, come," he said. To his surprise, and likely because the dog was more than happy to fuck with him, the husky came trotting over. "Sit."

She sat. Her blue eyes gleamed and he would swear she was laughing at him.

"Lie down." He pointed to the floor so it looked like he was making some effort and the dog did exactly as she was asked. "Roll over."

Molly performed a perfect roll and bounded back up into a seated position, ready to be rewarded.

"See," Leah said. "You've got all the basics down pat. I can show you the other things I've taught her. She's very smart."

"Smart when she wants to be," he muttered, narrowing his eyes at the dog. Molly narrowed hers back.

"You don't have to do it, Kea." Leah shook her head. "Forget I even asked. And I'm not saying that to be passive-aggressive—I genuinely mean it. I'll just cancel."

It would be the smart thing to do. Let her cancel and try to make it up to her some other way. Maybe he could treat her and Molly to a weekend away once Leah was feeling better. Or maybe he could get someone to redo the flooring in a way that would remove all the squeaks.

You mean, throw money at the problem instead of doing the actual thing she wants.

Shit.

"I'll do it," he said before he could fully think about the consequences of accepting the request. Was there such a thing as decision remorse? Because something that felt a heck of a lot like it coursed through his body.

But he could hardly say that his only goal in life was to take care of his family if he wasn't willing to back it up.

Leah held up a hand. "No, don't—"

"I'll do it," he said, more resolute this time. "I'll shuffle some stuff at work."

Thomas was going to *kill* him. And right around the time he was making a hard push for named partner as well…but none of that mattered if Leah wasn't happy. Besides, how difficult could a talent show be? He'd take the dog, make her sit, stay and howl at the moon, then he'd do his work through the night and grab a few hours' sleep in the early morning.

Easy peasy.

"Are you sure?" Leah's brow furrowed. "I know it's a huge ask."

"It's fine. I'm happy to do it." He nodded.

"You're not, but I appreciate it anyway." Leah reached

out her arms and he went over to envelop her in a hug. He cradled the back of her head as he felt her melt against him.

Nothing mattered as much as this. As much as her.

He pulled away when the kettle let out a shrill whistle. "Send me an email with the details, okay?"

"I will." A small smile brightened her face, masking some of the tiredness momentarily. "You could always ask August for help?"

Keaton poured the piping hot water into the mugs and brought them over to the table. "This better not be some elaborate setup scheme."

He knew his sister would *never* fake a flare-up for any reason, but he wouldn't put it past her to seize the chance to get him and August together should the opportunity present itself organically.

"Believe me, I'm so bummed to miss out on the competition." She shook her head. Molly whined for attention and Leah stroked her head. "I only suggested it because she might be able to give you a few pointers, given she has a background in dog training."

Molly snorted as if to say, *I don't need any help. I'm fabulous just as I am.*

"It would give you a leg up," Leah added.

Maybe it wouldn't be the worst thing in the world to ask for August's help. After all, Leah was right about her experience. And frankly, Keaton would need all the help he could get in putting up with Molly the Drama Queen's antics for a whole weekend.

As if sensing his disdain, the dog swung her head toward him and whined again.

"Trust me," he said, grimacing. "The feeling is mutual."

Yeah, he was definitely going to need all the help he could get.

***

August ran the clippers down the side of the miniature poodle's legs and the dog stayed still and calm. Cream-colored fur fell onto the table where she was working.

"Aren't you a good boy?" she cooed, grabbing her comb and running it over the section she'd just shaped to free any clumps of clipped hair. "So well-behaved. Not like your little brother—he's a real handful."

What did she expect from a house where all the dogs had silk bedding?

August's pet grooming business catered to a high-end clientele—she specialized in animal influencers, pets of celebrities and other folks of a high station in life, and she had a couple of former show dogs on her schedule as well. The people who hired her often preferred to have her groom the dogs in their home and paid a premium for it.

Several of her regulars even had a permanent grooming station set up in their homes, such as the client she was currently serving. Barbara Frank was a retired lawyer and the wife of a former New York senator, and she owned four poodles. Each of the dogs was a different color and sported a different cut.

"Now we're going to clean up those feet." She gently lifted the dog's paw and clipped the fur down around the pads. Then she reached for a pair of scissors to neaten and smooth the edges where the fur stopped at the ankle joint.

For this dog's lamb cut, the face, tail and feet were shaved down, with the rest of the coat left full everywhere else. It was important to keep the lines smooth so there were no harsh stops and starts.

August continued with the scissors, sculpting the dog's fur and shaping the little puff on the end of the tail and the topknot—which was the fur on top of the head. A client had once jokingly referred to this part of the grooming as "hedge trimming" and she could totally see the comparison. After she finished blending everything with thinning shears, she released the dog's ears from the little clips holding the long hair safely back and gave them a good comb and trimmed the ends.

"You're all done, my darling. What a good boy you've been today." August went into the cupboard where Barbara kept the dog treats and fished one out for him. The dog gobbled it up happily, and then she unclipped him from the harness that prevented him from jumping off the table and placed him onto the floor.

As August was cleaning up the grooming area, her phone rang and she reached into the deep pocket of her uniform apron to fish it out. Keaton's name flashed across the screen. Her heart leaped into her throat. Oh no! What if something had happened to Leah? What other reason would he have to call her?

"Hello?" she answered breathlessly.

"It's Keaton," he said unnecessarily, like she wouldn't have looked at her screen before answering.

"Is everything okay?"

"Yes." He sounded confused.

"Oh good. I just..." She shook her head. No wonder she needed a matchmaker; she was such an awkward turtle sometimes. "What's up?"

"Are you free tonight?"

She blinked. Now it was her turn to feel confused. "Why?"

"You eat dinner, don't you?" The question was delivered with his dry sense of humor, but there was nothing funny about it. "I thought we could eat together."

Dinner with Keaton? What on earth did he want? Maybe

to apologize for overstepping when they ran into one another at that fancy restaurant? That seemed unlikely. Apologies weren't exactly Keaton's strong suit.

"It's not a trick question," Keaton said.

"Uh, well... I've got another grooming appointment booked at four. But I should be free after that," she said. Whatever Keaton's motives, she was too curious not to say yes. But if he tried to put her off Asher, then she would shut it down like she did the last time. "Where should I meet you?"

"I'll bring food to your place," he said. "Don't worry, I won't cook it myself."

August narrowed her eyes. "It's kind of weird that you're just inviting yourself over."

"You know me," he said cheerfully. "I don't play by the rules."

A truer statement had never been spoken.

She supposed some people might be annoyed, or stressed at the thought of having to clean up their house. But August kept her place neat and tidy at all times, so a drop-in guest was never an issue. She also knew that Keaton had a thing about never inviting anyone to *his* apartment. His home was his sanctuary—or his prison, depending on how you looked at it. It was the place he'd shared with his wife, and she suspected he kept it like a tomb.

But in any case, she was too damn curious to refuse him.

"Sure," she said. "I'll be home by six thirty, give me half an hour to clean up."

"Done."

As she ended the call, she tried not to think about how her younger self would have been giddy at the thought of a dinner alone with Keaton.

Younger self your ass, you feel giddy right now.

But she would need to shut that down immediately. In fact, she was going to wear her most boring, unsexy outfit. No makeup, no perfume, sweatpants and a baggy T-shirt *and*, for good measure, underwear that she would never want another living human to see. Because there was no way she'd be able to feel even a glimmer of sexiness while wearing Bridget Jones–esque granny panties.

Whatever Keaton's game was, she would be prepared.

6

The granny panties were a solid strategy, but the second she opened her front door to find Keaton on her doorstep, August knew she had vastly underestimated how strong the man's pull on her was. Whatever feelings she'd banished when it came to her best friend's older brother, they were simply lurking in the background. And ushering him into her place while he was wearing a white T-shirt that clung delectably to his muscular shoulders and arms, while a pair of dark denim jeans rode low on his hips, dragged all those unwanted feelings back into the spotlight.

She *really* needed to get over Keaton Sax. Stat.

For a moment, she felt self-conscious about her apartment being so kitschy and homey. Her bright blue couch was decorated with throw cushions featuring animal faces and a blanket patterned with black paw prints. She had half a dozen succulents dotted around the room, all in pottery that was some shade of pink, a pile of romance novels teetering on the coffee table and a baby blue mug that said "thick thighs and pretty eyes"—a gift from one of the girls in her book club.

Keaton's place was probably all chrome and white and glass. Not that she would know, because she'd never seen it.

"So, to what do I owe the pleasure of your presence?" she asked, motioning for Keaton to hang his jacket by the front door.

"Can't a friend invite themselves over to enjoy a meal?" he asked, his smile sharp-edged.

"We're not friends. We're acquaintances joined by a mutual thread."

He pressed a hand to his chest, but the smile didn't fade. "You wound me."

"What do you want, Keaton?" She narrowed her eyes at him. "Because I can't remember the last time we saw each other on purpose. And it seems rather odd timing that this invite comes after we bump into one another at a restaurant and you tell me my date is a bad guy."

"You think I'm here so I can keep bad-mouthing Asher Benson?" Keaton snorted. "Please. I have far better things to do than waste any breath on that asshole."

August bristled. So far, from what she'd seen, Asher was far from being an asshole. He was smart, funny, charming, a total gentleman. Sure, if she was being one hundred percent honest—in a way she only ever could be in her own head—there weren't exactly major sparks between them. He was a little...polished. A little preppy.

And yes, there had been a teeny tiny little *whomp whomp* noise in the back of her head when they'd shared a kiss after the last date.

But that didn't matter, because she enjoyed Asher's company and he seemed genuinely interested in who she was as a person. Chemistry was not on the checklist. And the dates had gone smoothly—not a viral incident to speak of—and he was attentive and generous. They already had a third date lined up for tomorrow and it would have been sooner if not for their busy work schedules. What more could she ask for? Fireworks and tingles, perhaps?

Those could quite possibly come later, once they'd gotten physical. Maybe the sparks wouldn't fly until they took the next step. That was totally plausible, right?

"Then why did you come?" she asked. "And I'm sorry, but I don't buy the friend thing."

Keaton pulled out a bottle of wine from the canvas bag he'd carried with him—sauvignon blanc from New Zealand, August's favorite—and held it up in question. She nodded and retrieved two stemmed glasses from the kitchen. That's when she noticed he was holding the take-out menu for one of her most beloved little restaurants. Keaton was old-school and liked to have a paper menu, rather than ordering on Uber Eats, which August thought was a funny quirk.

But this was also a red flag. The request out of the blue, her favorite wine *and* her favorite food...he wanted something.

Going to skip right over the fact that he knows all of your favorite things, huh?

Yep. Because that would make her think about even more things that didn't deserve space in her brain, like how despite trying his hardest to act like a jerk, Keaton was actually one of the most kind and generous people she knew.

"So..." he said eventually, opening the wine when she placed two glasses on the countertop. "I have a favor to ask."

"Ahh. There it is."

He shot her a disarming smile and held his glass up to hers, and she couldn't resist clinking. The sound echoed through the quiet apartment and she was suddenly aware of how she'd never been alone with him before, aside from that fateful night. Most times when she saw Keaton, it was at Leah's house, formerly their family home.

But this felt different.

"So, Leah entered Molly into some silly competition thing," he said as he poured the wine.

"Yeah, the one being run by Paws in the City. I know all about it."

Isla and Scout were holding a contest to sign on a client who otherwise might not have a big enough social following to be considered, but the whole thing was being filmed as part of the *Put Your Best Paw Forward* documentary. The filmmakers were following three different animal-based businesses for a month each, and apparently they had some big streaming service signed on. It was going to be a *huge* opportunity for Isla's agency, and the competition would make for some great television.

"I figured you would probably know something about it," Keaton said.

"The woman who runs the agency is a friend of mine." August nodded, pausing to sip her wine. It was delicious. "It's somewhere upstate, right?"

"That's right."

August had originally offered to help Isla and Scout, and Isla had wanted her there as a groomer for the contestants. Unfortunately, however, the producer's niece was *also* a dog groomer and was one of the other businesses being featured in the documentary. It had been made clear that no other groomers would be involved, since they didn't want them outshining the niece. Shame. It would have been excellent promotion. But Isla had already felt terrible enough about not being able to include her, and August didn't want to make her feel worse.

August cocked her head, a little confused by the direction of the conversation. "What does any of this have to do with you?"

"I'm taking Molly to the competition."

It probably wasn't the best response she could have had, but August burst out laughing. "You…Molly…a team? Oh come on, you've got to be joking."

But when he didn't laugh, a stone settled into the pit of her stomach. Because if he was being serious, then…

"Leah is fine," he said, as if reading her mind. "She's having a flare-up and doesn't have the energy to take Molly herself. The drive is a few hours and she needs a lot of rest right now."

"So you're taking Molly in her place?" She shouldn't feel anything, but the devotion Keaton had to his sister really was the sweetest thing ever.

But the thought of him and the husky having to not only spend a weekend together, but work as a team…

Oh boy. That's a failure waiting to happen.

"Yes. I don't want Leah to miss out on this opportunity." He cleared his throat and then took a big glug of his wine. Okay, so at least he *knew* it was going to be a failure. "Obviously, she knows not to expect amazing results given how Molly and I…"

"Hate each other," August supplied.

"Yeah."

"And you want me to do what, exactly? Give you a crash course in how to get a dog to follow instructions?"

"I was hoping you'd come with me."

She blinked. "Oh."

"I know you're busy with work, of course. It's a last-minute request, but it really would mean a lot to me and to Leah."

The words were so sincere that August had to stop herself from throwing her arms around his neck. No doubt, cocky, teasing Keaton would be back in a heartbeat and those green eyes and perfect features would go back to being a thorn in her side.

She sighed and scrubbed a hand over her face. Would it be pathetic to admit that she'd kept those days entirely free in case the producer had a change of heart and Isla was allowed to have August come along? She'd have to stay behind the scenes, of course, so as not to get in the way of Isla's big opportunity by pissing off the producer. But she had the time *and* she wanted to help Leah.

Not to mention spending all that time with Keaton.

That was an item firmly in the "con" column.

"Please," he said, looking her right in the eye. "I forgot to add that."

Jeez. How was the guy so arrogant and yet so freaking sincere at the same time?

"Fine," she said with a sigh. "I'll help out. I'll come with you."

"You won't regret it!" he said with a beaming smile.

But August had a niggling suspicion that she would.

The following Thursday August and Keaton got a late start heading upstate for the weekend, because he was stuck at work trying to finish something. Now they were going to arrive at the venue sometime around 11:30 p.m. August, who prided herself on punctuality, looked as though she was trying not to be irritated.

She was not doing a very good job.

"The competition officially starts tomorrow morning at eight," she said, after they were on the road and out of the city. It was dark out and the flashes of light from oncoming vehicles lit up her red hair, making the edges glow like fire. "So, we'll need to make sure we don't screw around too much when we arrive. We want Molly settled in and feeling rested."

"Mmm-hmm." Keaton nodded, his hands resting on the steering wheel as they headed north along I-81.

"I would suggest we get up early so I can run you through some basic things with her. Maybe six."

Keaton glanced over at her, eyebrows raised.

"You're right. We'll probably need a bit more time," she said, nodding. "Let's say five thirty. I've gone over the itinerary that Isla and Scout provided, and I have some ideas for how we can make Molly shine. Now, I can't be too involved in front of the cameras but—"

"Cameras?" Keaton shook his head as if trying to rattle a thought around.

"Yeah, the film crew will be getting footage for the documentary."

"*What* documentary?" His hands tightened on the steering wheel. Funny how his sister hadn't mentioned that little detail. "I never heard anything about a documentary."

August held up the folder in her hand. "You mean the documentary that's literally mentioned on the first page of the welcome pack that Leah emailed you?"

The welcome pack, which he definitely had not read and which August had printed out, highlighted, applied sticky tabs to and had likely memorized by now.

That welcome pack.

"You didn't even open it, did you?" She shook her head. "Typical."

"Typical what?" His shoulders hiked up a bit. August was supposed to be here to help him, not bust his balls.

"Typical *you*. You always think you can breeze into a place and command the room without doing an ounce of preparation. You fly by the seat of your pants!"

He always tried to make it look that way. Because if he appeared to breeze in, people might think they could get one by him, and he'd found that the Wall Street Sharks tended to show their true colors when they thought you weren't fully prepared. It was advantageous to have people underestimate him. It had been like that since he was a kid.

Asher Benson had underestimated him—thinking Keaton was just some pauper who'd be so scared to lose his position at the firm that he'd put up with anything to keep it.

Wrong.

"So, has the matchmaker organized you another date?" he asked.

"You're trying to change the topic."

"Not trying," he said, shooting her a cocky grin. "Succeeding."

She rolled her eyes and, in the back, Molly let out a loud huff. The dog was mercifully docile tonight, but Keaton wasn't sure how long that luck would last. Something told him that grace tonight would mean a world of annoyance tomorrow. But right now, they had miles and miles of highway in front of them and nothing else to do.

He could figure out the dog competition when they arrived. For now, he wanted to know where August stood with Asher Benson.

"Did you wait until I was trapped in a car with you to bring this up?" she asked, burrowing back into the passenger-side seat.

"Of course not," he lied. "That's merely a coincidence."

"Why do you even care? And don't give me this 'we're friends' bullshit, okay? Because we've gone over that already."

Just because they didn't hang out, didn't mean they weren't friends, at least in his mind. But clearly she'd taken his teasing to heart.

"You're like family to me." That, at least, wasn't a lie. August might not be related to him by blood, but he'd known her since she was thirteen and she was important to Leah. Therefore, she was important to him.

"You think of me as a little sister?" August's expression was difficult to read.

"I didn't say that." As much as it would be easier if she fit squarely into that category, then he would feel even more gross about being attracted to her. "More like a distant second cousin twice removed..."

She snorted. "You're sending mixed messages."

I know.

"Why are you so reluctant to tell me about it?"

If she saw the tactic of switching the spotlight back to her, she didn't call it out.

"Are you going to judge me for using a matchmaker?" she asked.

"No. I mean, I don't really understand why you think you need one, but if that's what all the kids are doing today..."

She snorted. "You make it sound like you're *so* much older than me. Two years is nothing."

It wasn't his age that made him feel that way. It was the fact that he'd lived an entire life's worth of pain in his thirty-two years. While she, on the cusp of thirty, was still hopeful and eager and naive. It felt like an ocean between them.

"Why did you want to see a matchmaker?" he asked. "I'm genuinely curious."

"I'm sure you have no idea what this feels like, but..."

She glanced out of the window, as if trying to hide herself away from him. "Dating is scary. You don't know if the guy is going to be a creeper or if he's going to assume your only purpose in life is to pop out children or if he's going to think you need to lose weight to deserve him."

"I don't know which one of those things pisses me off more." Keaton frowned. "You've seriously had a guy tell you to lose weight?"

"Not directly," she said. "But you get the meaning behind the words. He was overly concerned about my health when there's nothing at all wrong with me. I'm healthy as a horse, according to my doctor. But he kept making comments about how being overweight leads to all kinds of problems."

August was a full-figured woman. He wasn't sure how you were supposed to describe that these days—curvy, plus-size or something else. All he knew was that he found her attractive and the idea that someone would think she needed to change her body to be "worth" their attention…

Oh boy. It made his blood boil like lava.

"People are assholes," Keaton grumbled. "You look great just as you are. Don't listen to anyone who tells you to change."

"You think I look great?" There was a hint of amusement in her voice, almost like she didn't believe him. Like he was pulling her leg.

He didn't want to do his usual joking thing now and brush off what he'd said, because it might make her feel bad about herself and she didn't deserve that. But if he backed the statement up…

Shit.

Why did he have to dig himself into these holes?

"Oh come on, August," he scoffed. "You know you're an attractive woman. Asher Benson clearly thinks so."

There, direct it back to the guy she's dating. Much safer.

"He does, and I feel the same about him." It sounded like she was trying to draw some barriers, too.

"You know they used to call him Egg Head in the bullpen, right?" He chuckled. "All that forehead and blond hair..."

"Stop it." She narrowed her eyes at him. "If you must know, we've had three dates so far and they all went well. I'm planning to see him after we get back."

For some reason, that made Keaton's skin crawl. She could do *so* much better.

It's none of your business. Stay out of it.

He'd do his best to keep his mouth shut, but the first hint he got that Egg Head wasn't treating her right, he would show up on that guy's doorstep to teach him a lesson.

What the hell was going on with Keaton? He was acting so weird lately.

After his persistent probing about the matchmaker, August changed the topic of conversation back to the activities that lay ahead of them—three days of competition, where entrants would be eliminated round by round until Paws in the City had their winner and newest client. She wanted Keaton to have his game face on, because this would *not* be an easy competition.

She'd spoken with Isla earlier to let her know that she was coming along to help out her best friend, while also promising that she would keep her mouth shut about the grooming business so she didn't piss of the documentary producer. Isla was delighted, since she'd wanted to include August from the beginning, but of course there would be no favorites played. She could never accept special treatment.

Molly would be standing on her own four paws...especially

since she was likely to get minimal help from Keaton. And Isla had hinted that they had some amazing contestants to be excited about.

It would be stiff competition.

August glanced over her shoulder to check on the dog, who was happily snoozing in the back seat, secured with a harness. Then she glanced at Keaton, whose eyes were fixed on the road ahead. He was impossibly handsome. Sharp jawed and green eyed and a smile that—on the rare occasion it was genuine—could power a hemisphere. She knew he hid himself behind layers and layers of self-defenses. He had ever since he was a teenager. Leah could be the same way.

Truthfully, so could August.

The misfit trio had been broken by things that'd happened in the past. For Keaton, it was the period of time where he went off the rails and lost his grip on who he was. For Leah, it was watching her mother fall apart after Keaton got sent away. For August, it was knowing that for her parents, she would never be enough.

He was right, they *were* like family. But that hadn't stopped years of very *un*-platonic urges on her part, even after he'd moved on and married someone else.

"Thank God," Keaton muttered as he flicked the indicator to turn off the highway. "I thought we were going to cross the border into Canada at any moment."

"Don't you trust your GPS?" she said.

"I don't trust anything."

The car navigated through increasingly smaller roads, until they found a few poorly lit signs indicating that they were heading to a place called Wild Woods Retreat.

The competition was being held at what was essentially a summer camp for adults and their furry BFFs, channeling nostalgic childhood vibes but with the adult luxuries of proper beds, rather than bunks, and private bathrooms and showers. And the animal patrons were in for a great time, including grooming and specialty home-cooked meals. All the staff were trained in animal handling and they had a vet on-site, too. There were fishing spots, hiking trails, campfires and a big hall where all the major activities and meals would take place.

It looked adorably rustic chic, in August's opinion. She wasn't exactly sure how Keaton—who thought five-star was the only rating that existed—was going to like it, however.

They pulled into the campground and found the only building with the lights on. That would likely be the reception area. A sign saying "humans and animals welcome" hung on the side of the building, where a mural of cats and dogs was painted. Leaving Molly to snooze in the car while they checked in, August followed Keaton inside.

"Hi there, welcome to Wild Woods Retreat." A woman stood behind the counter, wearing a polo shirt with the logo embroidered at her chest. She wore thick glasses and had a bright smile, despite the late hour. "You must be Keaton Sax."

Keaton blinked. "Uh, yes. That's right."

"No psychic powers, don't worry." She laughed. "You're just the last to check in. Now, I had a Leah Sax down originally for the booking, but I believe you're taking her place."

"That's right. I'm Leah's brother. My apologies for the late arrival." Like that, Keaton's smooth mode was turned on and the woman behind the counter had her eyes locked onto him.

August had seen it before. When he wanted to turn on the charm, people were magnetized to him and he eclipsed everyone else in the room. Oh to have that kind of social presence! She could only dream about it. Although, if she was being totally honest, she preferred Keaton when he was snarky and unpolished, because he had a wicked sense of humor…even if he did like to turn it on her frequently.

"That's no problem at all!" the woman simpered, flushing. "We're happy you made it here safe and sound."

"We'll need two rooms. One for myself and one for my associate, Ms. Merriweather."

Ms. Merriweather?

She raised an eyebrow but didn't say anything.

"Uh, that's um…" The woman behind the desk shook her head. "I'm afraid we're fully booked. There are no spare rooms."

August pressed her lips together to smother the words that nearly jumped out before she could stop them.

Oh shit.

7

"Excuse me?" August came around to stand next to Keaton. He could tell she was almost vibrating with stress. "I was under the impression that when Leah called to let you know about the change, she asked for two rooms."

At least, that's what had been agreed on. Leah said she would call ahead to let them know about the switch and ask for the extra room. It was certainly possible she *had* done all that and simply forgotten to tell him they were booked out.

It was also possible she'd chosen to keep that information to herself.

The woman flipped through a book at the front desk, looking flustered. "I don't have any record of that and we just gave our last room away two hours ago. I'm so sorry."

Right, so Leah hadn't asked about the extra room. It was

official. The second they got back to New York, Keaton was going to murder his little sister.

"Goddammit, Leah," he muttered under his breath, shaking his head.

Why on earth did August think she needed a matchmaker when his sister was subtle as a hammer? This was getting ridiculous.

"There are *no* rooms at all?" August's eyes pleaded with the woman behind the counter. "What about close by?"

"We're the only business around here for a few miles. The nearest town is forty to fifty minutes away, but..." She glanced at the clock on the wall. "Nothing will be open at this hour."

It wasn't exactly high tourism season as the summer rush was still a month away, which was probably why they were able to book the entire retreat for the competition.

"I can call your event organizer and see if there's any way we could shuffle some people around." The woman reached for the phone.

"It's fine." Keaton held up his hand and looked at August, whose eyes were wide. "It's almost midnight and we don't want anyone to get dragged out of bed at this hour. I'm sure we can deal with the situation for the evening and then when everyone is up tomorrow, we can look at solutions."

August didn't seem convinced, but she also didn't protest. She wasn't the type to want anyone else to be inconvenienced, either.

"I'm so sorry again," the woman said.

"We'll be fine," he reassured her, although inside his gut was already waving red flags like there was no tomorrow. Sharing a room with August? That was going to test his resolve to keep her at a distance.

The staff member looked visibly relieved. "Here's your key.

You're in cabin 19 and everything you need is already inside. Breakfast will be in the big hall, and if you need anything, you can simply dial 1 on the phone in your room and that will put you through to the front desk."

"Thank you very much," Keaton replied with a warm smile as he took the key and headed back out into the night. August followed.

"Your sister..." She shook her head.

"*Your* best friend," he replied. "Maybe you should get her a job at the matchmaking agency, because she clearly is showing an aptitude for it."

"No, she's *not.* We're the worst possible match!" August threw her hands in the air. "If this was a match she made for real, then she would be fired."

He stifled a laugh as she stomped toward the car, hands balled into fists.

"Me thinks the lady doth protest too much," he said under his breath.

For some reason, that made the inside of his chest feel warm where he'd felt nothing at all for the past ten years.

He got into the car and they drove slowly through the campground, counting the numbers of the cabins they drove past and following the pointed signs indicating whether they should go left or right. Eventually, they found their accommodation tucked into some dense trees. A single light was on outside to welcome them, and Molly grumbled when August woke her up. Keaton fetched the luggage from the trunk, and then he unlocked the cabin's front door.

A quick peek inside confirmed his suspicions that there was only one bed. Great.

"I'll sleep on the floor," he said, and he held the door open for August and Molly. The dog trotted inside, immediately spotted the cushy-looking dog bed that had been set up and made a beeline for it.

"Don't be ridiculous. It's hardwood flooring," August said. "You'll give yourself a bad back."

"You calling me old?"

"You called *yourself* old before."

August wheeled her suitcase into the room and he followed, closing the door behind them. Despite the charming and rustic nature of the cabin, the locks were electronic, hinting that although they were deep in the middle of nowhere, they weren't totally without technology. Still, glancing around the room with the exposed-beam details and bed that looked designed for snuggling—read, small—Keaton was regretting his desire to help his sister out with every fiber of his being.

How the heck was he going to get through a whole night of sleeping next to August? What if he accidentally touched her in the middle of the night? What if she rolled into him and he had a morning wood? What if—

Stop it. You're an adult. You can handle this. Just deal with the back pain tomorrow.

"You're not sleeping on the floor, Keaton," August said as if reading his mind. "I won't hear it."

"I didn't bring pajamas," he said.

She gulped. "I'd offer to lend you some of mine but..."

"Hello Kitty isn't really my style," he quipped.

"I don't wear Hello Kitty pajamas anymore," she said, her cheeks reddening. "That was... I was a kid."

Molly momentarily lifted her head up from the dog basket and then plopped it back down, as if deciding their angst was not enough to sustain her interest. Smart dog.

"I'm going to get changed in the bathroom," she said, walking away without looking at him. A second later, the door closed.

Keaton decided the best thing to do would be to get this over with as quickly as possible. He stripped down to his underwear—really, he *never* wore pajamas—and flicked off all the lights, except the lamp right next to the bed. Then he got under the covers and rolled so he was facing the wall. That way August could get in behind him and keep as much distance as she felt comfortable with.

He tried to fall asleep, but his mind was sharp and wired as though his body was plugged into an infinite energy source. Facing the wall, he couldn't see August when she climbed into bed beside him, but he felt the shift of the bed and the rustle of the sheets. He smelled the sweet fruity lotion on her skin and heard the soft, tense sound of her breath as she tried to get comfortable beside him.

Ignore everything. Do not react. Do not move. Play dead.

But Keaton's mind was alight. His head was filled with flickering images of August standing in the bathroom, peeling the clothes from her skin, revealing the curves that she said others didn't appreciate. He imagined her fair skin and long, red hair and the flush in her cheeks.

It was a damn good thing he wasn't lying on his back or else he'd be tenting the sheets.

Forcing himself to stare into the darkness, he remained still as a statue, not daring to move. Barely daring to breathe. He waited for the tension to ease in the air and the body next to him to melt into slumber. Only then could he even contemplate drifting off himself. Something told him the next few days were going to be far more difficult than he could have anticipated. Difficult in ways he never expected.

Because in that moment, he wanted the one thing he couldn't allow himself to want…

Her.

The following morning, August's body was so stiff it felt like she'd gone to the gym for the first time in years. Turned out doing your best impression of a log for eight hours straight was quite hard on the muscles. Or was it more like an impression of a hot dog?

Stop thinking about phallic objects.

Shaking her head, she strode through the retreat's large hall where everyone was currently having breakfast, looking for either Scout or Isla. Molly was back in the room, having already enjoyed a breakfast of gourmet homemade dog food that was supplied to each contestant. The plan was to listen to an opening address from Isla about how day one was going to work, and then they would go back and collect Molly for the first lot of activities.

August's idea to wake up early and run through some training exercises with Keaton had fallen by the wayside when he'd gotten up to shower and she'd pretended to still be asleep in order to preserve her sanity. She glanced back to where he was sitting, looking as though he'd slept about as well as she had. His dark hair was sticking up on one side and his jaw was coated in a wonderful shadow of stubble that gave him a dark edge and made his green eyes look even brighter. It seemed he'd already caught the attention of some female attendees, and two women had sat themselves down beside him, smiles wide and inviting.

It was almost disgusting how easily he attracted the opposite sex—and sometimes the same sex—and yet he seemed to make no effort at all. Meanwhile August felt like she had to comb, tweeze, wax, primp and pray her way into a compliment. It was patently unfair.

The hall was filled with long communal-style tables in the middle and a strip of trestle tables with breakfast foods on either side. They had a great selection, including three different types of toast, eggs that were soft and fluffy, bacon, homemade granola, yogurt and even a TIY—top it yourself—pancake station. But August's love of the most important meal of the day was currently stifled by her need to figure out where she was going to be sleeping the next few nights.

She spotted a familiar face across the room. "Isla!"

Her friend and fellow businesswoman looked up, smiling and waving. Isla's dark hair was pulled back into a sleek yet bouncy ponytail and her blue eyes were enhanced by expertly applied makeup. She wore a blue dress with white roses all over it and looked, as always, like a million bucks.

"You're so glamorous." August pressed a hand to her chest. "I *love* that dress."

"Thanks. I bought myself a few new pieces knowing this was all going to be filmed." Isla laughed and she sounded a little anxious. "Dear lord, please let this go well!"

August immediately felt guilty for bothering her friend with such a trivial problem when it was clear she was already stressed-out. But if she had any hope of getting through the next few days without losing her mind, she couldn't be sleeping next to Keaton each night. As it was, she'd sneaked a peek of him coming out of the bathroom shirtless, with a pair of jeans slung low on his hips, and water dotting his skin. If that image wasn't enough to fuel her self-love sessions for the rest of her life, she didn't know what was.

Which part of "off-limits" is not getting through your thick skull?

Never mind the fact that she was supposed to be lusting

after the guy who was a much better match for her: Asher Benson. And yet, mysteriously, he had not once entered her mind since she arrived here last night.

"I'm sure it will go amazingly. This is such an exciting opportunity." August looked around the room, catching a glimpse of a tall guy with a big camera hefted onto his shoulders following a woman with a microphone. "Excited to see your face on television?"

"Ack, don't remind me." Isla buried her face in her hands for a moment, before realizing that she shouldn't mess up her makeup and pulling out a compact from her pocket to double-check everything was in place. "You know me, I'm all about that 'behind the scenes' action. Never once have I wanted to be the subject of anyone's attention."

Understandable, since the entire catalyst for Isla starting her own agency had been a viral video that ousted her from her job and the entire social media industry for a while. If August thought the video of her bad date was bad, it was *nothing* compared to what Isla had gone through.

"This will do such amazing things for your business." August reached out and squeezed her friend's arm. "You're killing it, girl. It's inspiring."

"That really means a lot coming from you. I so admire what you've built with your grooming business." Isla's shoulders dropped a little and a smile brightened her face. "How's everything going? Did you sleep well last night?"

"Uhh…about that," August said, but before she could launch into her request, a woman August guessed was the producer approached Isla and completely butted in to the conversation.

"If we want to stick to the schedule, we'll need to start the morning address now," the woman said, a commanding, no-nonsense attitude radiating in the air around her.

"Sorry, August, I have to take a minute to prep for the welcome speech." Isla was back to looking anxious again. "But let's catch up later, okay? There's a fun trivia evening on the schedule for all the contestants tonight, but Scout and I were planning to slip off for a quiet dinner in our suite. You should join us."

Oh, a suite! Maybe she could bunk in with her friends.

"Theo and Lane are coming up tonight," Isla added. "It would be great to get our little group together."

August's heart sank. If the guys were bunking in the suite too, there was no way she could ask to crash. Maybe if she circled back to the reception area today, they might be able to sort something out.

"That sounds great," August replied with forced cheer, not wanting to stress her friend out.

"And bring you friend's brother, too. Keaton, right? I'd love to meet him outside all this chaos."

Before August could respond, Isla was whisked away. Great. For the moment, she was stuck sharing a room with Keaton, but hopefully not for too much longer.

She made her way back through the hall to where Keaton was sitting, looking like a deer in headlights as three women crowded his space, vying for his attention. When he saw August heading toward him, his gaze locked onto her as if trying to telepathically convince her to rescue him. It was funny to see him like that, looking so out of his element. Part of her wanted to leave him there to teach him a lesson for prying into her dating life, but she couldn't do that to him.

"Come on, Kea, let's get ourselves a coffee before the morning address starts." She came up behind him and placed a protective hand on his shoulder, leaning in close to his ear and saying softly, "You owe me one."

"Right. Coffee. Yes." He nodded, and August stepped back to let him get off the bench lining the table. "Please excuse me, caffeine calls."

August tried not to chuckle as the women deflated when Keaton hurried to leave. Poor things, they'd looked so enamored with him.

I know how you feel, ladies. But it's best not to get your hopes up.

"I should have left you there," she said as they headed toward the large urns of coffee set up on the side of the room. "If you shack up with someone, I'll get the room to myself."

He narrowed his eyes at her. "Not on your life. I'd rather sleep in the mud."

"Oh come on, they seemed lovely." August glanced back. "If a little…forward."

"One of them tried to convince me to invest in her 'fortune candle' business."

She wrinkled her nose. "Fortune-telling candles?"

"Not fortune like telling, fortune like cookies. The candles have a printed paper message inside them that's revealed when the candle is burned down." He shook his head. "Ridiculous."

"Isn't that a fire hazard?" It didn't seem like a wise idea. "And how do you get the piece of paper out without getting melted wax all over your fingers?"

"Thank you." He tossed his hands into the air. "Apparently asking those questions means I'm 'stifling creativity' or some bullshit."

August snorted. "Didn't seem to put them off talking to you."

"She thought she was on an episode of *Shark Tank*."

"Ah, that's what you get for wearing a Rolex."

Keaton glared at her. "I do *not* wear a Rolex. They're ostentatious."

"Right, better to pick an obscure luxury brand that screams wealth in a more subtle way." She chuckled as they reached the coffee station and grabbed a cup for each of them. "Much classier."

"I own literally one watch," he protested.

"And how much did it cost, huh? Feel free to round up to the nearest thousand, if you like," she teased.

He rolled his eyes. "Your ability to annoy is unparalleled."

"Oh, you don't like it when the tables are turned, huh?" she replied gleefully. "How does it feel to be on the receiving end for once?"

"You know me, I much prefer to give than to receive."

There was a dark edge in his voice and August got the impression she was treading on dangerous ground. But why the hell should she feel bad for teasing him when he did it all the damn time? She was going to hard pass on that double standard.

"Don't be a wimp, Keaton."

"*I'm* a wimp? Oh, that's rich." He held his coffee cup under the spout for the dark roast coffee. "I would say, even richer than my watch."

"What's that supposed to mean?"

"You were the one who went scampering off to your friend first thing this morning to see if they'd give us another room. Worried you can't control yourself for a few nights? I thought you had more willpower than that."

Oh, he did *not* just say that to her.

"For me to even think about engaging my willpower, a single cell in my entire body would need to be attracted to you, which sadly for you, is not the case," she retorted.

A lupine grin made his green eyes sparkle with mischievous delight. "Then stay tonight. Don't pressure the venue to shuffle everyone around. If you don't have any attraction to me at all, then it shouldn't be a problem to share a room, now should it?"

Damn him.

Keaton was so adept at laying out his spider's web that she didn't even know it was there until she stuck her big fly ass right onto it. She gritted her back teeth. "Don't you want a bed to yourself for comfort's sake?"

"I slept fine last night." He finished filling up his coffee cup and didn't put any milk or cream in. Masochist. "In fact, I would say I haven't slept that good in a while."

It was a bald-faced lie and they both knew it. He'd woken up with just as many bags under his eyes as she had—between them, they could open a luggage chain. But oh no, Keaton had to puff out his chest and make it a competition like he always did. The man couldn't back down in the face of a challenge. His ego was something else.

Be the bigger person and just admit you slept poorly, and then keep trying to get another room.

But something stopped her from being able to utter the words aloud. Clearly, he wasn't the only one with a stubborn, competitive streak. She hated that he thought he could always get one over on her, no matter the circumstance, and the last thing she wanted to do was *anything* that would feed his overinflated ego.

"I slept great, too," she replied airily. "It's lucky that talking with you has such a sedative effect on me. I should do it more often."

His jaw twitched and satisfaction surged through her. Screw Keaton and his teasing. The guy was going to get a taste of his own medicine this weekend, because she was sick of him always getting the upper hand.

"That's low," he said, narrowing his eyes.

"Not low enough." She shot him a saccharine smile, but instead of making him look more irritated, it seemed to have the opposite effect.

"Looks like we'll keep sharing the room, then." He held up his coffee cup for them to clink glasses. "That is, unless you change your mind."

"Not unless you change yours first." She touched her coffee cup to his. "Game on, Keaton."

"Game on, August."

8

Keaton was a man with many regrets, and yet he seemed to be throwing more on the pile with every second that passed. Agreeing to take his sister's place in this competition? Regret. Not having his assistant double-check that the accommodation was sorted out? Regret. Goading August into staying in the room with him? Regret.

Thinking even for a second that he could tell this damn husky what to do? Major regret.

Molly looked up at him with icy blue eyes as if to say, *If you think I'm going to listen to you, then you're even more of a fool than you look.*

"Don't get frustrated," August said. "Let's try again."

They were standing outside in an area that had been designated for owners to practice with their dogs, while contestants were brought in front of the judges one at a time. The grounds of the summer camp–style retreat were beautiful; even he could admit that. There were fir and spruce trees everywhere, adorable little cabins dotted around, and he could even spy black-and-red-check beanbag chairs placed around a firepit. It was a little too easy to imagine snuggling up with August on one while they roasted marshmallows.

But that was not what he was supposed to be concentrating on right now. They had only a minute to impress the judges with their "speed trick round," and August was convinced they could get Molly to shine like the star she supposedly was.

Keaton, however, was not convinced.

"Watch me." August stood in front of Molly, a small treat enclosed in her fist. "Molly, sit."

The dog sat, its eyes locked on the treat hand.

"Good girl. Now, lie down." She pointed to the floor and the dog complied. "Roll. Roll the other way. Up. Stay."

The dog sat on its hind legs, perfectly balanced and eye completely on the prize.

"Sit. Speak." The dog barked in response. "Sing for me, girl."

The husky threw her head back and let out an *oh wrow wrow* sound that had a few people around them laughing.

"Shake." August held out her free hand. "Good girl. Other paw."

The dog executed every command perfectly and happily gobbled up her treat when August opened her fist.

"See," she said. "She's smart and well trained."

"Too smart," Keaton muttered. Because she would only perform the commands when someone else asked. Which was a problem. Sixty seconds was not a long time to impress and the teams with the ten lowest scores would go into an elimination round.

He couldn't go home on the first day!

Why not? It would certainly solve the problem with the room. Molly would be happy to get away from you ASAP and you could head back to Manhattan tonight.

Flunking would solve *all* his problems. But there was something in Keaton that wouldn't allow him to blow it on purpose. Not just because it would feel wrong to let his sister down, but also because that wasn't how he was wired. Losing wasn't an option.

"Now you try." August put the treat in Keaton's hand.

Sighing, he looked at Molly. "Sit."

The dog remained standing.

"Fine, stand."

Molly flopped dramatically to the floor like a basketball player trying to draw a foul. Then she rolled on her back and stuck all her feet in the air, pretending to be dead.

August snorted. "She's a drama queen, that is for *sure.*"

"Molly, roll."

The dog raised her head at him, glared and then flopped back down onto the ground. Around them, a few people tittered, and Keaton scrubbed a hand over his face. The fact was, he might not have much of a say in whether he went home tonight—the dog could take care of it for him.

"Can't you do it?" Keaton asked. "She listens to you."

"I promised Isla I would stay in the background. Besides, I have a business relationship with Paws in the City…it would be unethical for me to be the key person handling Molly. I can't put Isla in that position."

He sighed. "Well, you might want to go back to your room and pack your bags. I suspect we'll be going home soon."

At that moment, a woman in a Wild Woods Retreat uniform came outside, holding a clipboard. "Can the final group of contestants please come inside?"

"That's us." Keaton clipped Molly's lead onto her collar and the dog reluctantly stood.

"Just do your best," August said. "Remember, commanding voice and strong, clear instructions. She knows what to do."

Keaton was grateful to be in the last group, because that had given him the maximum time to try to bond with Molly. Too bad the husky looked at him like he was a piece of gum stuck to her paw. He'd tried praise, pats, being authoritative. Nothing worked. Not even her favorite treats would get her to listen.

All the other animals here were *perfectly* well-behaved. Even Fortune Candle Lady seemed to have a masterful control of the small cotton ball dog at her feet. He'd seen the little thing dancing on its hind legs outside, pink tongue lolling out of its mouth. About seventy-five percent of the people here had dogs with them, but he'd also seen a guinea pig, a parrot, a cat and even some kind of lizard.

The Wild Woods Retreat staff member called on the first person in their group and Molly looked up at him. *"Wrow, wrow, wrow."*

"Save it for the judges," Keaton said.

This hall was slightly smaller than the one where they'd had breakfast. Cameras were set up around the area where the animals would be performing, and another was trained on the table where the judges were sitting. There were four in total—Isla and Scout, the two women who ran Paws in the City, a man named Alvin who ran a very successful Instagram account for his dog, an Italian greyhound named Minnie. The final judge was a woman who worked as an animal trainer in Hollywood, and had flown in after filming a series for Netflix.

The woman who'd been called to the stage was in her late forties or early fifties. Accompanying her was a cute little dog with enormous ears shaped like butterfly wings and one of those tails that could double as a feather duster. There was a ballerina vibe about her outfit, including a dress with a flippy skirt, pink tights and flat round-toed shoes with bows on top. The other contestants watched nervously as the woman and her dog paused in front of the judges.

"Please introduce yourself to the judges," the woman with the clipboard said.

"Hello, I'm Lisa and this is my dog, Mariposa. We're both from Connecticut." She smiled brightly. Her hair was slicked back into a bun so tight, Keaton thought it was a miracle she could still blink.

"What are you going to show us in your allocated minute?" Alvin asked. "Something tells me you're going with a dancing theme."

"That's right. Mariposa and I compete in Canine Freestyle Dancing. I've created a very short routine to show off her skills."

"Great." Isla clapped her hands together. "I can't wait to see. Play the music."

Some classical piano music played through a speaker and the sound was tinny, echoing off the high walls of the hall. It seemed to make it hard for Lisa to follow the beat, and the dog, taking her cues from her owner, struggled to follow instructions. The dog was cute—with a fluffy white body and mostly black head and ears—but she seemed a bit overwhelmed. There were a few times when it was clear she didn't know exactly what was going on and Lisa hissed the instructions repeatedly. Toward the end, they found a groove and the dog wove through her owner's legs effortlessly, her feather duster tail wagging with glee.

When the music came to a stop, Molly made a snorting sound. *Amateurs.*

Keaton had to stop himself from telling the husky not to judge, because he was still prepared for the dog to go all "selective hearing" on him. Although he had to admit, it eased his worries a little to see that maybe not *all* the contestants were as perfectly trained as he'd first thought. After asking a few questions, the judges bid Lisa and Mariposa farewell, and asked them to wait outside until the results were tallied.

The next few contestants went through the same schedule—a brief introduction, a one-minute spotlight of the animal's talents, more questions at the end and instructions to wait for results.

"Could Keaton and Molly please come through?"

"Let's go," Keaton said to Molly. "Are you going to do my sister proud? I sure hope so."

Molly's side-eye—which had been solidly at "turn a man to stone" status for the last twenty-four hours—didn't fill him with confidence. As Keaton walked toward the floor, he heard the other contestants talking quietly amongst themselves.

"...looks familiar? Reminds me of that guy who played Superman."

"...disaster waiting to happen. Did you see *that dog outside?"*

"...something tells me he's a plant... Too handsome for this..."

He shut the opinions out and walked calmly toward the judges, who greeted him warmly. When he explained he was there with Molly to help his sister out, everyone made an *aww* sound. Hopefully the friendly reception would put the husky at ease.

"Okay, please take the floor." Isla gestured for him to get started with their series of tricks.

The lenses of the cameras made sweat bead along Keaton's hairline. Earlier that morning, just after breakfast, they'd been required to sign release forms. Even though the cameras were there to focus on Isla's business and her quest to find a hot new client they could mold into a social media superstar, they were taking loads of footage of the competition…and Keaton *really* didn't like being the center of attention.

But his gut told him it would take a certified miracle to make it out of the first round. Perhaps it would be a blessing to be released from this personal hell.

"Ready?" he said under his breath to Molly, who was sitting regally by his side. Then he looked back at the judges, who were all waiting eagerly.

Keaton felt a stab of self-consciousness—which was something he hadn't felt for a long time. Not since he was the poor kid in the fancy private school where he didn't belong. Standing with lights shining on him, he had that same feeling of not belonging.

Curse you, Leah. Why am I such a sucker?

"Okay, Molly. Let's see how many different tricks we can do in sixty seconds." He waited for the woman keeping time to hit the stopwatch.

"Go!" she said.

"Molly, up." He started with something simple and the dog mercifully did as she was asked, standing up. "Shake."

He held out his hand and the husky looked at him, then at his hand, then back at him again. Then, because it was clear the husky was *not* going to let him be the one in charge, she turned in a circle.

"Okay, so we're turning. Now, drop down." He pointed

to the floor like August had shown him this morning, using his most commanding voice. But Molly didn't want to drop down, instead she sat back on her hind legs and brought her front paws up as if begging for a treat. "This isn't funny, girl. Drop."

The dog landed back down on all four paws, but instead of getting down on her belly, she put her paw up to shake. There was a giggle from the judges' table, and while not unkind, Keaton felt his cheeks go red.

"Sing," he commanded.

This time Molly dropped to the ground. Oh yeah, she was *really* fucking with him.

"Roll."

Molly got back to her feet.

"Play dead."

Molly howled at the sky.

Lord help him with this dog. The entire minute ticked by with excruciating slowness, while the husky performed an impressive array of tricks…though sadly not ever at the time they were requested. She jumped when he asked her to sit. She played dead when he asked her to smile. And she walked backward in a circle when he asked her to shake.

But by the end of the minute, all four judges were howling with laughter and clapping their hands.

"Oh my God," Isla said, wiping a tear from her eye. "I have never seen anything so funny. Who was expecting a comedy act today?"

"Not me." Scout shook her head, her eyes crinkled with amusement. She wore a fitted top that showed off her pregnant belly, which she cradled with one hand. "I have no idea how you taught her to do all those things but then do the opposite of the command you were giving her…but that was *genius*!"

"You have our attention," the Hollywood trainer said, nodding. "Thoroughly impressed."

Alvin whipped out a brightly colored silk pocket square from the pocket of his purple blazer and dabbed at his eye, still laughing. "That's a big thumbs-up from me. Hilarious!"

High praise that was absolutely *not* deserved. So much for getting laughed off the stage and heading home. He looked down at the husky and would have sworn that she winked at him.

Get a grip. Dogs do not wink.

"Looks like we might be staying here a while," he muttered to her as they walked offstage. "For better or worse."

Sure enough, when the bottom-scoring contestants were called to attend an additional session—where they would have a second chance to impress the judges before some were eliminated—Keaton and Molly were not on the list.

August realized that if several people were eliminated from the competition on the first day, there should be more rooms available! She hadn't even thought of that last night, but of course the knockout competition style would mean fewer people at the resort with each passing day. She *could* move into someone else's room now and do so without having to inconvenience any other contestants or the Paws in the City team.

Only…

Why did she have to get into a verbal sparring match with Keaton about the room thing? Because now, even though she had the perfect solution available, it would seem like she was the one backing down. Chickening out. Proving that she couldn't handle sharing a room and a bed with him.

In the worst-case scenario, it might make her look like she was attracted to him!

Over my dead body will I ever *admit that.*

What to do? What to do? An idea sparked as she was making herself a coffee in the main hall, while Keaton headed back to the room with Molly so he could squeeze in some work before he was required again for the competition. What if she made *him* want to get his own room? Perhaps that would require nothing more than her being a little obnoxious, and then he would have to be the one to back down.

She stifled a laugh. It would serve Keaton right, since he was always so happy to get her worked up with his teasing barbs. Maybe the man deserved a little of his own medicine. Buoyed, she enjoyed her coffee and a cookie from the snack table before heading back to the room. She wanted him to be deep in the zone when she started annoying him.

Walking slowly through the retreat's grounds, August sucked in the clean air and the fresh scent of earth and green leaves. A woman was kicking a ball around with a large shepherd dog of some kind, and another woman was lounging on the grass reading a book while her dog curled up by her side. Distant laughter carried on the breeze, but otherwise it was quiet. Peaceful. She couldn't remember the last time she'd gotten out of the city and enjoyed the lack of honking and flashing lights and the ever-present smell of street pretzels, car fumes and garbage.

"You need to do this more often," she said to herself, tipping her face up to the sun and letting it warm her skin.

But the life of a solo businesswoman didn't exactly make a lot of time for vacations. Part of that was her own fault, because August packed her schedule to the brim, working as hard as she could and squirreling the money away into her savings account so she could be independent.

Independent…but not alone.

Because years of aching loneliness inside her own family made her want to find a place to belong. To be welcomed and appreciated. To feel that she was enough.

And her best chance of success in finding someone like that was *without* relying on messy, unpredictable things like passion and chemistry and emotion.

A practical partnership, *that's* what she wanted.

That tingly, stomach-fluttery, make-your-cheeks-go-hot feeling she got from Keaton?

Absolutely *not* on her wish list.

9

August shut the cabin door quietly behind her and was surprised to find Keaton sitting on the bed, staring at Molly, who appeared to be glaring at him from across the room. His laptop was on the bed, shut, and he looked at August as she walked in.

"Work not going well?" she asked.

"It's going fine." Keaton frowned. "But I'm getting the 'I'm going to kill you in your sleep' eyes from this one."

He flicked his hand in Molly's direction and the dog snorted.

"If she wanted you dead, you'd *be* dead already," August said, biting down on her lip to stifle a laugh. Their hate-hate relationship was amusing. Keaton had never really been a dog person and Molly was...well, Molly.

She plopped down onto the bed beside him, letting her thigh brush against his and ignoring her instinct to put a little space between them. Since all his teasing and fake flirting—she was *sure* it was fake—was nothing more than sport to him, acting the same would put him on the back foot.

"Congratulations on not getting kicked out of the competition on the first day," she said. "That's exciting!"

"I'm ecstatic," he replied dryly.

"I can tell. You're practically bursting with joy." Holding her laugh in was even harder watching his less-than-impressed expression, but he didn't move away from her. *Why* wasn't he moving away? "But I think we should get in a little practice time with you and Molly. It's lucky the judges thought her whole 'you can't tell me what to do' shtick was a routine and not a personality trait."

Keaton snorted. "They'll find out the truth soon enough."

"You hoping to throw it so you can go home?"

"My life would certainly be easier if Molly threw a hissy fit and they sent us packing." He looked at her a little guiltily. "But I couldn't do that to Leah."

"Even if she conspired to have us in the same cabin?"

"To be fair, *I* was the one who asked you to come along and help me."

August rolled her eyes. "She told us she'd asked for an extra room when she clearly didn't."

She was going to have a word with her best friend about that.

"That's family for you." He lifted one shoulder into a shrug.

Must be nice to have someone care about you so much.

"And with people going home, some of the other cabins will be free," he said, echoing her thoughts from earlier. "If you feel that moving to another room would make you more comfortable."

He delivered the words with the same arrogant smirk he'd

used on her at breakfast—the one that said he was fully confident she would back down before him. Ooh it got under her skin!

"Why do you bring it up, Keaton? Feeling weird having me so close?" She leaned back on the bed, making her knee knock against his. No way was she going to be the one walking out of here with her tail between her legs. He'd had the upper hand for *way* too long.

"Not at all. I just figured in case you were bluffing this morning, I'd give you an out." The smirk blossomed into a full-blown grin. "Seeing as I'm such a good guy."

"I'm totally fine. Nothing about this bothers me even a little bit," she lied. "Now, if you're done trying to bait me, why don't we run through a few things with Molly?"

"If we must," he said with a sigh.

Molly grunted from the other side of the room as if to say, *I am just as annoyed about this as you are. Believe me, buddy.*

"Oh come on, you two, it's going to be fun!" August clapped her hands together and jumped off the bed. "Now, I've had a look over the schedule. After lunch, we've got a photo shoot where you can show the judges why Molly has the potential to be a social media star. So maybe have a think about that in advance."

"I don't need to think about it. I already know why she's perfect for social media."

"Oh yeah?"

"Because, like most people trying to make it big online, she's beautiful but egotistical."

August nudged him with her foot. "Don't say that."

"I can do one better." He snapped his fingers. "She has narcissistic tendencies and loves taking selfies."

He was just trying to wind her up now.

"First, dogs don't have opposable thumbs so they can't even take selfies. Second, your sister is trying to make it on social media! Do you think she's egotistical and narcissistic?"

"Of course not, but she's trying to make a difference and help people. Most content creators are only in it for the free shit."

She shook her head. The man was *so* cynical. "That's not true. Social media provides connection. It's a way to find people who like the same things you do and build friendships over shared passions."

"All while retouching your photos so that people only see a curated, distorted version of reality." He shot her a condescending look. "So much for human connection."

It was tough to argue with him there. August had fed her insecurities many times in her younger years while scrolling through picture after picture of women with appearances that were different from hers. She'd never been able to tan worth a damn, and she'd always been short and solidly built, even as a kid. Add to that her ginger hair, which in her late twenties was already speckled with glittering silver strands, and her short, stubby eyelashes, which were a pale gold and resistant to any kind of curling.

And Keaton was right; these days everything was retouched, and there were even filters on Instagram that changed the shape of your face in video! You could have bigger eyes, plumper lips and a less-rounded face with nothing more than the click of the button. She hated that. Hated that it made young girls think there was only one acceptable way to look. Hated that even as a successful businesswoman who'd worked hard to love herself, she still had days where she cringed looking in the mirror.

Social media had a lot to answer for.

"All the more reason to support Isla's business," August said. "Her whole mission is about making the internet a happier, furrier place. We love animals just as they are—weird and wonderful and in all shapes and sizes. It's a good lesson."

"I don't love that one and I suspect the feeling is mutual." Keaton eyed Molly. "But we should be prepared. Okay, so the photo shoot is after lunch. Then what?"

August grabbed the schedule from her bag and scanned it.

"There's going to be a social media workshop tomorrow morning, which you can skip because they've agreed to let Leah Skype in, since she would be the client and not you. For the afternoon, they've brought in a trainer to help assess how well the animals take instruction."

"Again? Why do they need to be so well trained if they're only taking a picture for Instagram?"

"It's *way* more than that." August shook her head. "They're booking animals for commercial shoots, and one of their clients recently got a cameo in a movie, so they need to know what the animal's capabilities are. It's one thing to have a dog sit and stay for a photo, but it's quite another to have them running around or doing things on command for film."

"Right." Keaton sighed, scrubbing a hand over his face. He was definitely in over his head. "Okay, what else is there?"

"Day three is the final ten contestants. There's another elimination round in the morning, but the schedule is a little vague on how that will run." She shrugged. "I guess they might want to see what other information they might need. There's time booked for the 'getting to know you' interviews as well. In the afternoon there's a proper photo shoot for a brand, which the top five animals will participate in."

Keaton nodded. "Well, we better get our shit together, then. Right, Molly?"

The husky lifted her head up and looked closely at him, as if assessing whether she should care about what he was saying. Or maybe it only seemed that way. Molly was a beautiful dog, but the black markings around her face *did* make it look like she had a permanently judgmental expression.

August had seen Leah's submission video for the competition and it totally played to Molly's strengths, giving off a *Gossip Girl*–esque kind of vibe, but from the POV of the dog. Now that was a reboot August would watch! And it appeared as though Leah had taken inspiration from the original The Dachshund Wears Prada Instagram account that had been the catalyst for Isla's business, back when she'd been a dog sitter for one of the richest men in Manhattan, her now husband, Theo.

But rather than feeling derivative, Leah had infused the video with her own unique flair. Unfortunately, Keaton and Molly did not have the same chemistry. In fact, they had *no* chemistry…and neither one of them seemed inclined to change that.

"Maybe we need to do some kind of a bonding exercise to get Molly to trust you," August said.

"Why don't we have an exercise to make *me* trust *her*?" Keaton grumbled.

"Um, how about because *you're* the adult in this situation."

"She's seven. That's forty-nine in dog years, so technically—"

August held up her hand. "Maybe this is the problem. You're expecting her to do all the work when she's the animal. Smart as she may be, she still takes her cues from us."

"Fine. What do I need to do?"

"For starters, you're going to be the one feeding her from now on. We'll even try some hand-feeding, too. Showing her that you provide something she wants and needs is an important way to build a bond. But since we're also on a time crunch, we need to do other things as well."

"Okay." He nodded. "Like what?"

"Since we've got a gap in the schedule while they do the first elimination round, we'll get you to spend some time with her. We can go for a walk around the grounds, find a quiet spot to play and work on some tricks." August motioned to where Molly's leash was hanging from a hook by the door—you could tell this was truly a pet-friendly vacation spot in all the small details. "You get her ready for the walk and I'll put some treats into a ziplock bag. But *you* need to give them to her, *you* need to issue the commands and *you* need to be her main point of connection. Forget I'm even here."

That would be difficult for two reasons. First, because August was not the kind of woman one could easily forget. Her wild red hair, bright smile and upbeat yet take-charge attitude demanded attention. And second, because Keaton didn't even want to think about how fast he'd be drowning in this situation if she wasn't here.

As he went to grab Molly's leash from the wall, his phone rang. Again. The unfortunate thing about working with other Wall Street types was that nobody knew how to take no for an answer. His out-of-office email message meant nothing, nor did the voicemail that basically said "I'm busy, don't call me" in corporate speak. Not even the instruction he'd given to his executive assistant—to turn away everyone except his researcher and Thomas—was keeping the sharks at bay.

He canceled the call but the phone started ringing again immediately.

"Wow, they're persistent." August made an *eek* face.

"Sadly, it's not just one person."

"You're popular."

Keaton snorted. "Far from it."

He walked over to Molly, feeling unsure of himself. Being here was like taking a trip to the Twilight Zone, because there was no other area of his life where he *ever* felt uncertain.

Oh, because there are so *many different parts of your life, huh? What do you have besides work and family?*

"Hey, Molly," he said, thinking it sounded ridiculous to talk to a dog like it was a human. "Want to go for a walk?"

Her ears flicked, indicating she was interested even if she didn't lift her head.

"Try again. Sound more confident," August said under her breath.

"Let's go for a walk." He spoke louder this time, jingling the leash so that the metal components made a tinkling sound.

That got the husky's attention. She jumped up to her feet and leaped gracefully out of the dog bed as if she were a show pony clearing a hedge. Molly looked at the leash, then up at Keaton, then back at the leash again. Then her head tilted to one side in confusion as if to say, *I normally like walks. Walks with* you, *however? Eh, I don't know about that.*

"We don't usually hang out very much, but guess what… we have to be friends for the next few days."

Molly made a whining noise as if Keaton had asked her to go without food for a week.

"I know, I feel exactly the same way," he said dryly, his gaze sliding to August.

"Don't be a baby. Clip her leash on and let's go."

"Bossy," he grumbled, but he bent forward and attached the leash to Molly's collar. Thankfully, she didn't kick up a stink. Clearly, the desire for fresh air trumped her desire not to spend time with Keaton.

* * *

The trio headed outside and August slipped Keaton the bag of dog treats. She'd also grabbed a few of Molly's toys that they might be able to use for tricks. August had a good idea what the dog could do, since she'd helped Leah with training her.

"Why are work people calling you so much?" she asked as they walked through the retreat.

They followed a path that wound through some fir trees, and the sunlight filtered down through leaves and branches, warming her skin. The ground was littered with twigs and other natural debris, and she caught some birds hopping around on the ground, scattering items to and fro as they looked for perfect nest-building items.

"That's just my job. It's nonstop. I also took this time off without giving any notice, so people are pissy about it." He grunted. "That's Wall Street for you—twenty-four seven and then some."

"Don't you ever…get tired of it?" she asked.

Molly padded ahead of them, tail swishing and nose sniffing. She seemed happy and relaxed, which was exactly how they needed her to be if they had any hopes of doing Leah proud over the next few days.

"Tired of working?" he asked, glancing at her. "Do *you* get tired of working?"

"I guess we're both workaholics." She laughed. As they walked side by side, an easy, comfortable silence fell over them. "It's been a while since I did this."

"What?"

"Got out of the city and enjoyed some fresh air."

"Asher would be happy to take you away," Keaton teased, nudging her with his elbow. "Pretty sure his folks have a house in the Hamptons."

August wrinkled her nose. For some reason, going to a big, fancy house in the Hamptons did *not* appeal to her anywhere near as much as walking through the forest with a handsome man by her side and a dog at her feet. She'd always been a bit more of a "dirt under the fingernails" kind of gal than someone who wanted glamorous vacations and designer swimwear and an expensive vacation home.

"What's with the face?" Trust eagle-eyed Keaton not to miss that detail.

"What face?"

"Don't play innocent with me, Augie. I say Hamptons and you screw your face up like I suggested you take a vacation in a dumpster. What gives?"

"I don't know, that's just a bit...pretentious, isn't it? Not my scene." She shrugged. "Would make my parents happy, though. I finally found a man that's the 'right caliber' to date. Ugh."

For some reason, that made the idea of Asher sour a little bit in her mind. Her parents would *love* him.

"They still pushing you to chase the upper middle-class dream, eh?" Keaton said, raising an eyebrow. "Climb that next societal rung?"

"You know what they're like. Everything is about status."

Her parents had been obsessed with keeping up with the Joneses for as long as August could remember, always so worried about what people would think—was their car good enough? What about the brand of her mother's purse? The place where she got her hair cut?

It was the reason they were so angry that August had defied their plan for her to become a doctor or a lawyer or something else worthy of bragging about to their friends. Apparently, dog grooming was a waste of her schooling, never mind that

August hadn't even wanted to go to that fancy-ass school in the first place.

"It's like, they can't even enjoy their lives because they're so focused on what they don't have." August shook her head. "Every decision they make is about what's going to impress their vapid friends and get them into the right circles. They only know how to want for more."

"That's a chronic disease in our world." Keaton grunted.

August glanced up at him and was struck by how handsome he looked in that moment—without the suit, without the styled hair, without his usual walls. The light made his green eyes look almost otherworldly and picked up on the fine stubble dusting his chin where he hadn't bothered to shave that morning.

"I find it sad," she said. "That people waste their lives chasing such superficial things."

"Me too."

The way he said those two words hit something in her chest. It had been a long time since August felt truly understood by a man. The vast majority of her dates had been somewhere on the scale of wet blanket to raging dumpster fire because the guys only seemed interested in talking about what they wanted out of life, assuming that she would fall in line. Asher had been better where that was concerned, but he was also from a different world. The whole "his family has a house in the Hamptons" was indication of that.

But Keaton knew. He knew what it was like to make mistakes and to struggle and fight for what you wanted. He knew what it meant to make tough decisions. Maybe she felt like he understood her because he *did*. They'd known each other since they were teens. They'd grown up together in a lot of ways.

She swallowed. There was something dangerous about him being here with her. Without all that custom Italian wool and leather for armor, he looked so much more touchable. So much more attainable.

Which was a lie, because Keaton Sax was about as far from attainable as a man could possibly get.

"Oh, look," she said, pointing and hoping her voice didn't sound as tight out loud as it did in her head. "There's somewhere we can stop and work with Molly."

Keaton might be the perfect guy in some ways, but she couldn't forget that the man he was now wasn't the same man she fell in love with all those years ago.

10

"I'm never going to get this," Keaton groaned.

They'd been working for a solid forty minutes, trying to get Molly to jump over a plastic rod. August was convinced she knew how to do the trick, but whenever Keaton asked Molly to do anything, she went rogue. *If* she did anything at all…

Which currently, she was not.

The husky lay on her side, flopped out as if she'd decided she couldn't possibly work under such conditions and had fainted like an actress in a bad daytime soap opera. Only she hadn't fainted, because he could feel her icy blue eyes on him the second she thought he'd turned away.

"This goddamn dog…" He let out a breath. "Do you know *I* was the one who suggested Leah get a dog? Great companionship, I said. Good for security, I said. People with dogs live longer, I said."

August was doing her very best not to laugh, but her cheeks were pink from the effort.

"Don't," he said, holding up a hand. "I know you think I'm being as dramatic as she is—"

"You are."

"I am *not*." He pointed to Molly. "That dog is a pain in my ass."

Molly snorted as if to say, *The feeling is mutual, asshole.*

"Well, if you take that attitude with her, then no wonder you're not working well together." August looked at him pointedly. "How would you feel if you had to work with people who were constantly complaining that you were a pain in their asses? And don't make a Wall Street crack, either."

"You know me too well," he grumbled.

"Come on." She motioned for him to follow her lead. "Let's try some basic bonding. Have you ever simply patted Molly or given her a good scratch to see if that makes her like you more?"

He shot her a look that said she should already know the answer to that question.

"Come here," she said firmly.

"Don't talk to me like I'm the dog." He folded his arms across his chest.

"Lord give me strength," she said, tipping her face up to the sky.

Molly glanced at Keaton as though smirking. He could practically hear her snarky voice in his head: *Who's the dramatic one now, bitch?*

"Do you want to help Leah or not?" August asked.

"Of course I want to help her. I agreed to come here, didn't I?"

"News flash, Keaton. Simply gracing people with your presence isn't enough. You have to put the effort in. If you want Molly to work with you, then you have to form a bond with her." August put her hands on her hips.

She was wearing a cute but casual outfit of cropped jeans, a pale green sweater that accentuated her small shoulders and ample bust, and white sneakers. Her hair was pulled back and secured with some bandana-tie thing that matched her sweater, but woe to anyone who assumed she was just some cute-as-a-button woman.

August was a boss, period.

Keaton really didn't like being told what to do. Never had, never would. Probably a leftover of his rebellious teen years.

"It's a dog," he said. "Aren't they bred to take commands?"

She rolled her eyes. "No wonder she hates you! You treat her like she's an inferior being."

"Who sits at the top of the food chain, huh?"

"Not humans, actually. We're not generally considered apex predators by scientific standards because of the diversity in our diet."

He growled. "Of *course* you would know that."

"It pays to be informed." Her gaze locked onto his, challenging him to fight her. The woman knew how to dig her heels in, that was for damn sure. "Now are you going to listen to me or not? I would like to point out that you were the one who came to me for help."

"Fine," he gritted out. "So what? I just need to pat her?"

"You need to form a bond through physical touch, if she'll allow it. Which, given your track record, she might not."

"What happens if she doesn't?" he asked.

"Then you're probably screwed and you'll get sent home in the next round of eliminations." She shrugged. "So, if you're fine losing, then don't worry about it."

He flattened his lips together. Damn. He'd dealt with a lot of people who liked to poke him over the years, but none were quite as effective as August. She knew exactly where to jab the end of her stick and how to sharpen it when you weren't looking.

"I don't want to lose," he said, feeling his competitive streak flare up.

"Ah, there's the Keaton I remember." She grinned. "I knew that petty AF shell-flinging sore *Mario Kart* loser was in there somewhere."

In spite of his frustrations, he chuckled. "You remember that, huh?"

"Oh, the dirty tricks? Like waiting until I was right behind you to toss a banana peel. Or letting me get past you, just so you could shove a shell up my ass."

His chuckle turned to full-blown laughter. "The fact that you're still hanging on to those things tells me you're no better at losing than I am."

At their feet, Molly whined. She might not like him, but she disliked not being the center of attention even more.

"You're right, I like winning." She nodded. "Which is why I don't want to have come all this way only to fail on day one. So can we work together, all three of us? Can we at least give it our best shot for Leah?"

God, hearing that fierce sense of competition and loyalty in her voice was enough to get something stirring below Keaton's belt. Which in itself, was a shock. *Nobody else* had stirred things down there in years. Not since his wife. Not since the life he thought he was working for crumbled like ash in his palm.

But August still had an effect on him. Even now. Even after everything.

"Yeah," he said, nodding and trying to swallow back the wave of attraction that crested inside him. "Let's try to win for Leah."

"Good." She nodded, satisfied that they were all on the same team. Well, at least the humans were. Molly still needed convincing. "Come crouch down by her and slowly put your hand out."

Keaton did as she instructed. He wasn't frightened of Molly biting him or anything like that. She might be a diva, but she was incredibly gentle with people. He'd seen it with his sister when she walked with her cane. Molly was almost hyper-aware of her and moved carefully around, making sure not to get underfoot. And one of Leah's friends had a little girl who was three, and Molly was very patient with the small grabbing hands and the squealing.

And he'd promised August that he would accept her help, so he was going to uphold his end of the bargain.

He held out his hand. Molly looked at him. He wasn't sure if dogs had eyebrows—it was kind of hard to tell since they were covered in fur anyway—but if she did have them, then one was currently raised sky-high.

"Can you just roll with it, please?" he said under his breath. "I'm making an effort."

He didn't dare look at August's face to see if she was laughing at him. Molly glanced down at Keaton's hand and stuck her head forward, nostrils twitching. Then she bumped his hand with her nose.

"Good," August said. "Now see if she'll let you pat her."

He felt like a bit of a fool, but he still needed to ask, "Where?"

"Well, you can pat her on the side of the body. She likes a pat on the head, too. Just stay away from her tail, feet, legs and...lady parts."

"Right, because I was planning to go straight for the genitals." He rolled his eyes. "Thanks, Captain Obvious."

She giggled. "Hey, you asked."

He reached out toward the dog and her eyes followed his hand, curious rather than concerned, and he stroked his palm along her side. Molly's fur was thick and soft. At first, she looked at him with narrowed eyes like she wasn't quite sure what was happening. But after a moment, her eyes fluttered shut and she let out a content sigh.

Turned out, a diva would allow herself to be pampered rather than refuse out of spite.

This went on for a few minutes, then August suggested they see if Molly might be willing to cooperate a bit more. "Tell her to get up and see if you can get her to do a couple of simple tricks—things she's already very familiar with. Then, when she does them, you have to praise her verbally, give her a treat and then some affection."

He opened his mouth to argue that it seemed overkill for a trick she'd already learned, but when he caught sight of August's no-nonsense expression, he decided to keep his trap shut.

"You're the boss," he replied with a nod.

"Yes, I am." She smiled.

He laughed. August had been bossing him around since she was a spunky thirteen-year-old who came over for regular hangouts at his house, making him set up the Nintendo for her and Leah, and getting him to help them hang fairy lights in the lounge room so they had the right "vibes" for their sleepovers.

He'd always been happy to do it, because August made Leah happy and that was all he cared about. Though he'd never admit it, she made him happy, too.

"Molly, sit." Keaton almost held his breath to see what the dog would do and, to his surprise, she got off the ground and plonked her fluffy ass down, head tilted up toward him and awaiting his next command.

He was about to issue it when August cleared her throat. Oh yeah, praise bomb time.

"Aren't you an…excellent girl!" Was that better than the standard good girl? "Here's a treat."

He palmed a hard little pellet—which looked more like a dried guinea pig poop than something edible—to the dog and she swiped it out of his hand with her pink tongue. Then he reached forward and ruffled the fur on her head, giving her a little scratch behind her left ear.

"Now ask her to do something else." August was slowly backing away from the dog, giving Molly and Keaton space to bond.

"Shake." He held out his hand and the dog obediently lifted a paw.

"You are not just a good girl. You are the *best* girl!" He produced another snack and then ruffled her head again.

There was something so sexy about watching a grown, hunky man play nice with a dog. Maybe this was how some women felt when they watched a man hold a baby. Since August didn't want kids, that image didn't do anything for her personally, but *this*—Keaton's adorably awkward praises and

Molly's wagging tail—Lordy! Someone stop her from stripping down right there in public and jumping the man's bones.

She supposed it wasn't fair to judge him for not knowing how to interact with animals, because it wasn't like he'd had any pets growing up. From what she knew, when Keaton and Leah were young, they'd lived in a tiny apartment where his mom and sister shared a bed, and he slept on the couch. The year before Leah was due to start high school, his mom ended up in a relationship with a wealthy businessman, and they'd all moved into a swanky brownstone near the private school they were put into.

But those years, despite having more creature comforts than ever, were not happy ones for Keaton and Leah. And she suspected his difficulty in bonding with people went back much further than him losing his wife. He kept people at arm's length, because it was safer that way.

If some people had walls around their hearts, he had a *Hunger Games*–style death trap arena around his.

So yeah, the image didn't just stir something in her heart because Keaton was hot and Molly was adorable. It was because she knew how hard it was for him to open himself up to connection.

"Keep going," August encouraged.

"Uh…drop." He pointed to the ground and Molly lowered herself down. "Now roll."

She rolled over with ease and popped back up onto her feet, tongue lolling happily out of her mouth.

"You are *so* good. A-plus!" Keaton palmed her another treat.

"That's probably enough treats for now, or else we're going to have to walk her back to Manhattan." August smiled. "But keep trying to have some physical touch with her, keep praising her, and she'll do what you need her to do."

"I will." He nodded.

"We should probably head back. They're serving lunch in the same place as breakfast, so we can let Molly have a snooze in the room and walk over together."

"I'm going to have to skip it." He raked a hand through his hair. "My phone's been going off this whole time."

He pulled the device out of his back pocket and showed the screen to her. Twenty missed calls.

"That's…" She shook her head. "Wow, they want their pound of flesh at your work, don't they?"

"Tell me about it."

For a moment, he looked…miserable. In the early days, she got the sense that Keaton thrived on the challenge and competitiveness of Wall Street. But now he looked exhausted and worn-out. It made her sad, because she believed that everyone deserved to enjoy their work rather than feeling like it was a prison sentence.

"But," he said with a sigh, "if I want my name on the front door, then I have to put the hours in."

"Are they thinking about making you named partner?" She blinked. "Wow."

"Not bad for the boy from juvie, eh?" He winked at her and she almost melted on the spot.

Stop it. You're supposed to be finding the perfect practical partner, and it's not *him.*

Keaton grabbed Molly's leash from the ground and clipped it to her collar. The dog made a whining noise and tossed her head back and forth. "I'm sorry. Playtime is over. But the good news is that you get to have a nap!"

Molly tilted her head to one side. *"Rarooooo."*

The sound was halfway between a whine and a howl. Keaton shrugged and started walking. Molly sulked for a minute, but as soon as she realized there were exciting things to sniff, she happily trotted ahead, tail wagging.

When they got back to the cabin, August paused by the door as Keaton let Molly inside. "Are you sure you can't come for a quick bite?"

"I really can't." Something flashed across his face.

Keaton never showed his stress, even though he must feel it. He worked so hard to take care of his family, but sometimes August wondered why he still acted like he needed to squirrel money away for a rainy day. He'd expanded and renovated Leah's house. He'd paid off his mother's debts and given her money to go back to school. He owned a beautiful apartment in Manhattan.

Yet there was still an undercurrent of duty, like he hadn't done enough. Like he was still repaying a debt. Like he believed he'd never make up for the past.

"How about I bring you back something?" she said, her eyes searching his face.

The stress melted away and there was a warmth in his green eyes. "That would be great."

For a moment, it felt like he might lean forward and kiss her, and August's lips parted in anticipation. A tingle of awareness rang through her body, a resounding *yes* echoing in her mind. She wanted him to kiss her.

What the hell are you doing? He's about as far from your practical partnership ideal as you could possibly get!

Why did it always feel like everything was a hop, skip and jump away from her falling back into old feelings. Falling back into being the naive, young woman who trailed after him like a rock star groupie. Falling back into wishing she could change the past.

You can't change the past.

Keaton leaned forward and she took a step back, as if trying to extricate herself from whatever force field encompassed him that made her act like a giddy schoolgirl. His brows creased, like he wasn't quite sure what had just happened.

"I can't kiss you because I've already kissed Asher," she blurted out.

There was something about hearing Asher's name that caused Keaton's competitive streak to flare up, and knowing that August had kissed him… Hell, no. It prickled under his skin. It was an itch he couldn't scratch. It *bothered* him on a deep level and he hated that. Because being bothered meant he cared, and he didn't want to care. He didn't want to be affected by her. He didn't want that sick green pulse of jealousy to ebb through his body like a poison.

But she could do so much better for herself.

Better…like you?

It was obvious she was attracted to him—had been since she was old enough to have such feelings. Back then it had been a silly crush and nothing more. But now when she looked at him…*oof.* He felt her wanting like a fist to the gut. It was intoxicating. Addicting. It made him feel real and alive and whole, like he wasn't a man made of broken parts haphazardly glued back together with cocky smirks and quippy one-liners.

It felt like he was the man he was *before.*

Her chest rose and fell in uneven bursts, as though she had to remind herself to continue breathing. The action strained the soft fabric of her sweater and flushed her cheeks pink. Her eyes glittered with frustration, but underneath that emotion was desire. Not a simmer, but a full rolling boil.

She wanted him.

"You kissed him?" Keaton nodded. "Tell me, what's it like locking lips with a wet fish?"

She narrowed her eyes. "He's not a wet fish."

"No? Because one of the interns at our first firm told me that it was like sucking face with a sea creature. I'd assumed fish, but maybe he was more like an octopus—hands everywhere, kinda slimy, weird smell."

The narrowed eyes turned to a glare. He'd never thought anyone could beat Molly's death stare, but August was giving her a run for her money. "Why do you even care?"

He shouldn't. But unfortunately for Keaton, he did. Because every time she looked at him with that undisguised need, it made his body misbehave. Made his mind misbehave. Made his brain sign a fucking hall pass so it could GTFO and shirk all responsibility.

This is a dangerous game. You don't want to go there.

Oh but he did. He wanted it very much.

"I just find it interesting that you stand here, looking like you want me to shove you up against a wall but then you chicken out because you're supposedly attracted to Asher Benson."

"There's nothing 'supposedly' about it." She frowned. "I like him."

"Maybe. But I bet you felt nothing when he kissed you. There's no chemistry between you, is there?" Keaton asked. The question was the equivalent of poking her with a stick to see if she'd react.

Her cheeks flamed even harder—he was right. Then why did she keep going on dates with the guy if there was no spark? It was very curious indeed.

"What I felt is *none* of your business." She folded her arms over her chest. "Besides, chemistry isn't everything."

"That's a red flag so early in the relationship."

"Spare me. For a man who's so resistant to human connection that he'd rather die alone than possibly risk getting close to someone, I don't think your opinion on chemistry matters very much."

If only she knew the truth, that the only parts of Keaton's day that felt real sometimes were the moments he shared with Leah and his mom. The rest—work, deals, the career climbing—helped to numb him from all the emotions he didn't want to feel.

"You don't know anything about me," he said.

Something flickered in August's eyes. Instead of being scared by that side of him, she came closer. Unfolded her arms. Reached a hand to his chest. Of course she would—she dealt with animals all the time. A little growling didn't scare her.

"I know more than you think," she said. "More, probably, than you'd prefer me to know."

"I doubt it." Control was in his grasp again, smirk firmly in place as he clasped her hand in his. *Gotcha.* "You see what I want you to see."

"Only a fool would take you at face value, Keaton." She tipped her face up to his. "And, for the record, you don't intimidate me."

"So in control of your emotions, August. So unaffected." His smile turned wolfish. "I bet if I tried to kiss you now, you'd melt like a stick of butter on a hundred-degree day."

"Dream on."

Satisfaction coursed through him when her nostrils flared, giving her true feelings away despite the cool response. He dipped his head lower so he could whisper right into her ear. "And I bet you'd cling to me like you were lost at sea."

Her breath stuttered. "You're not as attractive as you think you are."

"Maybe not to some people," he replied. "But I am to you."

It wasn't cocky if it was fact, right?

"I bet you'd feel a hundred times more chemistry with me than you felt with Asher," he said.

"I don't want chemistry," she said stubbornly. "Chemistry is unreliable. And you vastly overestimate your impact on me."

"Bullshit."

Defiance rolled off her in waves, but there was a flicker of vulnerability in her eyes. She was torn between being desperate to prove him wrong—to maintain the distance between them—and her fear that her own response was out of her control.

"Do something, then," she taunted. "Because I'm starting to feel like you're all talk and no action."

"Be careful what you wish for."

"Full permission. Do your worst and I promise you'll find my reaction disappointing. Maybe even a little ego bruising," she said. "I'm sick of your teasing. You never act on it, so it's all just hot air to me. In fact—"

She squeaked in surprise when he shoved her against the wall, trapping her with his chest, the palm of one hand planted beside her head and the other tipping her face up to his. He caught how her eyes widened when she realized that he was the spider and she was the fly—and that he fully intended to rise to her challenge.

"Full permission, huh? Well, I'm not going to waste such an opportunity."

"Keaton..." Her breath came in ragged bursts, but she

didn't tell him to stop. Instead she flattened her hands against the wall behind her and looked up at him. She wasn't backing down.

Her body was warm and soft against his, her curves pressing against him in all the best places. His lips hovered over hers, their breath mingling in that delicious pre-kiss limbo. As predicted, her lips parted in that final second, welcoming him in. He pressed against her, locking her down with his hips and his mouth.

She didn't kiss like a woman who had someone else she'd rather be kissing. Hell, no. She kissed like a woman starved. A woman who'd been denied what she wanted and finally had the go-ahead to take it all. Any pretense of resistance was crushed when her tongue slid along his, her hands coming up to his arms—not pushing away but pulling toward.

She ground her hips against him and his cock pulsed. No fear. No resistance. No demons shouting inside his head.

He felt like the old Keaton again.

He was tantalized by the thought of unzipping her pants so he could slide a hand into them. It would be oh-so easy to glide the zipper head down and feel her hot against his hand. To show her that he didn't want to stop at a kiss.

You're playing with fire. Redheaded, curvy fire.

He had to force himself not to wind the silken lengths around his fist so he could yank her head back and plunder that pouty little mouth further. What on earth was she doing to him? He *never* lost control.

Stand. Down. Now!

He pulled back—drinking in the sight of her lips, flushed and swollen, and her hair, mussed and vibrant. It was the most beautiful thing he'd seen in years. But before he could crow about proving his point…

"I have to go." August fled so quickly, he was left wondering whether he imagined the entire exchange.

From behind him, Molly made a noise of disgust.

"You might be right, girl," he said. "I am utterly despicable."

11

Fifteen minutes later, Keaton reached for a small savory pastry on the plate August had put together for him. When she'd come back from the food hall, she'd barely been able to look him in the eye. Not that he could blame her for that. But, true to her word—even with him being a dick—she'd brought him some lunch including all the things he liked and none of the stuff he didn't.

The woman was a shoo-in for sainthood.

For a moment, it made a memory flash in his mind, of Ellery bringing lunch into his office when he was working on a hard deal. They'd always done that for each other—when one person was in the trenches, the other picked up the slack and made sure they were watered and fed.

It was the ultimate show of care, to him.

In truth, August bringing him lunch had unsettled him

even more than the kiss. Because a steamy kiss was great, but it was more a battle of wills. Her looking after him was something else entirely.

"Keaton?" Thomas's clipped voice snapped him back to attention. "Have you frozen again? Do they have squirrels powering the internet out there?"

"I'm still here." He popped the bite-sized pastry into his mouth and chewed.

"What did you find out about the Waterline Press debt situation?"

"They owe fifty grand to a freight company." His research assistant had done some digging and found out that they were severely in arrears. Fifty grand might not sound like a lot to his boss or his colleagues, but for a small company that was a make-or-break amount. "We could offer to alleviate that debt if they play ball."

"Contact the freight company and encourage them to engage debt collectors," Thomas replied, as though Keaton hadn't suggested an action to the contrary.

"I don't understand why we can't agree to pay off the debt if the CEO lowers the selling price. Seems like a win-win to me," he said stubbornly. They could absolutely get this merger over the line without casualties, he was sure of it. "They avoid having their company name dragged through mud for not paying their accounts, and we help our client get the price they want for a company that will benefit their business."

"No."

Thomas believed that compromise was weakness. Why give up anything, when you can totally annihilate your opponent in the process of winning?

Keaton scrubbed a hand over his face. The stubble on his jaw felt oddly rough against his fingertips. He couldn't remember the last time he hadn't started the day with a clean shave.

"How do you think a named partner would handle this?" Thomas asked. The internet service was shitty being so far out of the city, and the image kept stalling and turning pixelated before clearing again.

His boss was sitting in his office, silver hair neatly styled and a sharp red tie standing out against the otherwise stark black and white of his suit and shirt. He looked ready for battle, like always.

But Keaton had seen another side to the man—the one who'd coaxed the whiskey bottle from his fingertips, who'd sat with him while he cried, who sent someone to patch the wall where Keaton's fist had slammed through plaster and paint. He'd recounted the pain of his own loss, shared the things that had helped him make it through those hard, early days alone. That man had shown compassion, kindness. He'd been the fatherly support that Keaton had never had. The rock to lean on when it felt like the world was slipping out from under his feet.

It was Thomas who'd gotten him through his darkest moment. Some days, Keaton was damn sure he owed Thomas his life.

"I think a named partner always looks for the most advantageous solution to a problem," he said.

"And you think spending fifty thousand dollars to fix someone else's mistakes is advantageous?" Thomas raised an eyebrow.

"I think a quick sale is advantageous. Time is money, is it not? I know you'd rather have the deal show up on this quarter's report."

"I need to know you're not getting soft," Thomas said, his tone ice hard.

Soft. It was a word that got bandied around like a hot potato on Wall Street—the ultimate insult. The corporate equivalent of flapping your arms and calling someone a chicken just to see how they'd react.

"Do you think I'm soft?" he asked, keeping his face neutral. He couldn't let the older man know how it stung when he said things like that—where he implied that Keaton was disappointing him. Because Keaton didn't care to impress others, generally. He didn't worry about what people thought of him or try winning them over.

Except Thomas.

"It's…different at the top," he said. "Now I can protect you. But once you're on this level, it's open water. I won't be able to shield you anymore."

For a brief moment, Keaton saw the man who'd sat by him and helped him with his grief. He saw the Thomas who cared about his pain and who'd taken him under his wing. He saw the man who'd come to his wife's funeral and laid a hand on his shoulder at the exact moment Keaton thought he might crumple to the ground.

"I can take care of myself," Keaton said, but Thomas didn't look convinced. "Give me the week. If I can't come up with another solution, then we'll speak with the freight company and do it your way."

"Fine. But remember where your priorities lie."

The screen went blank as he disconnected the call.

He closed the lid of his laptop. Fucking Thomas. Why did it feel like everything was a test lately? He'd been dangling the named partner thing over his head for a while, always dancing around it to keep Keaton "motivated." But now that there appeared to be serious talks about a promotion, it was like Thomas wanted to see how far he could push Keaton. How far he could bend him. Was this about loyalty? Did he want to see how much Keaton was willing to sacrifice of himself to make it to the top?

He wouldn't kibosh the Waterline Press deal, because that would be career suicide, but he wanted to be *sure* there wasn't another avenue that might save the owners of the small company from being totally decimated.

His client could afford to pay that fifty grand to smooth the way. And even if Thomas had to eat the cost in his budget, they could pad their fees out in other ways to make it back. There was no reason to bury the little guy.

The longer he did this work, the harder it felt to stay on the right side of the ethical line and the more pressure he felt to become like Thomas. He sat on the bed, staring out of the window.

"You really want to be a named partner one day?" he said, looking down at his wife. Ellery lay on the bed, her golden hair fanned out behind her, eyes twinkling.

"Of course I do." She grinned. "Who aims for second place?"

He laughed at her unabashed ambition. "Not my wife, Mrs. Win At All Costs."

"Don't you forget it." She looped her arm around his neck and brushed her lips against his. "Do you know how many people crash and burn on Wall Street? Who can't hack the pressure? I want to be one of the select few who climbs to the top."

"I know you'll get there." There wasn't a doubt in his mind.

Ellery had a determination that was unshakable. It was one of the things he loved most about her—that and some of the things she could do with her mouth. Good lord.

"We'll *get there," she corrected. "You and me. Race you to the top."*

The memory swam in front of his eyes for a moment, morphing and changing. Growing darker.

"Promise me you'll get to the top." Her hand was so weak she couldn't even squeeze him anymore. "For us. For our dreams."

The machines next to the hospital bed beeped softly and he looked away, unable to see through the hot, prickling tears in his eyes. He could feel his insides petrifying—hardening and crusting over, so brittle it felt like if anyone else tried to touch him he'd turn to dust.

Maybe that would be better. Then he could blow away on a breeze.

"Promise me, Keaton." Her voice was shaky, but there was no weakness to it. Even in her last breaths, Ellery was fighting for more.

"I promise." He turned back to her, steeling himself. He had to be strong for her. Had to keep going for her. Had to win for her. "I'll get to the top for us."

By the time Keaton entered the building where they'd conducted the first round of competition that morning, the memories were once again locked up tight.

Was it this latest acquisition that had his head swirling with memories? Maybe it was because Thomas was dangling the very thing Ellery wanted right in front of him. Not to mention that he was starting to face the question of "what comes next" after being made a named partner—a question that he had no idea how to answer.

Or maybe it was being here—away from the city—with the only woman he couldn't seem to hold at arm's length.

Molly whined at his feet. *"Row rowwwow."*

"Not you," he muttered. "I can definitely hold you at arm's length."

For the second event of the day, the contestants were once again brought through the activity a group at a time, to save all the animals being cooped up together. Not that Molly seemed to mind. She wasn't one of those dogs that had an issue with other animals because Leah put Molly into a doggy day care for one day every week and took her to the local dog park whenever she was able to manage it. So Molly had been well socialized.

He spotted August chatting with a woman who had a smaller dog—one of those little rat ones with the big ears—and he waved.

She came over, still seeming to avoid eye contact with him. Great. Now he'd gone and made everything awkward between them by letting his ego take the driver's seat. Why should he give a shit if she'd kissed Asher? That was her business. Not his.

"Hey." She smiled, but it looked a little forced.

"Hey."

The silence felt like a thick soup.

"I, uh..." He raked a hand through his hair, trying to figure out the best way to apologize for how he'd behaved earlier.

She got under his skin without even trying. But it was his fault that he couldn't seem to ignore that feeling. It was his fault that he was also so tempted to taunt her.

"About before," he began.

"We don't need to talk about it." She set her lips into a firm line.

"I wanted to say—"

"We. Don't. Need. To. Talk. About. It."

He nodded. "Okay."

"Are you ready for the next activity?" she asked, her voice falsely bright.

Message received.

Keaton scanned the immediate area, which appeared to have several stations set up with backdrops, costumes, props and lighting. There was a beach scene, a bright blue background with bubbles printed on it and more.

"So, we take Molly around and snap some photos?" He wrinkled his nose. "That doesn't seem very difficult."

August snorted. "You've clearly never tried to take a picture of an animal before."

They walked toward the blonde woman, whose lanyard said Scout Myers, Paws in the City. Her willowy legs were made to look even longer by black jeans and heeled boots. On top she wore a hot-pink T-shirt with the company logo printed on the front that stretched across her pregnant belly, and her hair was pulled back into a loose blond ponytail.

Scout smiled and waved as they headed over. "I don't think we've officially met." She reached her hand toward him. "I'm Scout."

"Keaton."

"It's great to finally meet you." She beamed.

Finally? He glanced at August, who was studiously avoiding him. "It's great to meet you, too."

"How's your sister doing?" she asked, an empathetic expression on her face. Usually that kind of a question would make him bristle, because it felt like something private that was nobody's business. But for some reason, Scout struck him as genuinely caring, perhaps because she was friends with August.

"She's okay." He nodded. "I was texting with her earlier and my mom is staying overnight to help her around the house. Then her boyfriend is coming tomorrow."

"That's good." Scout looked genuinely relieved. "If there's anything we can do for her, please let me know. I can only imagine how disappointed she must feel not being here in person. But we've set up some virtual facilities for her so that she can join us online for the workshop, at least. I know it's not the same, but we still wanted her to feel included as much as possible. And we'll have some fun promo items and stuff for you to take home for her."

"That's very kind."

"I think we're going to be having dinner tonight as well?" she said, her eyes bright. "Mine and Isla's husbands are both coming up from the city, so we thought it would be fun to have a meal together. Lane suggested a restaurant in one of the nearby towns, while the rest of the contestants have their trivia night."

"Oh." Keaton blinked. This was the first he'd heard about it.

"I was going to mention that," August said, her laugh a little thin, like she absolutely was *not* going to mention it.

Did Scout think they were…together? He opened his mouth to make it clear they weren't, but before he could get a word out, they were interrupted by a yelp coming from one of the photo areas.

"Excuse me, I need to check on that." Scout darted off, leaving him and August alone in the waiting area.

August crouched and ruffled Molly's fur, making the husky groan with pleasure. He watched her for an entire minute and not once did August look up at him, despite the fact that her cheeks grew steadily pinker so she *knew* he was looking.

What the hell was going on with her?

"So, dinner, huh?" he said. "Planning to go without me?"

"I didn't think you'd want to come." She cooed at Molly.

"And eat a restaurant meal over something they cooked up in the canteen here?" He raised an eyebrow. Not to say that the food was bad, because it wasn't. But it was still summer camp–style serve-yourself fare, and Keaton had gotten a little too used to white tablecloth dining.

"It was more the 'spending time with people' aspect I thought you would dislike." She stood and brushed the strands of white and black husky fur from her jeans.

"I doubt I'd be lucky enough to get two meals delivered to my room in one day. So I'll gladly take a small dinner over a hall full of strangers."

August's lip quirked and she finally made eye contact with him. "Stranger danger, huh?"

"You know it. I barely tolerate the people I know, let alone the ones I don't," he quipped, thankful they were back to bantering again instead of wondering how to deal with the awkward silence.

"I can't tell which lie you prefer more—the Wall Street winer and diner, or the grouchy hermit."

"One of those isn't a lie."

"Hmm." She nodded, clearly biting back a response.

"Say it," he said, gesturing to her. "I'd rather you take a swipe than do this holier-than-thou *hmm* response."

"I don't want to take a swipe, Keaton. Not everyone is looking to attack you." She wrapped her arms around herself. "You can let go of the defensive stance around me."

"Take a look at yourself." He laughed. "Arms positioned like you need a shield in front of you. And you've barely been able to look me in the eye for some reason. What's up with that?"

She made a *pfft* sound. "Don't be ridiculous. I can look you in the eye."

"You can try to bullshit me, Augie. But I see right through you."

"Don't call me that." She shook her head. "Augie. It makes me sound like a child."

With a head for business and a body made for long, sweaty nights in bed—he did *not* need the reminder that she wasn't a child anymore. The sharp snap of attraction that gripped him by the throat made guilt rush through him. How could he be thinking about his dead wife one minute and wanting to kiss his little sister's best friend the next?

It's been ten years. You don't have to berate yourself for being attracted to someone.

But it wasn't "someone" like an anonymous actor in a dirty movie or a hot woman passing him by on the street. It wasn't the idea of attraction and a fleeting feeling. It was *her.* August. And the feeling wasn't fleeting. Far from it.

"The next group will be coming through in a few minutes. So get prepared!" The retreat's event coordinator waved to get everyone's attention. "We're going to give you a station to start at, and everyone will have five minutes to take a great shot to submit to the judges. Then the bell will ring with a one-minute warning before everyone will need to rotate to the right, until you have completed all the stations."

"This sounds like my version of hell," Keaton said under his breath while shooting a glance in August's direction. "This is to simulate posting on social media, right? I don't even know *what* people post on social media. Who cares what people had at their boring brunch? You like avocado toast, so what?"

August burst out laughing. "Gee, Keaton. I remember a time when you were fun."

"Social media is *not* fun. It's performance." He wrinkled his nose. "People feel like they need to prove their lives are relevant and amazing, so they take a carefully curated selection of things and post them online so other nobodies will think they're cool. If their lives were actually good, they wouldn't bother wasting time trying to convince strangers online."

"That is *so* cynical!"

"It's not. I don't count Leah in all this, because she's creating educational content. That's different." He huffed. "I'm talking about the people who go to the Eiffel Tower or the Tower of Pisa and spend all their time looking at it through their iPhone instead of experiencing it firsthand. Or worse, using one of those selfie stick things because they have to insert themselves into a landscape to enjoy it."

"Wow." August shook her head. "I don't even know what to say to that."

"Not everybody will get to experience those things. I have no time for people who waste such precious opportunities."

He saw the moment that the penny dropped for August and turned away, not wanting to see her pity. He shouldn't have said anything. It made him feel weak to still be so bitter about his wife's passing. Ellery would be ashamed of him for behaving this way, because she'd had a zest for life and believed that everyone should be left to enjoy things as they pleased.

But it killed him that she wouldn't get to see all the wonders of the world that she'd wanted to see.

Right before she died, he'd created a "virtual trip around the world" for her as she lay in her hospital bed. He'd brought his laptop in and they'd visited the pyramids of Giza and the Sydney Opera House and the Acropolis and the Colosseum, all through pictures and video.

It occurred to him then that he was only able to do that with Ellery thanks to the people who'd taken the footage at those places. So maybe his view on social media was a little skewed. Maybe he didn't hate that behavior at all.

Perhaps he simply mourned the fact that Ellery never got to do those things herself.

12

"Come on," August said brightly, grabbing Keaton's arm. "It's our turn to go through."

The previous group—which smartly contained all the "non dog" animals, like cats and lizards, et cetera—trooped out of the space through a door on the far side of the room. Keaton, Molly and August were assigned to start their first five-minute photo shoot at station number three, which was the beach-themed area.

The backdrop showed an artistic representation of a beach, with soft azure sky, blue-green water and yellow sand. As a husky, Molly looked woefully out of place. If they had any chance of creating one of the top photos—which would earn someone a bonus prize of an hour social media assessment and consultation with Isla herself—they needed to get creative. August *wanted* that prize for Leah.

And also working toward a goal is a great *distraction from thinking about the fact that you* FREAKING KISSED KEATON SAX!!

Ugh, her brain was so annoying sometimes.

"Look, Keaton," she said, choosing to focus on the issue in front of her rather than the ones in her head. "It's clear that you're working through some stuff right now and I totally appreciate that. Maybe this whole thing has dredged up some bad memories. Or maybe it's because this is the first time you haven't been working yourself into the ground in a long time and the clear air is making you think."

He looked at her, surprise flickering in his green eyes. It had taken everything in her a moment ago, when vulnerability flashed across his face like lightning, not to pull the big grump into her arms and kiss him until he couldn't think anymore.

It *hurt* to see him like that. Because Keaton had grit and resilience and a pick-yourself-up-ness that she deeply admired.

Seeing his pain…oh boy. It made her tender heart ache. Not only because of what he'd lost, but because she suspected that he couldn't lean on anyone else, because being the pillar was *his* job. Being the supporter and the giver and the rock was who he was.

And she wanted to be that person for him, if only to give him a break from carrying the world on his shoulders.

However, they couldn't be distracted from their goal right now. Goals were safe. Emotions and kissing…not so much. Especially not since she already had her ideal guy in mind: her perfectly practical partnership, where chemistry and emotion took a back seat to safer things, like common goals and shared interests and mutually beneficial checklists.

Yes, maybe she wanted the "granny panties" of relationships and that made her boring. But while a "red thong relationship" might seem like the sexier option, it would ultimately end up being a pain in her ass.

"Even if you don't believe in any of this social media stuff, I know one thing about you." She grinned. "You like to win."

He chuckled, the expression crinkling the edges of his beautiful green eyes. "I *do* like to win."

"So let's win, okay?" She held her hand up for a high five. "Let's win that bonus prize for Leah."

She could tell the exact moment that Keaton's competition mode clicked into place. The shift in his face was stark and…exciting.

"Everybody ready?" the coordinator called from the front of the room. "Your first five minutes starts…now!"

"Okay, a beach scene with Molly." Keaton unclipped her leash and slung it over his shoulder, then got Molly to follow him in front of the backdrop. "Sit."

Molly did what she was told, albeit reluctantly. August could practically hear her voice. *You expect me to do what? Pretend I'm at the beach? Have you* seen *this fur, people? Do you know what I'm bred for?*

Hmm, hopefully there was a snowy scene. Then she'd look less out of place.

"What props can we use?" August looked through some items that were messily scattered on the ground from the last group. There was a bucket and spade, a stuffed lobster toy, a shark fin, some plastic starfish, an inflatable beach ball.

"How about this?" Keaton held up a floppy sun hat.

"Perfect!"

He walked over to Molly, but she tossed her head and stamped her paws. *"Nooooo."*

"Did she just say no?" Keaton looked at August.

"Ah, she's just being dramatic. Try buttering her up."

Keaton approached the dog, the floppy sun hat dangling from one hand. Molly eyed it with extreme suspicion. She didn't love wearing hats but tolerated one of those cone-shaped party hats with the glittery pom-poms each year for her birthday because it made Leah happy. For Keaton and August, however, she was not so tolerant.

"No no no no no." The dog's noises really did sound like a toddler throwing a temper tantrum.

"Oh come on, Molly. You'll look so pretty." Keaton crouched in front of her and tried to pat her head, but the dog tossed his hand off and glared at him.

You were just buttering me up earlier. Betrayal!

August clamped a hand over her mouth to stifle a giggle, because she didn't want Keaton to lose heart. But this was not going to be an easy exercise. Leah would have been able to get Molly to do whatever she wanted—despite Keaton thinking that the dog had his sister wrapped around her paw, it was quite the opposite. Molly *adored* Leah and always wanted to make her happy.

"Pretty please with gross doggy treats on top?" Keaton pleaded.

Molly snorted. *No, thank you, sir.*

"Come on, do it for Leah? You love Leah, don't you?"

At the sound of her owner's name, the dog's ears pricked up and Keaton caught on.

"That's right, these photos are for Leah. It will make her so happy to see you enjoying yourself at the beach." He held the hat up and the dog eyed it with wariness, but she didn't protest this time. "Good girl. Now, I'm going to place this hat on your head and I want you to smile for the camera, okay?"

He gingerly placed the floppy hat down on the dog's head. It slipped forward over Molly's eyes and Keaton carefully readjusted it so you could see her face. But smile, she did not. In fact, Molly's resting bitch face had never been more prominent than it was now. August reached forward to place the bucket and spade at Molly's feet, stepping out of the shot so Keaton could snap a few photos with his phone.

Later, they would have to pick their five best shots and send them to the coordinator, who would project them all onto a wall in the main hall, along with their submitted captions, so the judges could pick their favorite and eliminate a few more contestants.

"Smile, Molly," he tried again, but the dog continued to glare.

Nothing worked. Not waving a treat in front of her face, not trying to get her to shake or high-five. Not doing a funny little dance. Her tail stayed stock-still as if it were made of concrete and her eyes bored into Keaton with unmatched disdain as he snapped some photos from a few different angles.

"I think I'm going to call this one *Molly hates the beach*," he said, snorting as he swiped through the photos with August.

"Oh dear, she looks..."

"Like she wants to commit homicide?" he suggested.

"Yeah, kinda."

"And you all thought I was being dramatic when I said I felt like she was going to kill me in my sleep," he said smugly.

A bell sounded near the front of the room. The first five minutes was up and they needed to move to the next station. As if sensing this was her cue to be free from the beach hat of doom, Molly tossed it off and gave her whole body a shake. Taking a moment to give Keaton a stare down, she trotted off toward the next booth.

"Did you see that look?" Keaton said as they walked over. "Premeditation."

August chuckled. "She *does* have a vindictive streak. One time Leah wouldn't give her any treats, so she found the bag and ripped it open, then proceeded to sprinkle the treats all over the kitchen floor. She didn't even eat them! She just wanted to prove she could get to them."

Keaton shook his head. "This is why I don't want kids. I couldn't handle the mess and the constant boundary testing."

August blinked. "I didn't know that you don't want kids."

"Nah, never have. Maybe it's because I felt like Leah and I were such a burden to Mom when she was going through her tough times. There were days where I had to be the parent and make sure we had dinner on the table because Mom struggled to get out of bed and…so I feel like I already lived that experience." He shrugged. "Most people think I don't want kids because Ellery died, but it was set a long time before that."

August nodded. "Right."

"Isn't this the part where you say, 'Oh but you'd be such a good dad'?" he said in a high-pitched voice, rolling his eyes.

"Hell, no, I hate it when people say that." She wrinkled her nose. "Not being a parent is a perfectly legitimate life choice."

Keaton looked surprised by her answer, but they didn't have time to expand on the conversation because the whistle blew for the next five-minute photo shoot. This time they were at the bubble bath station. The background was blue with bubbles on it, and there were all sorts of bubble-making implements, including the traditional ring wand, and some automatic bubble blowers. There were also clear balloons with confetti in them and other cute props, like shower caps and rubber duckies.

"I don't think we should attempt a hat a second time," Keaton said.

Molly looked at him as if to say, *Wise move, buddy.*

"How about I blow some bubbles and you take the photos?" August suggested.

"Good idea."

August found one of the little automatic bubble guns and filled the water chamber with the bubble-making liquid. "Ready, Molly? Here come the bubbles!"

She fired the gun and bubbles streamed into the air. Keaton snapped some photos and asked August to try shooting the bubbles this way and that. They even did one of those long exposure photos while August shot the bubble stream in all different directions, with Molly sitting stock-still in the center. It turned out so cool…except for Molly's utterly unimpressed expression.

"Well, if the last one was *Molly hates the beach* then this one can be *Molly hates bath time.*" Keaton laughed heartily. His eyes twinkled with delight and his face was relaxed, showing off his handsome features to their full potential.

It was like the moment when sunshine broke through storm clouds, and good lord it was beautiful. Keaton could be so intense sometimes. But she loved this side of him—it reminded her of how he used to be. Playful, fun, lighthearted. Even in the tough times when his mom was struggling and he hated his stepdad, he still smiled readily. Cheekily. He managed to balance the intense and easygoing sides of himself better than he did now.

In some ways, he and Molly were *a lot* alike. But she figured saying that out loud would probably piss either one of them off, if not both.

"What are we going to do for the rest of these photos?" Keaton scrubbed a hand over his face. "She won't do anything except look grumpy."

August tapped a fingertip to her chin. The second lot of five minutes was almost up and they didn't exactly have a lot to work with. Nothing seemed to budge Molly's disgruntled expression.

"Well, maybe we lean into it?" August shrugged. "If she's going to be miserable, then we can make it funny? The comedy angle seemed to work for you in the first round, so maybe it will work again."

"You're right." He snapped his fingers together. "Wasn't there that grumpy cat that everyone liked?"

"The one literally called Grumpy Cat."

"Oh, that was actually his name? I didn't know that." He seemed completely serious.

"Don't you know *anything* about the internet? You're only thirty-two, there is literally no excuse to be such a Luddite." She laughed. "Do you even know what a meme is?"

"Of course I know what a meme is." He waved her off. "I'm not living under a rock."

"I'm not sure I believe that, but I *do* like the idea. A collection of pictures of all the things that Molly hates." She giggled. "It's fun."

"Maybe I could even be in the last photo with her. Because I'm the number one thing she hates." He grinned, and Molly made a noise of agreement down at his feet.

That's the first accurate thing you've ever said, human.

"I think it might work out great." Hope filled her heart. Maybe they *would* win this prize for Leah! "Great work, team."

She held out her hand to Molly and the dog reluctantly lifted her paw up halfway. August met her there, deciding an attempt to follow the instruction was better than nothing. They might not be the perfect team, but they were doing the best they could with what they had.

★★★

Fifteen minutes later they had an entire series of Molly hating things. Aside from the beach and the bubble bath, she also hated birthday parties, pumpkin patches and romantic candlelit dinners. Keaton had jumped into one photo, holding out a rose to Molly, who looked at him as though he were some disgusting bug who'd dared invade her space. They decided not to use that shot for the final submission, because the aesthetic looked better with only pictures of Molly, but August texted the photo to Leah, who responded with a string of laughing, crying emojis.

And it worked! Molly scored the top spot for that round of the competition, and he'd slung an arm around August's shoulders, the two of them reveling in the feeling of winning as a team. Even better, Leah would get to have a one-on-one session with Isla to help improve her social media game. She'd squealed with excitement when Keaton rang her to share the good news.

Now they were back in the cabin to get ready for dinner.

"Uh, you go first," August said, motioning to the bathroom.

Now that the euphoria of winning the photo contest had died down, some of the awkwardness was creeping back in. It was hard to look at his face and not remember the scratch of his stubble over her skin. To not remember the heat of his hands on her body and the firm instances of his lips against hers.

"You sure?" he asked. "I don't need long."

"Not going to make an effort, huh?" she teased.

He laughed. "Doesn't take me long to look good, is all."

"Asshole," she muttered. Molly made a sound of agreement from her doggy basket. She was currently curled up with a stuffed toy that had been part of the prize, the little plush lobster firmly secured under one leg.

"Fine, I'll go. No peeking." He winked at her.

Yep, they were back to teasing alright. Probably for the best—the last thing she needed was Keaton looking at her like he might want round two of that kiss. Or more.

Think you won't be able to say no?

She wasn't confident.

Keaton disappeared into the bathroom and music blasted from his phone, then the sound of rushing water followed.

"Don't forget the fan," she called out, and a second later the whirring sound started up.

August smiled. She remembered Leah shouting the same thing at him when they were kids, because he'd always take hot showers without turning the fan on, leaving the girls with a fogged-up mirror. Leah had loved to stay in the bathroom for hours playing with makeup, and that was impossible when you couldn't see your own reflection.

August plopped down onto the bed and dropped her head into her hands. The thought of him being fully naked with water streaming down his body mere feet away was doing funny things to her insides. Maybe she should just concede defeat and move to another room.

Or maybe you need to try harder to convince him *to move rooms?*

It was clear she had as much willpower resisting Keaton as she did a fresh batch of chocolate chip cookies. It was futile. No matter how much time passed, there would always be some part of her that yearned for him.

Before she could decide on the room situation, her phone rang. Talk about a welcome distraction! She fished the buzzing device out of her purse and blinked in surprise. It was the matchmaking agency.

She swiped her thumb across the screen. "Hello?"

"Hi, August, it's Maxine Diamond. Is this a good time to talk?"

"Uh, sure."

For some reason, her heart started to beat a little faster. Was something wrong? Had Asher called the agency to say he wasn't interested in another date with her? Everything *felt* like it had gone according to her expectations. Sure, there was no real spark, but even that was still in line with her plans. What if—

Stop spiraling.

"Great," Maxine said. Her voice was deep for a woman, and a little gravelly, and she spoke with a warmth and confidence that made you want to listen to her. "I need to talk to you about Asher."

"Okay." Something about Maxine's tone didn't feel right, almost like she was leading up to something.

"I've come across the unfortunate information that he's registered with more than one agency. I found this out by accident when talking with a former staff member of mine who now runs her own matchmaking business."

"The implication of that is…?"

"Well, he's been matched with different women at each agency." She sighed. "It turns out that he was in talks with the producers for that reality TV show, *The Bachelor*, but they ended up going with someone else in the end. He apparently still wants to live that fantasy, however, so he approached several agencies and is making the experience for himself, all while writing an article for *New York Magazine* about running his own 'red rose experience,' as he called it."

"What?" August's stomach dropped suddenly as if she was on a theme park ride.

"I'm *so* sorry about this. I obviously would not have paired you if I had *any* idea that this was happening. It's a huge breach of the agreement he signed with us, and my legal team is currently looking at how we can block the publication of his article."

August pressed her palm to her forehead.

Don't vomit. Don't vomit. Don't vomit.

Keaton was going to have a field day with this. He'd warned her about Asher from the moment he found out they were dating. Well…going on dates. That felt like an important distinction. They *weren't* technically in a relationship yet. But she'd hoped it was moving in that direction.

So, it still felt like a betrayal. An embarrassment. Another black mark on her disastrous dating record.

"August?" Maxine sighed. "Are you still there?"

"Yes," she croaked in response. "I, uh… I need a moment to process this."

"Of course, please take all the time you need. I am already compiling some new matches for you, because I don't want this to stop you from finding the right partner. I assure you that I will go over every single one of them with a fine-tooth comb. This will *not* happen again."

"Thank you." August ended the call before Maxine had a chance to say anything else.

For a moment, she could only stare at the phone in her hands, her mind whirring.

What if they couldn't stop Asher from writing his article? What if August was the victim in yet *another* viral dating disaster? What if this was merely a grim preview of what her dating life would always be—from the frying pan into the dumpster fire?

Why, oh why, did she push Keaton away that fateful Christmas Eve?

13

On the drive over to the restaurant, following along behind the car containing Isla, Scout and their respective partners, Keaton was convinced something was up with August. She'd barely said a word the whole time—which was long enough that her silence was *definitely* noticeable. He'd tried a few times to get her talking, but she stared out of the window, as if transfixed by the scenery, which, while nice, wasn't *that* interesting.

"Is everything okay?" he asked as they pulled into the main strip of a small town. It was a picturesque place, with old buildings and colorful awnings capping the entrances of ice cream parlors, bakeries and bookstores. The kind of place you'd expect to see as the backdrop in one of those Hallmark Christmas movies his sister loved so much. "You've been quiet as a mouse."

"It's been a long day," she replied.

"I know you work ridiculous hours. This is nothing."

"Maybe it's all the fresh air." She gave a weak laugh. "City girl isn't used to breathing in something that doesn't smell like gasoline and burned pretzels."

He frowned. She was dodging, which wasn't like August. Usually if she had a problem with him, she had no issue telling him to shove it.

"I certainly don't smell gasoline or burned pretzels out here, but I *do* smell some bullshit."

Her head snapped toward him. "Excuse me?"

"You're excused."

She frowned. "What are you trying to say?"

"That something is going on and you're being weird. I suspect it has to do with the kiss, but you don't want to talk about it, which leaves us in an uncomfortable position of being awkward around one another." He let out a breath. "And I don't like it."

"Being awkward?"

"Not with you." He shook his head. "And not when we need to spend not only the rest of the night together, but the rest of the weekend as well."

It was Friday evening now, and they had the whole weekend together ahead of them. The last thing he wanted was August and him having to tiptoe around one another instead of just having a conversation.

"So why don't you change rooms?" she said, her voice laced with challenge. "That might help the awkwardness."

His shoulders immediately hiked up. "Why don't *you* change rooms?"

If she thought he was going to give up winning their little game simply because she wanted an easy out, then she was shit out of luck.

It was *so* childish, such a silly competition. But bantering with August was sometimes the only thing that felt real to him anymore. The rest of the time he was lost in his work, forgetting all his own needs, burying his memories. With her, things were…comfortable.

Except not right now, and that pissed him off.

"It's not the kiss," she said with a huff, folding her arms across her chest.

"Then what is it?"

"Nothing I want to talk about."

Keaton watched the road as the car in front of them started flashing its turn signal light and pulled into a side street. He followed and parked his car. Outside, he could hear Scout's and Isla's laughter as they exited the other car. When he killed the engine, he turned to look at August.

She'd dressed up for dinner, although it was dressed up for a meal in a small town, rather than the kind of dressed up he usually witnessed in Manhattan. She wore a pretty yellow top with some white embroidery at the neckline and those puffy sleeves that made her look like a sexy Swedish milkmaid.

There's a fantasy I didn't even know I needed in my life.

Her hair was soft and bouncy from some weird hair dryer attachment she'd used to do her hair, and her eyelids sparkled with something soft and golden. August wasn't the kind of girl who wore much makeup—she'd said once that she didn't feel the need because her four-legged clients didn't care how she looked. But seeing her like this—looking glowing, and a little made-up, and smelling like something sweet and delectable—it reminded him of *that* night. That fateful, memorable, change-everything night.

"I appreciate the concern, Keaton," she said. "But you don't need to worry about me. I'm not your little sister, okay? I'm not someone you need to feel obligated to care about."

"I don't feel obligated to care about you," he said. "And I most certainly *don't* view you like a sister."

Much to the detriment of his resolve to remain unentangled, unfortunately.

"I don't mean literally," she said, shaking her head. "But I thought you always viewed me as that annoying little kid type. A hanger-on."

"I've *never* viewed you as a hanger-on, August. Not once." What on earth was going on with her right now? Could she not tell that the kiss was a poorly disguised attempt to have something he'd wanted a long time ago? That he might want again now?

You don't want to start anything with her. Or anyone else.

Then why did it feel like there was something brewing. Like a storm was coming. Like lightning was about to strike.

"I know we banter and stuff, but..." He shook his head. The teasing was always to keep her from getting too close, but it was never meant to push her away entirely. He didn't want that. "I respect you."

She bit down on her lip. Something had well and truly rattled her.

"We should get going. They're waiting for us." She pushed the car door open and stepped outside, leaving Keaton baffled.

"It's not your problem," he said to himself. But as he got out of the car and saw that August was waiting for him, so they could walk over to the group together, he knew it would be a burr under his skin until he figured out what was up with her.

"I'm so glad you two could join us," Scout said with a bright smile as he and August approached them outside the restaurant. It was a cute mom-and-pop place, with red-and-white-striped awnings and a chalkboard sign stating the evening's specials. "Keaton, this is my husband, Lane."

She indicated a tall man with red-tinted brown hair and an easy, friendly smile. "Nice to meet you."

"And this is my husband, Theo," Isla said, smiling up at the man standing next to her, who looked serious though not unfriendly.

Keaton knew who Theo Garrison was immediately. Old money Manhattan royalty, a figure he'd only ever seen as a name printed in papers under his picture or someone whispered about in exclusive venues. Keaton wasn't one to get starstruck, but it was strange to meet a man in person when he had such a larger-than-life reputation.

He stuck his hand out to each of the men. "Thanks for including us."

"Of course. It's good to see you, August." Lane reached in and gave her a warm hug. Theo followed with a peck on the cheek. It seemed the two men had quite different personalities—Lane, like Scout, was laid-back and open. But Theo would probably take a little warming up.

"Shall we head inside?" Isla asked, ever the leader.

The group followed her and they were quickly seated at a corner table with a banquette on one side and wooden chairs on the other. Tea light candles were dotted along the table, along with small bottles of balsamic vinegar and olive oil. Wine and food were ordered, and bread appeared at the table with small bowls for dipping. Isla poured the oil and vinegar into the bowls and made sure everyone had access.

When the wine came, Theo took a small taste and then it was poured for the table.

"So, I'm confused about how you're involved in this whole

thing," Lane said to August, who was sitting across from him, next to Keaton. "You're not working with Scout and Isla?"

"No, I'm here as a…helper."

"It's a long story," Isla said. "But the producer of the documentary got the idea from her niece, who's a dog groomer. They're following three women-run businesses in the animal space, including the niece."

"Ah." Lane nodded. "So August is competition."

August laughed. "I guess so."

"Frankly, I think they would have been better following August," Isla said. She tucked a strand of long, dark hair behind one ear. "She has a much more successful business and she even grooms the pets of several celebrities."

"Really?" Lane's eyebrows shot up. "Like who?"

"Technically I'm not supposed to say too much," August replied, pausing to take a sip of her wine. The deep red color left a slight stain on her lips and Keaton caught himself staring. "But I may have groomed the pet of a certain *Game of Thrones* actor."

Scout gasped. "Which one? I used to love that show."

"The one who drank a lot."

"That does *not* narrow it down," Theo replied with a dry chuckle. "I swear, everyone who lives in a fantasy realm must have pickled insides."

August laughed. "True. I usually sign an NDA for the really big-name clients, but I've got all kinds of people on my list. Some politicians, a supreme court judge, a fashion designer, and then some regular people as well."

"How did you end up with such an impressive list of clients?" Lane asked.

"Recommendations. Once you prove you're punctual and do good work and that the animals like you, word spreads."

August seemed to glow under the attention and genuine interest. It was wonderful to see her passion for her work shine through. "But enough about me!"

"How is the filming and the competition going?" Lane asked.

"You mean other than us crushing it in the photo challenge," Keaton said, winking at August and pretending to dust off his shoulders.

She turned to him and grinned. "We *totally* crushed it."

"Oh, you should have seen it, Theo." Isla grabbed his arm. When his wife was in close proximity, Theo's reserved outer shell seemed to dissolve and he looked like any normal guy who was utterly smitten with his partner. "The photos of this husky were hilarious. They called the series 'Molly Hates Everything' and it was just photos of her looking unimpressed."

"Sounds like my kind of dog." He chuckled.

"I think Molly and Camilla would totally be BFFs," Scout chimed in, nodding.

Theo's Dachshund might be the only other dog to rival Molly in levels of sassiness.

"They would." Isla nodded. "The filming crew has been shadowing us for a full week already. We had them along to a campaign we were shooting with one of our biggest TikTok stars, Sasha Frise."

"The *real* Sasha Frise," Scout said, looking at Lane.

"They also filmed me doing an interview with a local news station and even came to the office one day, to see us doing all the boring admin bits." Isla shook her head. "I don't know why they wanted that, but it was no skin off my nose."

"They take hours and hours of footage, and only a small portion will make it into the documentary," Theo said. "Sometimes they don't know exactly what they need, so better to get more rather than less."

"They must have a ton, since they're also following the other two business owners." Isla sipped her wine. "I have no idea how they go through all that footage to decide what to keep and what to discard. It must be an incredible amount of work."

"And you're taking part in the talent competition?" Lane asked, looking at Keaton. "With August's help?"

"That's right. Molly is my sister's dog, but Leah is unwell at the moment. I'm here on her behalf so she didn't miss out," he said. "And August and my sister went to school together, so we've all known each other a long time."

"Keaton is doing a great job," August said encouragingly. "Especially since Molly can be a little difficult at times."

"I know that feeling." Theo shot him a look of respect. "They can be stubborn animals."

"But worth it, right?" Isla beamed up at her husband and pressed a hand to his cheek.

"Yeah." He leaned down and brushed his lips against hers. "Totally worth it."

The whole way through the dinner, August tried her best to stay engaged. But all she could think about was freaking Asher Benson and his egotistical DIY *The Bachelor.* Who even *did* something like that? What an absolute dick.

She should have taken Keaton seriously the night they bumped into one another. But oh no, she had to be all pissy because it felt like a slight against her independence and her ability to make good choices for herself. Like he was a big brother teasing her. Like he was her parents questioning her every move. Like he was that little doubtful voice in the back of her head brought to life.

If only she'd listened.

Was she destined to be single forever? Maybe life would be better that way.

But as she looked at her friends being supported by their amazing partners, her heart panged. She wanted that. Not because she thought finding a man would make her whole—she was already whole. But August was a deeply social creature and she wanted someone to share her life with.

Because sharing was the cherry on top of the sundae of life.

"Hey." Keaton nudged her with his elbow. "Earth to August."

She blinked. "Sorry, I'm totally zoning out."

The rest of the table was in discussion. The owner had come out to see how the meal had gone, and he and Theo were chatting about their favorite Italian wines. Scout, meanwhile, had Lane and Isla in peals of laughter about something funny that had happened at her prenatal checkup last week.

"You can try to act like it's nothing, but something is up," he said.

"I never denied that. I simply said I didn't want to talk about it."

He turned to her in the banquette seat, and the action caused his knee to brush against her thigh. He slid his arm along the back of the seat, not around her shoulders, but it still made part of her want to sigh and lean into him.

"I might be able to help," he said. "I know you think I'm just some emotionless robot, but I do give good advice."

"I don't think you're a robot."

"You'd be wrong, then," he said, leaning forward slightly. His stubble had grown even darker through the day, and she'd never seen him look so rough-and-tumble sexy. "I'm actually a bionic weapon of annoyance."

She snorted. "Now *that* I would believe."

"Look, I understand you think we're not friends, but rather 'acquaintances joined by a mutual thread' and all…" He cocked his head. "But I *do* consider you a friend. If someone is being an asshole to you, I can have a quiet word with them."

She couldn't help but smile. "Sounds like that 'quiet word' has some baseball-bat-to-the-knees connotations."

"Not required. I'm *very* persuasive with my mouth alone."

She gulped. He probably didn't mean those words to have such a strong sexual undertone, but August was feeling at least fifty degrees hotter all of a sudden. She took a swig of her red wine, but it didn't help at all. The sensual berry notes of the alcohol were going to her head, and suddenly she was finding it hard to fight back all the usual things that held her at a distance.

He's emotionally unavailable.

But was he, though? He seemed genuine now.

He's already broken your heart once.

Technically, that was her fault. Not his.

He's not looking for commitment.

Were any men? It felt like every time she tried to find someone who was looking for the same thing as her, she ran into a dead end. Doing the same thing over and over was like slamming her head against a brick wall.

He's not the practical choice.

He really wasn't. There was so much baggage. So much history. He was guarded and wary and he had the potential to break her heart clean in two. Because she'd already loved him for very nonpractical reasons, for chemistry reasons.

All the things she'd struck off her checklist.

Yet, for some reason—maybe the wine and good meal and the warmth of being around the people she cared about—the checklist suddenly felt like a burden, rather than an aid.

"Tell you what," she said. "I don't want to get into it here, but we'll talk in the car, okay?"

"Told you I'm persuasive," he said.

Across the table, August caught Scout nudging Isla, and then both women looked in their direction, giggling. It must be written all over her face how much she wanted him, even when she knew better.

But she'd drunk enough that her tongue felt loose and her ability to put her brain in charge was slowly slipping through her fingers. She was tired of trying to make good decisions, only to face humiliation. She was tired of pretending that she didn't feel the chemistry she had with Keaton. And, most of all, she was tired of feeling like the partnership she wanted was completely out of her reach.

What if, for one night, she just…had a good time?

14

On the drive back to the retreat, Keaton was at the wheel. He'd only had a small glass of wine, and the espresso he'd drunk with dessert made him feel like a spring wound tight. It was probably a bad idea, given sharing a bed with August was already making it tough to sleep. But at least he was feeling wide-awake and super alert for the drive back in the dark.

They'd spent the first leg of the journey chatting about her friendship with Scout and Isla, who seemed like fun and interesting women. August made friends so easily.

Add that to a list of skills I definitely do not have.

Keaton was more of a closed-circle kinda guy. He loved his family fiercely, but that left little room for anyone else. Usually that didn't bother him, but when he saw how easily August attracted people to her genuine and warm personality, it made him wonder if something in him was missing.

Just outside the turnoff for the retreat, he realized that she'd been skirting the topic they were supposed to be talking about.

"So," he said. "Tell me why your attention has been MIA tonight."

For a few heartbeats, she said nothing, then, "Remember how you told me that Asher was a bad guy and to stay away from him…and how I didn't listen?"

"Yeah." He glanced over to her, but it was hard to see anything. The road leading into the retreat was dark and he had to concentrate on making sure he wasn't veering off the edge. "What about it?"

"Turns out you were right." Her voice was tight.

"What did he do?" Keaton felt his lip curl back as if he were about to snarl. But he held himself in check. The last thing he wanted was August clamming up. "He didn't hurt you, did he? Because I swear to God—"

"No, nothing like that." She shook her head. "We only got as far as a kiss and I wanted it."

Hearing her say those words made his stomach twist.

"But earlier today I got a call from the matchmaking agency and…"

He waited a few breaths before asking, "And?"

"Apparently Asher is registered with several different agencies."

He wasn't quite sure if that was a bad thing, or if there was more to come, but he kept his eyes on the road and his mouth shut.

"That means he's been matched with different women at each place and has been going on dates with a few people at once." She blew out a breath. "Which I guess isn't *so* bad, even though it technically breaks the contract with the matchmaking agency. But I mean, who's to say there aren't some clients also using Tinder or an equivalent dating app at the same time? Going on a date by itself doesn't mean exclusivity. We never even got to that point in our conversations, so it wasn't like he was breaking a promise."

"Right." The sucker punch was coming; he could feel in the tone of her voice how she was dancing around it.

"Apparently he sold the idea of a DIY *The Bachelor* experience to *New York Magazine*. At least, I think they know about it. Maybe he was going to write it first and then pitch it... I can't remember exactly what she said." August was picking up pace, the words tumbling out quicker and quicker. "And if I'm one of the people he matched with, then he might try to put me in the article! I can't have that. It could damage my business, especially since many of my clients are particular about their security. At the very least it will make me look gullible and—"

"August, breathe."

She drew in a shaky breath. "I believed him."

Good lord how he wanted to turn this car around right now and drive back to New York so he could find Asher Benson and make his face unpresentable for television. That privileged asshole never thought about anyone but himself.

But that wouldn't help the situation.

"He's a good liar," Keaton said, keeping his voice even. "Don't beat yourself up."

"I should know that already, though. You *told* me and I didn't listen."

Silence settled over the car as they continued along the winding road, black shadows moving outside the car as moonlight filtered down. Ahead of them, the headlights bounced on the road, catching on the vehicle in front of them.

"Say it," August said, her voice heavy.

"What?"

"I told you so."

"There's no satisfaction in saying that," he said, shaking his head. "I wish I wasn't right."

That's a lie. You're fucking over the moon that she won't be running back to lock lips with Asher after you get back to Manhattan.

"I want to find someone who has the same goals as me," she said quietly. "That's all. Just a decent human with a nice smile and a good sense of humor who wants to build a life together and who won't ghost me the next morning. Is that too much to ask?"

Usually Keaton would have made a joke, but she sounded so utterly dejected that he couldn't bring himself to make light of the situation. Besides, if he claimed they were friends—which he did—then it was his job to act like one in this moment.

"Any man would be lucky to have you, August," he said. "Don't let one egomaniac dent your confidence."

"Oh, you think it's just one?" She let out a humorless laugh. "I wish."

He raised an eyebrow.

"I once had a guy leave halfway through a date by telling me I was one of three dates he had lined up that night and I was too 'pasty' for him. Another guy said he would take me on a second date…to the gym." She ticked the experiences off with her fingers. "Oh, and then another guy said he didn't believe women when they said they didn't want to have kids, because they just hadn't, and I quote, 'found the right dick yet.'"

"Where are you finding these men?"

"Online."

"Well, there's your problem," he said. "The internet is for trolls."

"People don't meet the old-fashioned way anymore. Dating apps are the norm now." She huffed. "And yeah, I've been on dates with some more polite guys, but they weren't much better in the end. A couple ghosted me for no reason. One guy at least tried to explain himself, but it ended up with the same result. I'm starting to think there's something wrong with me."

"There's *nothing* wrong with you, August. These guys, they're just..." He made a sound of disgust. "Men are bastards."

"Where do I find the ones who aren't?"

"Why do you even want to date, anyway? People are awful." Keaton wrinkled his nose. "They have emotions and they're complicated and then in the end you die."

She blinked. "Wow. I don't even know *what* to say to that."

"It's true."

"Yeah, but by that logic you'd never do anything. Might as well not bother making any friends, because I'm going to die one day. Might as well not bother traveling or taking up hobbies or going on adventures because...imminent mortality."

Wasn't that exactly how he lived his life—without friends or hobbies or travel for pleasure?

"That's a terrible way to live," she said, without waiting for him to respond. "And I want to date because I'm lonely."

The word was like a javelin being thrown right at his chest. It lanced him. Hit him somewhere soft that he'd been *sure* was covered by armor only moments ago.

"You're lonely?" he asked.

"Yeah." She looked down. "Leah and Scout and Isla are all paired up now. Yes, I still see them all regularly, but I'm also conscious of not wanting to intrude on their time too much.

And I see how happy and supported they are and… I want that. And I want to give those things to someone as well."

This is exactly *why you've been keeping her at arm's length. You are the antithesis of what she needs. At best, you're a distraction. At worst…you're another scar on her heart. Another bad news story for her to share when she eventually finds The One.*

The car ahead of them peeled off toward the large cabin where Scout, Isla and their husbands were staying, and he turned the opposite direction. The headlights glanced over trees and other vehicles, and after a moment, their cabin came into view.

He parked the car and killed the engine. Trying to gather himself, he wanted to say something meaningful. Something helpful. But August unbuckled her belt and got out of the car, a sniffle cutting through the night air.

"Shit." He hung his head.

Why did he have to be so crap at dealing with emotions?

August strode up to the cabin and opened the front door, letting it swing shut behind her. An emotional August was totally outside the realm of his experience. For as long as he could remember, she was the girl with gold stars in her eyes. The ambitious, driven, stubborn one. Even as kids, if she fell, she would get right back up and dust herself off. She was quick to comfort others. Quick to show compassion.

But there was a guardedness in her. A protectiveness.

Did you have to be such *a dick? Couldn't you just say the things she wanted to hear instead of projecting your own issues onto her?*

He should walk away. Let her cry it out and emerge with her mask intact. Wasn't that what she'd want?

Why did he even agree to be here? It was a silly dog competition and nothing more. He could have told Leah he was too busy with work and hired someone to step in. At the very least, he could have done it on his own instead of dragging August into the situation.

He got out of the car and locked the doors. Outside, the air was crisp and moonlight shone down through a gap in the trees.

He wasn't sure how long he stayed outside, trying to figure out what to do. Five minutes? Ten minutes? Half an hour? Ellery had always told him that his emotions were like tadpoles, slippery and impossible to catch. That's why August scared the shit out of him.

She was…open. Like a wound waiting for some salt to be poured in. Like sunshine, bright and warm, just waiting for someone to drown her out with their rain clouds.

Around him, insects chirruped as he paced back and forth. But he couldn't stay out here all night. He walked to the cabin, pausing at the threshold, hand hovering the room key in front of the door's scanner panel while he wrestled with himself.

Turn around and walk away. Get another cabin. Hide. Isn't that what you do best?

Keaton gritted his teeth and tapped the room key down. The lock clicked inside the door and he eased it open. All the lights were off, except for the bathroom, with the door cracked open so that he'd be able to see. And the blinds were open, allowing moonlight to flood in through the window, casting silvery bands across the bed and floor. They revealed the outline of her form—the curve of her shoulder and hip, and the gentle dip at her waist. The gleam of her fiery red hair spilling across the pillow like ribbons.

He toed off his sneakers and nudged them to one side with his foot. Then he carefully set his wallet and keys down on the little table by the door, trying not to make any noise. A soft muffled sound broke through the otherwise silent room. Was she…?

"Augie?" He let the door shut softly behind him.

In the corner, Molly raised her head sleepily, barely cracking one eye open, before she dropped back down and resumed her light snoring.

There was a soft sniffling, but then it stopped abruptly. She must have realized he'd come inside and was trying to hold it together. He respected her for that.

Is that only because you think emotions make you weak? Vulnerable?

He shook off the inconvenient question as his eyes adjusted to the dim light. August faced away from him, her body curled up in the center of the bed, shuddering slightly.

"Augie?" He let out a breath. "I'm sorry."

"It's not you."

He padded to the bed and sank his knees into the mattress, so he could check on her. Her cheeks were damp, the moisture catching the silvery moonlight. He swallowed. Inside him there was a war—one part of him desperately wanted to comfort her and the other part was screaming at him to walk away. He brushed his knuckles along her arm, his breath sticking in his throat when she shivered at his touch. But he couldn't seem to pry himself away like he had every other time he'd thought about his feelings for August.

Every time he'd remembered how much he wanted to do more than kiss her that fateful night.

"I shouldn't put my misanthropic shit onto you. That's not fair." It felt like there was a fist around his throat, trying to stop him from saying more. "I feel bad for saying those things, because…shit. I didn't mean to belittle your dreams."

Get out of here.

"But let's not get into that now. It's late. I'll let you sleep." He pulled away, but she rolled, her hand reaching out for him. The movement caused the sheet to slip further down, revealing a pale shoulder and arm, the curve of her bust pressing against the slightly twisted fabric of the T-shirt she slept in. "I can… I can find another room."

"Stay," she said. "There's not going to be anyone at the front desk now."

"I should…" Should what? He had no idea how to navigate this situation. What was he going to do, sleep outside? In the car?

"Get into the bed." She tugged him to her. "We did it last night, we can do it again."

Lord he was being tested right now.

But the tremor in her voice was one he'd never heard before. Usually he could find sense enough to back away, but now he was stripping down to his jocks. Then he lowered himself down onto the bed. The mattress shifted under the additional weight and he kept a slight distance between them.

But the urge to touch her was too much. He rubbed his hand up and down her arm, hoping it might soothe her enough that she would fall back to sleep. Her skin was like silk.

Get her to sleep and then you can go back to your original plan of sleeping on the floor. Tomorrow, you'll both pretend like this never happened.

That would be the smart thing to do.

He'd tried to maintain a little distance between them, but she wriggled until her back lined his chest, the curve of her ass cradled perfectly in his lap. A jolt of arousal shot through him, but he held his breath and stifled the reaction. It was like trying to swallow a pill without water.

"Do you ever wonder what life would be like if things had turned out differently?" she asked groggily.

"Constantly."

What if August had kissed him back that night? What if he'd never met Ellery? What if she hadn't been stolen from him in such a cruel and unpredictable way?

"Me too."

The instinct to ask her what she would change surged through him, but he held his tongue. There was no point getting into such things. The what-ifs of life could eat you alive. It was better to put your head down and keep going.

Wondering was dangerous.

"I think about that night a lot."

He didn't need to ask which night she was talking about.

"What might have happened if I hadn't been so fucking afraid."

Her whispered voice prickled at his resolve, but he resisted. This conversation could go nowhere good. His brain scrambled to find the right thing to say, but emotions had never been his forte. He was a blunt instrument, a greyhound chasing a marker.

He only knew forward. Speed. Focus.

"Shh." He brushed his hand over her hair, smoothing his fingertips over her temple with each stroke. "It's a busy day tomorrow. You should sleep."

For a moment, he thought she'd drifted off, her breathing turning even and her body becoming soft and pliable. Holding his breath, he didn't dare move until he was sure.

Ten, nine, eight…

He'd been holding himself in check—holding every basal, lustful urge in check—because he wasn't here to put a move on her in a vulnerable moment. He cared about August as a person. He wanted good things for her…which didn't include him.

But it was getting harder and harder to deny the fact that when he looked at her, there was nothing platonic about it. That those feelings he once had, all those years ago, were still as alive as ever.

She sighed and shifted position on the bed, the gentlest brush of her ass against his crotch yanking open the floodgates. He hardened in an instant and a groan stuck in his throat.

Balling his hands into fists, he willed himself to remember why he didn't want to get involved with anyone ever again. As he was about to extricate himself from the bed, she moved again. This time the action was absolutely and undeniably on purpose, and knowing that made him even harder. The smarter part of him screamed to get the hell out of there, but she felt so damn good in his arms.

Soft, smooth, warm.

"We shouldn't…"

"We shouldn't or you don't want to?" Her soft voice was like a whisper of smoke disappearing into the air.

"It's not about what I want," he said, closing his eyes. How could he be so weak to end up in this position again? "If it was, then…"

No, don't say that.

She was still in his arms. "Then?"

Dammit. He rested his cheek against her hair, his arm lying over her body where she'd placed it. He could feel the gentle rise and fall of her rib cage, the slight hitch in her breath, the warmth radiating from her skin.

"If it was about what I want, then I wouldn't be hesitating." He bit back a curse. "I wouldn't be wrestling with myself."

"Can it be about what *I* want, then?" She let out a shaky

breath. "Because I don't want you to hesitate. I don't want you to walk away."

Need coursed through his veins and he found himself rocking against her, the desperate need for friction like a chant in his blood. It had been so long. Too long.

Not long enough.

But it would never be long enough, in his mind. It would never be long enough until he was six feet under.

"You don't want this, though," he said. "You want someone with shared goals and aligned needs and who will give you the stable, happy life you deserve."

"I do," she admitted.

Could she hear the raging protests in his head? The security guards that kept his heart locked up tight shouting at him to remember why he couldn't fall for anyone ever again. Because grief was a relentless bitch. Because he'd loved with everything he had and it still wasn't enough to keep her alive. Because good things would be ripped from your hands the second you felt comfortable.

He had no idea how to voice any of that. Even after therapy and grief counseling, he still wasn't good at talking about his feelings. About voicing his fears. It was easier to keep it all in, put his head down and work, work, work.

"I'm not asking you to put a ring on my finger," she said gently. "I understand why you don't want to do the relationship thing again."

They'd never explicitly talked about Ellery's death. August had been there for him the whole time, however, showing her support even if she didn't verbalize it. She came to the funeral and the wake. She dropped food at his apartment because she knew he couldn't cook for shit. She would check on him through Leah, wanting to know how he was coping and if there was anything she could do to help.

"Sex doesn't have to be..." She shook her head. "Sometimes it can just be a moment between two people."

But it wasn't, with her. That was the problem. Sex with August could never be casual, no matter how many boundaries they put up.

"I don't want to... I don't want to ruin things," he said.

"I appreciate that. But we can act on something that's been there a long time without drawing up a lifelong contract. I'm not trying to say it doesn't mean anything, but... I just... I respect your boundaries, that's all."

Good lord, this woman. This bighearted, intelligent, perfect woman.

"Keaton..." She sighed. "I'm lonely and I know you are, too. Maybe we don't have to be lonely tonight is all I'm saying."

She was right. He *was* lonely. By choice, admittedly, but he still felt the yawning void in his life that Ellery had left behind. It was why he filled his time with work and family, keeping busy so he could ignore the festering wound in his heart.

But tonight she was offering him a salve. A balm. A moment.

And the raw honesty in her voice frayed the last vestiges of his control. He leaned forward, brushing his lips against hers. The first kiss was brief. Testing. Like he wanted to see if God would smite him down on the spot for betraying the promise he'd made, even if it was one Ellery hadn't wanted.

Nothing.

August blinked, her mouth parted in anticipation and moonlight dancing on her freckle-dusted skin. Her eyelashes were still damp, and they stuck together in little spikes.

He brought his head down again and she wound her arms around his neck, keeping him in place so he knew this wasn't over. Not yet. Not by a long shot. He pressed his lips to hers again, opening her this time and slipping his tongue into her mouth. His mind went blank, fingers thrusting into her hair, pulling her head back so he could take more, demand more. Taste more.

He was about to cross a line he'd never thought he'd cross, and there was no going back.

15

Unable to stop herself, August pressed her hips against Keaton, rocking back and forth until a wonderfully primal sound came from the back of his throat. He was like steel against her and he wedged a muscular thigh between her legs, forcing an echoing sound from her lips.

She'd dreamed about this for so damn long.

For a second, it was almost like having an out-of-body experience and looking down on herself instead of experiencing the moment. His dark hair was a stark contrast to her pale fingers, and the stubble scratched deliciously against her cheek as he kissed her. His hands traversed her body, over her shoulders and down her arms, cupping her hips and then finally digging into her backside.

He pulled her tight against him and she gasped.

"Is this what you want?" His voice was rough as tarmac.

"You want me to finally give in to you after all these years. After I've been so goddamn determined to stay away from you."

The words socked her in her chest. *Had* he found it hard to stay away? All this time she'd thought he wasn't interested, that whatever spark caused him to try to kiss her that night had fizzled and died for good. He'd seemed amused and irritated by Leah's matchmaking attempts, but never interested.

She shook herself, as if remembering why she was here. This was sex. Yes, she cared about Keaton. Yes, she wanted to sleep with him. But there was no way she'd *ever* fool herself into thinking it would go anywhere. He was too damaged for that. Too broken. Too walled off. And she deserved to find someone who would commit to a partnership wholeheartedly and without games or reservations.

Keaton was not that man.

This was simply a release of emotion, checking off a fantasy from her sexual bucket list, satisfying a raw, human need. Nothing more.

"Then walk away," she said, challenging him. "I'm not forcing you to be here."

"No, you're not," he replied, opening her mouth with his thumb so he could kiss her harsh and swift.

The air left her lungs as Keaton reached for the hem of her T-shirt and pulled it up. She wriggled, allowing him to get the fabric over her head. It didn't make a sound as it landed on the floor. Then his hands were on her, cupping her breasts.

"Keaton," she sighed, and pressed her hands against his bare chest. "Yes."

But he didn't linger. His fingers crept under the waistband of her underwear and she levered her hips up so he could finish undressing her. They were really going to do this. Her heart fluttered wildly as she looked up at him, the moonlight highlighting the beautiful yet hard angles of his face. The strong jaw, proud nose, heavy brow. His eyes seemed to shift color, turning almost like platinum in the moonlight.

He looked at her, drinking in every inch of her body, all the curves and dips and dimples. She didn't feel self-conscious like she might have with another man. She trusted Keaton. Felt safe with him. They knew all each other's flaws, so there was nothing left to hide.

"Your turn," she said softly.

Keaton swung his legs over the edge of the bed and stood. For a second, he didn't move—was he savoring the moment or thinking about whether he should continue? Whatever was running through his mind, August wasn't sure she'd ever know. The moonlight caught on the ridges of his ab muscles, turning him into a sharper version of himself. He hooked his thumbs into the waistband of his boxer briefs and drew them down. The fabric pooled on the floor. If August had thought Keaton looked intimidating in a suit, it was nothing compared to him naked. And it was nothing to do with his body, gorgeous as it was.

Oh no. It was the look in his eyes—the raw, untamed heat. But his emotions were tucked away, every brick in his walls firmly in place.

You're not here to break down his walls. Put the chisel down.

"Can you pass me my wallet?" she asked, pointing to where her bag was slung over the back of a chair.

He fished it out and handed it over, so she could pluck out the condom inside. For some reason, this part made her blush. Which was silly, given they both knew what was about to happen.

"Who knew you were such a Girl Scout," he said as he tossed the wallet to the floor and climbed back into bed.

"Don't you keep one on hand?" she asked, blushing.

"No."

Of course not. He never anticipated connecting with someone.

Fearing that she was on the verge of losing her nerve, she pushed Keaton back against the bed and crawled over him, her knees digging into the soft mattress on either side of his hips. She leaned forward, her breasts brushing his chest. Reaching for him, she wrapped her fingers around his erection in a way that drew a deep moan from the back of Keaton's throat.

His eyes were no longer platinum with moonlight. They were twin black holes. An abyss of lust and feeling.

He planted one hand against her thigh, fingers digging into her flesh. "Wait."

August stilled, ice water sliding through her veins. If he changed his mind now, she wasn't sure she'd ever get over the shame. She'd never be able to look him in the eye again.

"I want to look at you first." His voice was rough and his eyes traveled over her body. "You've been tempting me all this time with these curves."

"You don't need to flatter me, Keaton."

"It's not flattery. It's fact." He looked up at her, a wicked grin curving his lips. "You know I don't sugarcoat things."

"No?"

"No." He shook his head. "So when I say I dread summer rolling around because I know you'll be wearing those strappy little tank tops and I'll have to stand under freezing water in my shower until my dick behaves, I am *not* exaggerating."

She leaned forward, letting her breasts trail along his chest, feeling warmth grow in her belly. "That's payback for all the times you used to mow the lawn with your shirt off. So I guess we're even."

"Not even close." His chuckle was dark and rich. "What about those skinny jeans that make your ass look like a peach? And those little white T-shirts that cling to you?"

"You like that?"

"You have no idea." He brought a hand up to her face. "Now you either get properly on top of me or I'm going to flip you on your back. But frankly, I'd rather you be on top so I can see every part of you."

Warmth pulsed through August's body. She felt truly desired, truly wanted. Keaton had that effect—his intensity could make you feel like you were the only person in the world. And knowing that he'd been watching her, lusting after her…

She tore the foil packet open and rolled the condom down the length of him. He made a delightful little grunt as she handled his erection, excitement filling her with sparkling, crackling energy.

This was it. She was really going to do this.

She really *wanted* to do this.

"You might have to go slow." She sucked in a breath, a little flash of uncertainty rippling through her. "It's, uh…been a while."

His eyes were smoky and intense. "Same."

She leaned forward to brush her lips against his, needing to connect with him. They were in this together—in this moment, crossing this line.

Keaton smoothed his hands over her hips. "Say stop if you need to, okay?"

She nodded.

He reached his hands to the inside of her thighs and slid his palms up her skin, delving between her legs. As his fingertips brushed her sex, endorphins rocketed through her. The touch was so soft, she could have imagined it, but in seconds Keaton had her panting. Her forearms came up to brace against the bed, so she could bring her face close to his, her hair falling in a sheet around them and blocking out the world.

"More," she gasped against his ear.

He pressed one finger inside, then two. The gentle rocking of her hips matched the timing of his strokes, and she quivered. "August…you feel incredible."

"That's good." August's lips grazed his neck. "So good."

She turned liquid. Molten.

His hands were all over her—cupping her breasts, grabbing her hips, parting her sex. She panted, her head dropping down so that her forehead rested against his. Keaton touched her like he already knew everything about her—her wants, her needs, her pleasure points.

It was so familiar, it was like they'd been here before.

She reached down between them and filled her palm with him, and Keaton groaned. The sound echoed in the room and she smothered it with her mouth, their tongues tangling as she pleasured him.

"August." He thrust slowly into her palm. "I need to be inside you."

"I'm ready."

Gliding his hand over her backside, he guided her down onto him. When he pushed inside, easing them into position and giving her a moment to adjust, her eyes fluttered shut. The feeling of fullness was all-encompassing, and it was hard to remember to breathe.

"You feel even better than I'd imagined," he said, his voice so soft for a moment she thought she might have imagined him speaking.

Emotion swirled up inside her, driven by something far greater and more powerful than lust, but she tamped it down by crushing her mouth against his, greedily seeking his tongue. Nipping at his lips. Encouraging him. Teasing him.

He sank his fingers into her backside and thrust up into her, burying himself over and over.

"Keaton," she moaned, rocking back and forth to meet his pace. "I think I'm going to…oh God."

She clenched around him as she came, her moans turning to cries as she tipped over the edge and buried her face into his neck to mute the sound. His arms wrapped around her, holding her tight to him as he followed her into oblivion.

When he woke up the next morning, August and Molly were both gone. He sat bolt upright for a moment, panic seizing his chest as he tried to blink the foggy clutches of sleep from his mind. Did he screw everything up? Had she taken Molly and gotten the hell out of Dodge?

His eyes drifted to something bright pink on the nightstand—a Post-it note.

Molly was whining, so I took her for a walk.

Molly. She'd been right there the whole time he and August…

"Shit." He scrubbed a hand over his face.

Were dogs traumatized by that kind of thing? He'd been so caught up with August that he totally forgot about the snoozing animal in the corner of the little cabin. Maybe she slept through it all. *Hopefully* she slept through it all. Was that just the ultimate in bad animal parenting?

Keaton flopped back against the pillow and let out a sigh. Where did they go from here? Where did he *want* to go from here? He wasn't quite sure. Because there was no way that he could possibly classify last night as a "scratching an itch" kind of thing—whether he'd been breaking a sexual drought or finally being with someone he'd had feelings for, on some level, for a long time.

Keaton, despite always taking pains to be seen out and about in Manhattan, didn't have the raging social life or sex life people assumed. That he *let* them assume. Casual sex was not a thing in his life. Sex meant something to him.

August meant something to him.

"Ugh." He let out a long bellowing sound of frustration.

At that moment, the door swung open and August and Molly stood there, twin looks of concern on their faces. Okay, maybe Molly's was less concern for him and more concern about what she was going to find inside the love shack.

It is not *a love shack.*

"Everything okay?" August asked as she walked Molly inside and unclipped her leash. The dog did a happy trot around in a circle, and then went to find her new BFF—the stuffed lobster.

Sunlight streamed in through the window and made August's hair glow like embers in a fireplace. Her fair cheeks were lightly flushed from her walk and the fresh air outside, and she looked…

Beautiful.

The kind of beauty that you appreciated when you were in a relationship and you really knew *why* someone was beautiful—the real reasons. Not that they had a perfectly symmetrical face or a banging body or great eyes, although she did have those things. But the beauty that went beyond the surface. Like how her kindness shone through her eyes and how she snorted when she laughed really hard and how she was always ready with a smile when someone needed encouragement.

That kind of beautiful.

Those are the things that cut you most when that person is gone.

He had to remember that. Because the better something was, the more it hurt when you didn't have it anymore.

"Kea?" She stepped forward and he realized that he hadn't responded.

"Yeah, fine. Everything's fine. Super fine." *Three fines means everything is categorically not fucking fine.* "I'm going to have a shower."

He got out of bed, not missing the way August's eyes were instantly glued to his naked body as he beelined for the bathroom. Oops. He'd forgotten that he wasn't wearing anything.

He turned the taps on and stepped into the shower, the drumming water drowning out some muffled words from the other room. In spite of feeling all kinds of awkward about the whole thing—and having no idea at all how people normally handled this kind of shit—Keaton couldn't help the goofy grin from spreading across his face.

Dammit. He liked her a lot.

Even more than he remembered.

16

The second day started with a social media workshop, which August attended while Keaton used the time to catch up on work back in the cabin. Before Leah joined the workshop virtually, she and August talked on the phone, and August was relieved to hear her friend was doing a little better. The flare-up had been a nasty one, leaving her completely drained the past few days, but her boyfriend, Will, was coming over to help out.

The workshop was a welcome distraction, even if it wasn't one hundred percent effective at stopping her from thinking about last night. Sleeping with Keaton was like going back for another handful of candy when your teeth were already aching. It might feel good in the moment, but afterward there was an air of regret.

There's no point regretting it...especially not when it was the best sex of your entire life.

Ugh, why did it have to be so damn good? She tapped her pen against her notepad as Isla wrapped up the workshop with some inspiring words about chasing your dreams. But August was struggling to stop her mind from ping-ponging back to Keaton.

A night of great sex is a lovely diversion from life…and nothing more.

It shouldn't change her goals or her plans or what she was going to do next. Maxine Diamond had already emailed with some new potential matches. When they took a break later today she would read through them and pick someone to have a date with.

You've always been good at picking yourself up and dusting yourself off, so keep doing that. Last night is nothing more than a memory.

This was the resolve August wanted to embody. Because the next activity of the competition sounded like a doozy and she *really* needed to get her head in the game to help Keaton and Molly do their best.

After the workshop she'd met up with the two of them to prepare. The competition was down five contestants from the elimination yesterday, which left them with fifteen animal and human pairings in total. Another five would go home at the end of today, and a further five would go home after another elimination round the morning of day three. Only five animals would make it to the end and August wanted one of those spots.

But Molly had some *big* competition.

The top performers included a white-and-beige Chihuahua whose tongue permanently dangled out of its mouth and a Hungarian sheepdog—which was one of those dogs that looked like a mop—named Swish.

"Welcome, everyone, come on through." Isla stood in front

of the group and August buzzed with excitement to see what she had in store for them.

Keaton, on the other hand, radiated tension.

She could understand why. Smart as Molly was, she was prone to mood swings, temper tantrums, dramatic outbursts and all other manner of husky-type behavior.

It was lucky that for both the speed talent showcase and the photo shoot, they'd been able to use those personality traits for comedic relief. But now, however, she wasn't so sure.

"I'll walk you through today's elimination activity." She clapped her hands and waited until the four groups of contestants were settled. "You're the first lot of contestants to come through. We'll have our smaller dogs come through after you, and then we have an even smaller version of this activity set up for our more pint-sized contestants later this afternoon. As you can see, we have something fun planned today."

Isla's arm swept in an arc, gesturing at the room. Beside her, Scout looked on, her face lit up with anticipation. One camera was trained on the women, and another focused on the group of contestants.

Behind everyone, four identical short obstacle courses were set up, with each roped off and consisting of a small ramp, a blow-up kiddie pool with shallow water, a beach ball and a large inflated rubber duckie.

"One of the things we do at Paws in the City is book clients for commercials. We've even had one client book a movie recently. Our hope is to move more into film and television, in addition to our social media work, since we already have interest from several film studios looking for talented animals."

August gasped. That was so exciting! Isla caught sight of August's wide-eyed expression and winked. Paws in the City was growing like wildflowers and she was so thrilled to see it.

"We love a client who can do it all!" Isla turned to Scout.

"Yes, we do." Scout grinned. "And with the increase in streaming services creating their own content, the demand for animal talent is bigger than ever. So, today we're going to put your pets to the test. Our lovely demonstrators—Zuri and her dog, Maple—will show you what we want your pets to do."

Everyone turned to see a woman in the retreat's uniform holding a leash attached to a gorgeous dog with long fur the same shade as a shiny copper penny. The woman had close-cropped black hair and brown skin, and she held herself with a strong, authoritative posture. August had spoken with her the previous day, during one of the breaks, and she was the head animal activity coordinator for the retreat, and also had a background in dog training.

"Maple, come." Zuri gestured to the dog, who obediently trotted to the foot of the ramp next to her owner. "Wait."

The dog seemed raring to go, but she held herself in check, waiting for the signal.

"Go."

The dog trotted up the ramp—which was only a foot off the ground—and then jumped into the kiddie pool, splashing gracefully into the water. She bent down and knocked the beach ball with her nose, sending it out of the pool. Then she jumped out of the pool, went over to the large inflated rubber duck and raised one paw, bopping it lightly on the head.

"Good girl." Zuri crouched and ruffled the dog's fur, praising her for a job well done.

"A round of applause for Zuri and Maple, everyone!" Isla said, bringing her hands together.

After the clapping died down, Isla spoke again. "You've got an hour to get your pet familiar with the activity and then everyone will have three attempts to complete it in front of the judges. We know that great training, like you've seen with Maple, takes time. And we want this to be fun! Feel free to add your own flair, but we want to see your pets get as close to the four main points as possible."

"We have several staff on hand to help you out with tips and tricks—Zuri, whom you've already seen, plus Bobby and Willow," Scout added.

She gestured to where the three retreat staff stood, waving their hands at the group. Nervous rumblings went through the contestants, so Keaton clearly wasn't the only person who was a bit apprehensive.

"We've put your pet's name on a sign at the front so you know which station is yours. Once everyone is situated, we'll start the timer," Isla said. "At any time you can raise your hand if you need help, and someone will come over to you. We can't wait to see how well your pets do!"

Keaton raked both hands through his hair at once. "I don't have a good feeling about this."

"Think positive," August said, holding on to Molly's leash and leading her over to their section. "The trick is to break it down step-by-step, so that she feels comfortable with each component. Move the pool away from the ramp, and we'll tackle this bit first."

For a moment, August wondered if she was barging in and taking charge—something she'd been accused of in the past—but Keaton looked relieved that she had some idea of how to approach things.

He moved to the pool and dragged it away from the ramp. Molly wanted to see what was going on, but August still had her on the leash so she couldn't run amok.

"Molly, sit." With a reluctant huff, the dog did what she was told. When Keaton returned, she handed over the leash.

"Okay, so you're going to walk her to the top of the ramp, give her a treat and then come back down. We'll do that a few times, until she comes up the ramp on her own."

He nodded. August unclipped the leash and Molly sat, her head turned upward with interest. Keaton still had the little bag of treats that August had given him, and he pulled one out, immediately catching Molly's attention.

"Come," he said, holding his hand over the ramp and walking up the side. She followed him, at first a little uncertain of the ramp beneath her feet, but when it became clear the ramp was steady, she walked up to the edge. "Such a good girl."

He palmed her the treat and she gobbled it down. Then she jumped off and he instructed her to come back to the start of the ramp so they could do it over again. In only a few attempts, Molly walked up the ramp as soon as he asked her to.

Progress!

The ramp, however, was the easy bit. Getting her to jump off into a kiddie pool with some water in the bottom would be harder. It wasn't the depth of the water—which would barely come over the top of her paw—but more that Molly tended to associate water with bath time.

And Molly and bath time were *not* friends.

"Do we get her to put a paw into the water so she knows what's coming or just get her to jump over and find out for herself?" Keaton scratched his head.

Glancing around, the other groups were having mixed success. A group with an adorable bulldog was struggling because the dog had decided the ramp was his own personal nap location. Another group with an Australian shepherd, however, was already working with the beach ball.

"Either way is going to be tough." August planted her hands on her hips. "Maybe if *you* have a little splash in the pool and she can see you doing it, then she won't be as scared by it?"

"You want me to splash around in the kiddie pool?" He raised an eyebrow. "Seriously?"

"I don't mean strip down and jump in, Keaton." As soon as the words were out of her mouth, heat shot into her cheeks. That was so *not* what she needed to imagine right now. "Just make a little splash with your hand."

"Thanks for clarifying that," he grumbled, rolling his eyes. "Or else I would totally have taken my pants off in front of all these people."

She let out a snort laugh and tried to cover it with her hand, but it didn't do any good. He still heard and narrowed his eyes at her. But, being the trouper he was, he got down on all fours, peach-perfection ass in the air, and called for the dog.

"Hey, Molly, come here. Come!" He motioned and the husky trotted over, her treat-seeking nose sniffing. "Look at this awesome pool. It's got water in it."

He made a little splash with his hands and Molly backed up a step. *"Waa waa waa."*

Her doggy noise sounded a lot like "why? why? why?"

"Don't worry," he said, still splashing. "You're not going to have a bath."

Uh-oh.

At the sound of the B-word, Molly flattened her ears and crouched down low, eyes narrowed at Keaton. *"Wrooooooo."*

Noooooo.

"I said *no* bath." But his correction went ignored, as Molly skittered backward, bumping into August, who grabbed her collar so she didn't flee.

"Stop saying that word! She doesn't understand the use of it in the negative." August let out a sigh. "It was clever of them to use a little water. That will separate the men from the boys, so to speak."

"Or the dramatic huskies from the..." He looked toward the Australian shepherd, who was bounding around, doing everything required of it. "Whatever that unicorn of a dog is. Maybe we can put the treat *in* the water?"

"Would you like to eat something that had been submerged in a blow-up pool?" August asked.

"Mmm. Good point."

They both looked at Molly, who wore an expression that August jokingly called "the face of betrayal." Molly liked to pull it out whenever she knew she was going to be asked to do something she didn't want to do—go to bed when it was early, stop asking for treats, come home from the park or take a bath.

"Maybe we take the ball out of the water and try that next. Then we come back to this once she's forgotten about your liberal use of the B-word," August said. "Divert her attention for a bit."

"Sounds like a plan."

Twenty minutes later they had not made much progress. Molly continued to eye the kiddie pool like it was a black hole waiting to suck her down and spit her out into hell, where endless bath times and other such horrors awaited her.

Keaton was getting frustrated.

As a competitive person by nature, he liked to win. But needing to be in control at all times meant he *hated* relying on other people. Or animals. Most people couldn't be trusted, and the ones that could usually had an ulterior motive.

Do you think August has an ulterior motive?

No. She was one of a kind. A person who genuinely wanted

to help others, who was caring and smart and witty and sensual and—

He mentally cut himself off. This was not the time to be mooning over the sexy thorn in his side. August was a distraction. A redheaded, ample-bottomed, bighearted, quick-witted distraction. The *exact* type of distraction that would disarm him, if he wasn't careful.

Last night had been heaven. Now, working together and watching her in her element—despite Molly being a pain in both their asses—was actually kind of…fun.

"Okay, so she'll go up the ramp." August ticked the to-do list items off her fingers. "She'll jump off the ramp when the pool is removed *and* she'll knock the ball with her nose when it's not in water. We're, like, sixty percent of the way there."

He glanced at the clock. "So we're on track…mostly."

"Rubber duck?" August suggested.

"Let's do it."

They led Molly to where the big rubber duck was seated at the end of the course. The duck came up to the middle of Keaton's calf, so it was decently sized, and it stared unblinkingly with its beak open. Molly eyed the duck with caution.

"Don't tell me she has a problem with ducks, too," he said. Thankfully, this time there was no reaction to his choice of words. *Bath* was a no-go, but *duck* was fine. "How do we get her to touch the duck?"

"Let's try this." August crouched in front of Molly and put her hand out. "Shake."

Molly raised her paw. But instead of shaking, August guided her paw to the duck head and tapped it on the beak.

"Good girl!" she praised, and provided a treat. "Shake."

They tried that a few more times, with success.

Keaton had come to realize that much of dog training was

simple repetitive actions and positive reinforcement. Doing the same action, over and over and over, while providing treats and praise and then eventually weaning the dog off those things so they would perform the action when commanded.

August was very good at it. She was patient and kind, but firm when she needed to be. More fool anyone that took her freckled cheeks and friendly smile and positive, upbeat demeanor to mean she was a pushover. She absolutely was *not.*

"Shake." She did it again, and this time August didn't put her own hand out. Molly touched the top of the duck by herself. "Good girl!"

"She really is a smart dog," Keaton said, nodding. The last few days had given him newfound respect for the husky and her abilities. "She'd be amazing if she weren't so stubborn."

"True of us all," August replied with a wink.

He chuckled. "Good point."

Keaton tried the trick with her and it worked again. "Now all we have to do is figure out how to get her in the water."

Molly swung her head toward him, eyes narrowed, as if to say, *I don't know what you're up to, human. But I don't like it.*

"What if you get her to go up the ramp and I push the pool underneath at the last minute?" he suggested.

August scratched her head. "I don't like the idea of shocking her."

"But maybe if she sees that the water level is so low, it's nothing like a ba—body of water in which to bathe, then she'll be okay? I've seen her run through puddles like it's nothing, so I know it's not the water itself that's the issue."

Molly continued to glare like she knew they were plotting something.

Dogs didn't hold grudges…did they? But if any dog were to hold a grudge, it would be Molly.

But time was ticking down and Keaton could tell they were starting to get behind the others. He watched a terrier mix jump off the ramp and into the pool with surprising grace, then it splashed around, jumping over the ball and looking adorable. Shit.

"Why can't you do that?" he asked Molly, gesturing to the other dog. Molly snorted, not even bothering to glance in their direction.

Because I'm not your puppet, human. I do what I want!

"We have to do *something*," Keaton said, sighing. "Or we're as good as done in this competition."

"Think, think, think," August muttered to herself. "The ticking clock is driving me nuts! I don't want to shock her by sliding the pool in at the last minute. So put the pool in place and we'll have her do the trick while being able to see the pool is there. She knows there's water in it, so she might back out. We'll just have to see."

He nodded. "Okay, boss."

"I'm not the boss," she protested.

"Yes, you are. You're the one who knows what's going on here and has the skills and experience to actually get Molly to do what she needs to do. I'm happy to take orders." He winked over his shoulder as he moved the pool, unable to help teasing August just a little. "I like a woman who knows what she wants."

Rolling her eyes and turning the approximate color of a strawberry, August got into position and called Molly over. "You'll need to instruct her from now on, because we haven't got much time left and she needs to know you're the one issuing orders."

"Great, just when we get to the hard bit you start delegating."

"You *did* say I was the boss." She grinned. "What do we have to lose?"

"Our good standing in this competition…not to mention our dignity." He scrubbed a hand over his chin. "But there's no choice. Okay, let's see how she goes."

Keaton stood at the base of the ramp. "Molly, go."

He walked alongside the ramp, hand out with a treat as he'd done many times in the last hour. She went up the ramp, tail wagging…until she saw the pool below. Then she stopped dead in her tracks and turned to Keaton, snorting, before trotting back down the ramp and sitting next to August. The dog let out an irritated whine.

Look what the bad man tried to make me do. He wants me to take a bath!! The gall of him.

"Dramatic freaking dog," he muttered. "Molly, go."

She sat still.

"We're never going to get this," he moaned.

Molly stomped away from August and went over to the big rubber duck. For a moment, Keaton thought she might perform the trick to earn herself a treat. But before either August or Keaton could get over to her, she clamped her jaws down on the duck's head, puncturing the inflated plastic, then she tossed him back and forth as if trying to murder the damn thing.

"Molly, no!" August ran over, hand outstretched, but Keaton got there first.

"Drop it," he commanded in a strong voice.

To his surprise, Molly dropped the duck. But everyone in the room was looking at them, hands covering amused smiles and laughter. The duck landed on the ground, the air already escaping its poor punctured head, which tipped to the side as the air drained out of it in a sad little *wheeze*, one eye looking at Keaton accusingly for causing its murder.

"Uh-oh." August pressed her hands to her cheeks. "I hope they have more ducks."

The duck deflated like a sad, forgotten birthday balloon, leaving only a puddle of bright yellow plastic behind. Sighing, he looked at the dog. Molly looked up at him with intense eye contact and zero degrees of remorse.

You brought this on yourself, human. Actions have consequences.

For some reason, the lesson felt very appropriate.

17

The commercial shoot challenge was…kind of a disaster. For their team, anyway. While a few of the dogs happily trotted their way through the obstacles to enthusiastic applause from the judges, August and Keaton had to request a new inflatable duck and completed the task without the kiddie pool.

Molly did her best, but it wasn't a great showing.

Had they blown their chances of Molly winning the competition? Perhaps. But she'd still managed to avoid elimination for one more day.

And working with Keaton, trying to problem solve and achieve a shared goal had felt…nice. Rewarding, even if the outcome wasn't as good as they'd wanted it to be. It had been a long time since she'd worked with anyone toward a shared goal, and it really played into her feelings of wanting a partner in life. If trying to win a competition with someone made her feel connected and part of a cohesive unit, then having a partner in life would be like that times a million.

Scout had invited August for a drink in their cabin, but she'd had to decline because she had plans. Reviewing the files that Maxine had sent through and then a meeting with the woman herself. All the contestants were taking part in headshots—proper ones this time and not DIY stuff—so Keaton had to stay with Molly for the next hour or so while she was groomed and photographed, which would give August complete privacy.

She headed back to the cabin, trying to perk herself up and get excited about the matchmaking meeting. There was absolutely *no* reason to be dreading it. The idea of a perfectly selected match being presented to her felt so much safer than doing it herself.

Yet the doubts still niggled.

What if the next guy was a disaster, too? What if Asher Benson wasn't a one-off? What if she was still doing this dance for the next ten years? Or fifteen? Or twenty?

What if she was destined to come home to empty houses her whole life?

"Worrying never solved anything," she said to herself as she reached the front door of the cabin.

Once inside, she checked her appearance in the mirror. Her skin was pink from the sun shining down on the walk over and it made her hazel eyes appear slightly greener and the freckles along her forehead and nose more pronounced. She looked…good. Healthy. Vibrant.

"Sunshine and sex will do that to you," she muttered at her reflection. It had been a while since she'd indulged in either of those things. "It's all the endorphins."

Grabbing her laptop, she positioned herself on the bed and started making her way through the files, reading each one over carefully, looking for any possible red flags. When the alarm eventually went off on her phone, she logged into the Zoom call that Maxine had set up. A second later, the older woman's face appeared on-screen.

"Hi, Maxine."

Maxine Diamond was something of a Manhattan legend. A self-made millionaire with humble beginnings who found fame on television, hosting a popular dating show in the eighties before having her own talk show that focused on love and relationships. She then went on to start her own matchmaking company, using her skills but also employing technologists to help her build a patented matchmaking algorithm that had led to thousands of love matches.

Maxine *looked* like the kind of person who'd hosted a dating TV show in the eighties. She was in her sixties and her hair still had that "fuzzy perm" style, with fluffy brown curls surrounding her heart-shaped face. Her lashes were coated in electric-blue mascara and she wore a pink-and-black houndstooth blazer with *serious* shoulder pads. Chunky gold hoops dangled from her ears.

"Hello, August." She smiled warmly. "Is this still a good time to chat?"

"Yes."

The first time August had met with Maxine, her stomach had been filled with butterflies. Now it felt like she'd eaten a lead tennis ball.

This is supposed to be exciting. You're working toward something you want.

For some reason, the first thing that flashed into her mind was a picture of Keaton from last night. The way his eyes had darkened with intensity as he'd drunk her in. The raw and naked want displayed like a flashing neon sign across his face. The utter peacefulness as she'd drifted off in his arms.

You can't have that…not with him.

"Great." Maxine gave an efficient nod. "Have you had a chance to look through the profiles I sent you? I've got an idea of who would be a great first option, but I want to hear your thoughts."

For a moment, August's mind went completely blank. She couldn't think of a single one of their names or anything she'd read, despite looking at the profiles only moments ago. It was like Keaton had taken up all the space in her head and now there was no room for anyone else. Feeling slightly panicked, August reached for her phone and opened her email app so she could jog her memory. That's right.

There was Brad, the banker. Thirty-eight, divorced without kids. Liked to go hiking and camping.

Next was Kai, the dental surgeon. Forty-three, never married. Liked vintage cinema and going for day trips to farmer's markets.

Then there was Darius, the sales executive. Thirty-nine, never married. Liked something equally as bland and uninspiring as the first two.

Keaton would laugh all three of these guys out of the room.

"Uh…" August shook her head, trying to gather herself.

"It's okay to say none of them are taking your fancy," Maxine said gently.

"I guess I'm still feeling a little gun-shy after what happened with Asher." It sounded plausible coming out of her mouth. But August wondered if it was nothing more than a convenient lie.

A convenient lie that covered up a very uncomfortable truth: that she still had feelings for Keaton.

Why couldn't she get it through her thick skull that he didn't want a relationship? How was she supposed to achieve her goal of shared companionship and practical support when he wouldn't even let anyone into his home? Let alone his life?

"That is completely understandable." Maxine nodded. "I'm hoping to have an update from my lawyers soon on what our next steps will be, but they seem confident we can prevent Asher from mentioning us in his article, as it would be a breach of the contract he signed. If we need to take him to court, we will."

August let out a long breath and her shoulders sagged. "That's a relief."

"But I don't want you to let one bad egg put you off your goals, August. He doesn't deserve to take that from you." Maxine looked concerned and August felt a lump form in the back of her throat.

In some ways, Maxine had a nurturing vibe about her. Or maybe that was simply because August's own mother was the human embodiment of a lump of ice and so anyone with warmth, by comparison, felt like a nurturing presence. Maybe that's why August was so terrible at dating and figuring out whether a man had good intentions or not—it wasn't like she'd had *any* guidance. Ever.

Her grandmother had died before she was born and her mother had zero empathy or people skills from which to learn. With no sisters or female cousins to help her out, August had been left to wade through the dating waters alone—without support or advice—until she'd had more relationship false starts than a lawn mower with no gas in it.

"I can see you feel conflicted," Maxine said. "Why don't

we go back to basics here? Let's leave the matches to one side for a moment. Tell me about a time when you *really* connected with someone and what it was about them that made that connection."

"There's one guy..." She looked down at her hands, where they were twisting up the bedcovers. "He's chronically unavailable. But when we're together it feels like...like I've let out a breath I've been holding. I can be myself, unfiltered."

"Authenticity is very important."

She released the covers and smoothed her palms down her thighs. "I want the kind of relationship where everything is aligned. I don't need it to be full of hearts and roses and candlelit dinners, you know? I'm not a romantic at heart. But I want someone to *share* my life with, to not have it be one-sided."

Maxine nodded, her head bowed as she was taking some notes.

"It's not like I think I'm perfect or anything, so I don't expect someone I date to be perfect, either. But at least someone who actually wants commitment and a long-term future. I feel like I'm seeing smoke and mirrors and falsehoods with these guys." Her lip quivered. "I'm sick of being on the outside all the time."

"This might sound a bit odd, but trust me for a moment," Maxine said. "Tell me a little about your parents. It will help me understand the relationships that have shaped you, because our familial influence is usually a strong one. Are they still together? Are they deeply in love?"

August sighed. "They're deeply invested in climbing the ladder together and furthering their social standing. But love? They were never affectionate in front of me...ever. Or with me, for that matter."

For a moment, she felt incredibly vulnerable, like she'd

walked into the middle of Fifth Avenue completely naked. Plenty of people knew her relationship with her parents was strained, but no one besides Leah knew the intricacies of it.

That her parents had never once said they loved her. That she'd cried in bed some nights, wishing she could have been born to a different family.

Maybe that was why passion scared her, because it was wildly unfamiliar. Foreign. If her own parents didn't show her love and affection, how could she ever expect it from a romantic partner?

"My mom is a doctor at a family practice and dad is a surgeon. They were never home much when I was a kid."

Coming home day after day to the silent house had worn on August. She needed to be around people, needed the social interaction and the feeling of belonging. But often she'd have to cook dinner for herself, since her parents got home late, and she detested the way the house creaked and groaned in the quiet.

"I've learned to accept myself instead of needing acceptance from them," she said. "I'm proud of who I've become."

"As you should be." Maxine nodded. "You're an exceptional young woman."

"Thank you." She swallowed. "My dad in particular…he has always held me at a distance, and I'm not sure why. It's like I'm on the outside, looking in. Never truly being seen for who I really am."

Maxine's head was bowed again, as she took notes.

"I don't want someone like him, you know. I don't want to be with someone who's going to hold themselves back the way he does. Who's not capable of letting people in."

Now that they were done with the headshots, Keaton walked Molly through the grounds of the retreat, back toward the cabin. Molly's nose was glued to the ground, sniffing every little thing and tugging on her leash whenever she wanted to follow a trail or chase a bug. The sunshine warmed his skin and the sight of Molly's wagging tail put a smile on his lips.

Who'd have thought there would ever be a day where anything *to do with that dog made you smile!*

"You did a good job today, Molly," he said as they walked. The husky paused to look over her shoulder at him, tongue lolling out of her mouth. "You are the most excellent girl."

He wasn't sure that huskies—or any dogs for that matter—could actually smile, but he *felt* her smile. In his heart.

Two days out of the city and you're turning into a fucking sap.

Maybe he should get a dog of his own?

He dismissed the idea as quickly as it popped into his head. One, he worked *long* hours and it would be cruel to keep a dog home alone for that much time every day. And the chance of Thomas allowing pets in the office was slimmer than a single sheet of paper. Two, getting attached to someone—even a canine someone—was a bad idea, as dogs lived even less time than humans.

But maybe whenever he visited Leah, he would spend some time with Molly instead of trying to ignore her like he usually did.

Molly tugged on the leash, clearly captured by something. *I want to go here.*

"Okay, okay. Don't choke yourself."

There was no rush to get back, since August had some Zoom thing she needed to do. She'd been a little vague about it, which was unlike her.

The cabin was up ahead, and Molly was still sniffing something. Then she caught sight of an orange-and-black butterfly. Lurching forward, she yanked on the leash and it slipped out of his hand. Molly took off running.

"Shit." He righted himself and started after her. "Molly, stop! Heel!"

But the dog didn't listen. She galloped like a freaking horse toward the cabin, changing direction at the last minute to go around the side, the leash flapping behind her and whacking everything in its path.

"Sit, Molly."

But his command went unheeded. He jogged across the grass and rounded the corner of the cabin, his heart sticking in his throat. If anything happened to this damn dog, his sister would *kill* him.

Thankfully, Molly had slowed and was sticking her nose against a leaf containing another butterfly. She watched in spellbound wonder as the butterfly flittered up into the air and landed on her nose. For a moment, the dog didn't move a single hair. Then she turned to Keaton, mouth open in a huge smile, as if to say: *Look what's happening right now!*

Grinning like a goof, Keaton slowly crept forward and snatched the leash off the ground, causing the butterfly to take flight again. Snorting in annoyance, Molly glared at Keaton.

"Sorry, girl, that's what you get for bolting on me."

Now that his heart had stopped thundering in his head, Keaton noticed the sound of August's voice floating through the open window around the side of the cabin. He'd opened it earlier to air out the smell of sex, just in case the staff came through to change the sheets or replace the towels. There was another voice, but it sounded much softer and farther away. It must be whomever she was talking to on the other end of the call.

"…he has always held me at a distance, and I'm not sure why. It's like I'm on the outside, looking in. Never truly being seen for who I am."

She was talking to the matchmaker!

Keaton stilled. Shit. If he tried to walk away now and made a noise, she would think he'd been listening on purpose! Molly tugged, so he slackened the leash a little so she could sniff around. But he held a finger up to his lips. *Shh.*

She tossed her head and went back to sniffing.

He dithered for a moment about what to do, stepping forward and cringing when a twig snapped loudly beneath his feet.

"I don't want someone like him, you know. I don't want to be with someone who's going to hold themselves back the way he does. Who's not capable of letting people in."

Oof.

Keaton felt the blow right in his chest. Was she…was she talking about him? The voice on the computer was muffled and he couldn't quite hear all the words.

"…the way he was…it's not…you deserve…"

"I know." August sighed. "I seem to attract people like that. They want me to be a certain way with no regard for what I want out of life."

Had he done that very thing by sleeping with her? *She* was the one who'd set the boundaries and initiated things. But if he thought back, they were only in the room together because he'd decided to bait her into a challenge of wills. A challenge, deep down, he knew they would fail. And as much as it made him feel like a terrible person, being with her had done something to him. The sun felt brighter, the trees looked greener and the air felt easier to breathe.

"It's gotten to the point where I don't trust myself to make the right decision." August sounded so frustrated he wanted to leap through the window and pull her into his arms. She was impossibly competent and capable, and the fact that she didn't feel that way was a crime. "I know in my brain what I want and what I need, but…my heart wants to go in another direction and I don't know how to force it to stop."

"…getting to know…gathering data…no pressure just…"

He inched closer to the window, trying to catch what the matchmaker was saying.

"You can do a meet and greet with each of these men. I'll let them know it's not an official date, and you could even do it online if that feels more comfortable." The voice was suddenly clearer, as if August were walking around with her laptop and had gotten closer to the window.

"I like that idea," she responded. "I need to build my confidence back up."

"Send me an email with your schedule for the next week and I'll set them up for you. When I showed your profile to each of these three men, they were *very* keen to meet you. You're a catch, August. Don't forget it."

"Thank you."

It sounded like the call had ended. Now Keaton needed to figure out how to get Molly back around to the front of the cabin so he could make out like they'd just returned and that he hadn't heard her private conversation.

He started to creep away from the window, trying not to step on anything that might snap or make a loud noise.

"Come on, Molly," he whispered, tugging the dog away from something that had caught her attention. But the damn dog wouldn't budge. "Don't do this to me now."

Molly turned and looked at him. He smiled, trying to remind the husky that they were friends now, and not enemies.

If only he'd kept a few of those treats in his pocket, he might be able to lure her away. But when he tugged on the leash again, she stood her ground, eyes narrowed at him.

Can't you see I'm busy, human?

"Come on, you stubborn dog." He tried again and this time Molly had enough with being told what to do.

She threw her head back and howled at the top of her lungs, as if she were a damn werewolf in a B-grade horror movie. Keaton immediately caught movement in the window of the cabin, and August's face appeared there.

"Kea, is that you?"

Sighing, he looked down at Molly, who stared back at him smugly.

That's what you get for telling me what to do, human. I'm in charge here.

Shit.

18

"How long have you been outside?" she asked as he walked into the cabin and unclipped Molly's leash, hoping that her voice didn't betray the anxious energy inside her. For some reason, she felt uncomfortable at the idea of Keaton hearing her talk to the matchmaker.

It felt...wrong. Like she was betraying him.

Except she wasn't. He didn't want a relationship and she didn't want to settle for booty calls. Not that what they shared was a booty call exactly, but the whole "just sex" thing wasn't her. She wanted more. She *needed* more. And she respected that he didn't.

"Not that long," he replied, but he wasn't making eye contact.

That's not a good sign.

"How much did you hear?" She toyed with the hem of her T-shirt.

For a moment, he didn't say anything, instead busying himself hanging the leash on the hook by the door.

"Kea?"

"Just about how you seem to attract people who want you to be a certain way with no regard for what you want out of life," he mumbled.

He thinks you were talking about him.

Her heart clenched. "Yeah, people like my parents and all the bad dates I've been on."

He looked at her, wary. "Anyone else?"

"Not you, if that's what you were thinking." She walked over to him. "You were holding back last night because you were worried about our mismatched needs. That's pretty much the exact opposite of someone who doesn't care about my feelings."

"You were talking to the matchmaker?" he asked, his shoulders dropping slightly.

"Yeah." She looked at the ground.

"You don't have to be ashamed about it," he said. "I mean, I stand by my assessment that people are awful, but if you want to find Mr. Right, then I'm not going to judge you for it."

She snorted. "You'll judge me, alright, but you'll be smart enough to keep it to yourself."

A genuine smile tugged at the corner of his lips. "You know me so well."

"I didn't want it to seem like I got what I wanted last night and then I was back to checking out other men." She cringed. "Which I guess is exactly what it is, but that sounds so callous and I don't mean it that way. It wasn't nothing, but..."

"It's not something, either."

She nodded. "Yeah."

Except it absolutely was something. Or worse, everything.

"We don't have to make this weird." Keaton clamped a hand on her shoulder in a way that was probably intended to feel platonic, but it still sent a tingle of awareness down the length of her spine, therefore making it…weird. He withdrew his hand, frowning. "It's weird, isn't it."

"Yep."

"Shit." He scratched his head. "Maybe you should find another room tonight."

August narrowed her eyes. Oh, they were *still* playing this game? "Why should I move rooms? I've already unpacked."

"So have I," he replied stubbornly, folding his arms over his chest.

Molly swung her head between them like she was watching a tennis match.

"How about you be a gentleman and take one for the team?" she suggested, matching his stance by folding her arms over her chest. Two could play at this game.

"If you're the one who's not comfortable, then it's on you to do something about it. I'm sure the staff would be happy to turn over one of the other rooms for you." His eyes met hers in challenge.

Why did they do this? Ever since they were kids there'd been this push and pull between them, this competitive have-to-prove-myself energy.

The worst thing of all was…she liked it.

"That way you can have all the private conversations with as many of your dial-a-man options that you want. Don't let me get in the way of finding true love." He smirked. The walls were up again, that was for damn sure.

Goddamn Keaton and his too-sexy smirk and his amused green eyes.

"You're just jealous that I don't want to date you." The

words shot out of her, fueled by shame and other prickly emotions, rather than any shred of sense. Poking the bear was not a good idea.

"You want *something* from me, that much I know." He didn't look ruffled at all, the bastard. "Tell you what, you can stew on it while I take a shower."

He headed toward the bathroom and didn't even bother to look over his shoulder before he slipped inside. He *knew* she'd be looking.

You're pathetic.

The sound of a zipper being lowered cut through the quiet air. He'd even left the door open just a crack, not enough that she could see anything—and therefore, he could claim he'd closed it—but enough that the sound trickled through. And the sound of Keaton showering was a low-key form of torture. Because now she knew what he looked like totally naked and the combination of fantasy and memory was a potent one. As a lover…

Holy smokes.

He made her feel all the things. Sexy yet respected. Cared for yet an object of desire. Desperate yet safe. It was perfect… which was a huge problem. What other guy stood a snowball's chance in Florida of living up to that? A guy she'd known most of her life, whom she'd crushed on that *entire* time and whom she now knew had the route to Pleasuretown tattooed onto his brain.

Nobody could match him.

"I think he ruined me, Molly." She sighed and sat on the edge of the bed.

The dog came over, tail swishing back and forth, and her head cocked to the side in sympathy. *"Roaooow?"*

"I'm *so* attracted to him." She groaned. "And I hate myself for it."

Molly snorted and gave a little shake.

"I *know* he's unavailable. You don't have to tell me that." She reached out and ruffled the husky's fur. Molly came closer and plopped her head on August's knee, her icy blue eyes looking up lovingly. "I wish I could just get a dog as awesome as you and be happy with that."

Molly made a noise as if to say, *I am pretty amazing. Too bad you can't clone me.*

"That would be a good solution, wouldn't it?" She found tears gathering in her eyes—frustration? Sadness? Regret? She wasn't sure. "I need more. God, I'm so clueless. If I'd just kissed him back that night, then I know we'd be together right now. I know I'd be happy with him, because back then he was so determined and full of light and...he wanted love. *Craved* it, even. I could have had that with him."

A tear dropped onto her cheek and she whisked it away. Molly sat down and tipped her face up, letting a long, mournful howl into the air.

"I can't change the past and I can't change how he is now—that's not right. You have to love a person as they are, flaws and all." She smoothed her thumb between the dog's eyes, smiling as they fluttered shut in enjoyment. "You're such a good dog, aren't you? I know how much Leah loves you and how much you love her. You're doing such a good job in this competition. How about we kick some butt tomorrow, huh? You and me and Keaton, we make a good team."

Molly let out a bark of agreement.

"Good girl."

The running water continued to taunt her from the bathroom. The door was slightly ajar, and steam billowed out through the sliver of space. Seemed like her previous reminder about him needing to turn on the exhaust fan hadn't stuck. There was even a sign on the bathroom mirror telling guests to do so!

Keaton never was very good at following instructions.

Huffing, she rose from the bed and walked over, reaching inside and feeling around with the intention of flipping the fan's switch, but her arm bumped the door open a little farther. The mirror was quickly being consumed by fog, but a small, clear space reflected slick bare skin.

Her senses hummed in awareness and every change in the rushing sound caused by him moving under the spray brought a dirty image to her mind. She flicked the fan switch and then withdrew her hand, sagging back against the bedroom wall.

The water was still running but it sounded sharper now, like he'd opened the sliding door to the shower and had poked his head out. "August?"

"I turned the fan on because you forgot." She cringed. Did he think she was trying to sneak a peek at him? She'd *wanted* to.

Because no matter how many times she told herself today that last night was a onetime deal, something about the words seemed to slide out of her brain like a foot over a banana peel.

It'll end up hurting you like stepping on a banana peel, too. Emotional injury incoming.

"Why don't you join me?" he asked, his voice full of teasing. He thought she wouldn't do it, the asshole. "Roomie."

This was what Keaton *always* did. He put barriers in place by challenging her and feeling confident she wouldn't take the bait, because then she'd pull away and the distance between them would be maintained. He made himself safe by getting *her* to enforce the boundaries. She wasn't naive. Keaton's games were as transparent as glass with the sun shining through it.

"The water's fine." His dark, raspy chuckle made her bristle. "Or are you heading off to find yourself a new room?"

"I hate you," she muttered under her breath.

Yet a shiver still went through her. The thought of being with Keaton again sent fire through her veins. The way he touched her...it was like no man who'd touched her before. With him she felt new and whole and blissfully content.

It was a feeling she'd craved all her life. A feeling she'd decided to give up on when faced with the chaos of dating, because it felt like reaching for the moon and asking for magic. That's why she wanted something that wasn't based on intangible things like chemistry and spark and sexual attraction.

Those things could blow up in your face. Shared goals and dreams and hobbies were so much safer.

Maybe she just needed to prove that he didn't have an effect on her—even if that was totally a lie. But she could act, right? She could pretend.

Against her better judgment, she pushed the door to the bathroom open wider. The steam billowed out and the heavy, warm air created immediate dampness on her bare arms. She stepped into the bathroom, a knot of anticipation in her stomach. The standing shower was made of textured glass, and it offered a hazy view of Keaton from head to toe, except the gap where he'd stuck his head out before and water was splattered on the tiles.

That sliver showed smooth water-speckled skin, cut muscles and one-half of the most wicked smile August had ever seen.

"What are you doing?" she asked, being careful to keep her eyes high. But it was useless. Keaton naked was a sight to behold.

"Trying to save water." He grinned.

He braced one forearm against the wall near where the

door opened and stood there, body partially exposed through the gap. He was like a modern-day David, his perfect body sculpted as if from marble with every muscle toned and taut, every line clean and smooth.

And lower… She gulped.

You can't blame this on the heat of the moment. This is premeditated.

If she joined him now, there would be nothing on which to blame her actions.

Her brain was so good at drawing boundaries but her heart wasn't always so good at following them. She bit down on her lip, movement stalled by the wave of desire that washed through her. Keaton grabbed a bar of soap, eyes meeting hers.

The muscles in his arms and his chest flexed as he worked the white bar over his skin, leaving trails of lather everywhere. His hand dipped lower. He wouldn't…

Oh.

Keaton ran the soap over himself, from the soft trail of hair from his belly button down to the hard, strong length of him. The fog and textured glass hid some of the details, giving her only a sliver of the action, but her mind could easily sketch in the rest.

"I can soap you up, too, August." Fire burned in his green eyes.

This was a power move. He wanted to be back in charge, because he felt like she'd gotten one over on him last night. He wanted to be back where he belonged. Keaton, king of the world. No weakness for anyone to see.

August should know better than to give in. But she knew in that moment there was no way she could resist him—not when she was already becoming addicted to the way he made her feel. So safe and secure and known.

Like she truly was enough, without changing a thing.

Her hands came to the hem of her T-shirt, like her limbs were on puppet strings and someone was controlling her actions. She dragged the fabric up over her stomach, over her breasts and over her head. Then she drew the zipper down on her jean shorts and shoved the fabric over her hips, taking her underwear along with it. The mirror to her side reflected the flush in her skin and the tangle of red hair creating a halo around her head. She could see every lump and bump in this light, the little bit of cellulite on her thighs and all the bits she'd once wished to change about herself.

But the way Keaton was looking at her, she felt like a goddess. It was impossible to judge herself when a man she adored was looking at her like that. August unhooked her bra and slipped her arms out, letting it fall to the floor with her other discarded garments. Keaton's gaze was locked on her and his erection bobbed in front of him.

"Make room," she said, meeting his eye contact with her chin lifted into the air.

She wasn't going to let him have the upper hand.

"I love it when you talk to me like that," he said, stepping back into the cloud of steam and pulling the door open for her.

Inside it felt like they were encased in their own private bubble.

"You thought I wouldn't do it," she said, sliding the door shut behind her.

"I don't underestimate you," he replied, reaching for her hand. "Ever."

His tone was calm, but the flare of darkness in his eyes was saying something else entirely. He wanted her. He still felt guilty about it. And he might not underestimate her, but he certainly thought he could keep this to the physical.

I want more.

The pain of wanting a person in a way you could never have them was unique. You either had to walk away or you had to settle. Was she settling now, by being with him? Was she just taking what she could get, knowing that later it would leave her hungry for more?

Keaton turned August around and swept her hair over her shoulder, so it trailed down her front. Then he worked the bar of soap over her skin, enjoying the way she gave a little shiver when he brushed against her. There was something so intimate about showering together, and it made him feel closer to her.

You're not supposed to want that.

But he did. The time they'd spent here together had opened his eyes to who she was now—as a woman, as a friend, as a lover. This wasn't the adorable and awkward girl on the verge of adulthood he'd almost kissed. This was a woman who'd come into her power, who knew what she wanted and wouldn't settle.

If she's with you, then she will *be settling.*

"Are you getting me back for initiating things last night?" she asked.

"Why would I do that?" He smoothed the soap down the side of her body, gliding it over the flare of her hips.

"Because you like to be in control."

"I can't argue with that, but no. I don't believe in living life tit for tat."

She sighed as he brought his hands around to the front of her, running the soap over the gentle roundness of her belly and up toward her breasts. "You're trying to set up a joke about tits, aren't you?"

He chuckled. “I love your sense of humor, you know that?”

“I’m pretty amazing.”

Hmm, that was a wall. August wasn’t a cocky kind of person who often sang her own praises. She was the kind of person who preferred to work her ass off and let her actions do the talking. Even now, naked in front of him, she was holding part of herself back.

It’s for the best.

But instead of listening to his head, he listened to something else. His heart. He let himself get sucked in to the desire of wanting more of her. Wanting to go deeper. To get under her armor. Standing under the spray, holding her but without seeing her hazel eyes bore into him, he felt emboldened.

“I’ve always thought you were pretty amazing, actually.”

She turned to look at him over her shoulder, but he dipped his hand lower to distract her and she sagged back against him. “I thought you were pretty amazing, too, Keaton.”

The teenage fuckup? The kid who put so much strain on his mother that she almost had a nervous breakdown when he got locked up? The man who worked for a company that preyed on the little guy?

Some days it felt like there weren’t enough good deeds in the world for him to atone for what he’d done.

“I…that night at Christmas…”

Don’t say it.

Please say it.

No…don’t say it.

“I think about it a lot,” she finished. Her unsaid words lingered in the air, riding the steam up and away. “What might have been.”

He drew her hair back so he could work some shampoo

into the ruby lengths. She hummed her pleasure as he massaged her head. "The road to hell is paved in what-ifs."

"Yes, it is," she whispered.

This is a very bad idea. Repeat: this is a very fucking bad idea.

They switched places so she could finish her hair, and he was more than happy to watch. She didn't seem shy and he loved that—confidence was something he found supremely sexy, and it took all his willpower to let her finish cleaning. But when she was done, she looked him in the eye.

"So that's it?" she said. "Just a shower and nothing more."

He backed August against the tiles, leaning one forearm against the wall next to her head. His body lined hers, the warm softness of her breasts and belly and thighs pressing against him, and stirring him below the belt.

"I'm not done with you yet," he said.

"Good."

It felt like they were playing a game of chicken. To see who would whip out a white flag and beg for mercy. So far, neither side showed signs of admitting defeat.

"You're so beautiful." He lowered his head to hers. "So stubborn and beautiful."

Her head rolled back against the tiles and she chuckled. "You told me once you didn't like people who let go of things too easily. Is that why you're attracted to me?"

"What are you not letting go of?" he asked.

"You."

Her lashes were dewy, her eyes wide and luminous. She knew exactly how badly her answer would slay him. How it would cut him down the middle and stick him in the part he tried so damn hard to hide. He'd made it easy, too. He'd walked right into it.

Tell her she doesn't have you and she never will.

But the words wouldn't form. Because knowing August wanted him—all of him—was like slathering balm on some roughed-up, chewed-up, scratched-up part of him. It softened his edges, like water neutralizing the fire of anger and resentment that normally fueled him.

He lowered his head toward her and kissed her. She met him, hungry and willing, and the feel of her was so achingly familiar. Not because he'd been with her enough to know her every taste and scent.

But because he knew this feeling. This completeness. He'd experienced it before.

The rightness of it made him want to crumble. But there was no way he could let on that this was anything more than sex. That it was anything more than primal need and pent-up lust and the consequences of too much work and not enough play.

This was what he needed to focus on. The here and now. The pleasure.

Keaton wrapped his fingers around her wrists and pressed her arms back to the tiled shower wall, holding her still. The muscles in her wrists flexed under his hard grip, as if testing him. As if reminding him that she couldn't be controlled.

"Do your worst," she whispered. "I can take it."

"I know you can. You're stronger than I am."

He slipped his hand between her legs and found her ready. She gasped as he touched her, her eyes fluttering shut and her mouth hanging open. Touching her was as much to give him time to calm down as it was to wrench some of his power back. To put them on even footing.

Because they weren't playing for keeps. Not now, not ever.

"More," she gasped as he teased her. "Please, Keaton. I want you inside me."

The thought of burying himself inside her was like a lit match to a bonfire. It was so wrong and so right. So perfectly right.

"I, uh..." He shook his head. "Did you bring any more condoms?"

They both knew he didn't have any.

"I'm safe." That's when her mask slipped and he caught a rare glimpse of her vulnerability. No hard outer shell, no piercing glare. Just August. "I got tested before I signed up with the matchmaking agency."

Oh yeah...*that.*

He didn't want to feel jealous thinking about her preparing to sleep with some random "match approved" guy. But fucking hell it made him want to snap something with his bare hands.

"I'm still on the pill, too." She looked like she wanted to explain more, but instead she bit down on her lip as if trying to trap the words inside.

But these things were important.

"I'm safe, too...which I'm sure you would have guessed." It was hard to catch anything when you didn't have sex.

August cupped his face with both hands and, for a brief moment, it felt like she could see into his soul—all the charred and blackened parts of him, the emotional wasteland he kept under lock and key. It was too much. A rejection bubbled up the back of his throat, but before he could say anything at all, she brushed her lips across his. So gentle, like a reassurance she wasn't going to break him. She wasn't going to hurt him.

"I know it's a big deal, Keaton," she said softly. "I'm honored that you trust me."

He wanted to scream, to shake off her tenderness because

it felt like it could physically burn him. He didn't want to trust her. Or for her to feel honored.

And yet…

God, how he'd missed those things. The real connection. Having someone care for him. Having someone look at him and see past all the smoke and mirrors.

He pushed forward, yanking one of her thighs over his hip and dragging the head of his erection through her sex until he found the right spot. When he slid inside her, the tight heat made his head swim. It felt like coming home. Like letting out a breath he'd been holding for a decade.

"Yes…" Her breath was hot on his ear.

He brought his hand to her ass, digging his fingers into her smooth, firm flesh, and drove up into her, primal need fueling him. Warm water sprayed against them and the tile was mercifully cool against his palm. He thrust into her, lazy and slow at first, enjoying the sound of her gasps in his ear and the feel of them skin to skin. Everywhere.

He never wanted this moment to finish. He never wanted to leave the steamy bubble of perfection.

His mouth covered hers, his tongue driving between her lips, and she met his intensity with ease. Her hands grabbed at him, nails lightly scratching his skin and her teeth nipping at his lower lip. Her face was wet from the spray of the shower, the water droplets sliding along her cheeks and catching on her lips.

"I'm there," she mewled into his neck as the first wave of her orgasm hit hard, making her arms tighten around him like a vise. She buried her face against his chest and he held her to make sure she stayed upright. "I've never stopped wanting you."

Rushing water and the smack of skin on skin drowned out his response. But the words echoed in his head.

I've never stopped wanting you, either.

August's body was heaven in his arms, the way she opened herself up to him like a balm to his weather-beaten soul. With one last thrust, he seated himself deep inside her and came hard, cradling her head with his hands and pressing their foreheads together.

19

After their shower, Keaton and August went to the hall to grab dinner. Neither one of them mentioned changing rooms again, and for some reason it hung over August's head. It was almost like an invisible line that they were walking up to but refusing to cross. Or maybe it felt more like limbo.

Wasn't that their relationship in a nutshell? It felt like they'd had a lifetime of sniffing out each other's boundaries but always failing to take the next step.

As they walked back to the cabin after a simple but yummy camp-style meal, it had grown dark. Stars were strewn across the sky like shards of a broken mirror, glinting and sharp. The air was cool, and goose bumps skittered across her skin and she drew closer to Keaton as they walked.

In some ways, it felt even more intimate than sex. Being together in the dim light, fingertips brushing, need lingering in the air. Unfulfilled desires, unspoken feelings, the lines blurred by their actions.

"Any updates on the Asher situation?" Keaton asked. "Tell me that asshole isn't going to get away with his DIY *Bachelor* experiment."

"The matchmaker's lawyers seem confident they can prevent him from speaking in any specific terms about the agency and, therefore, me. It might not be enough to stop him publishing the article, but at least my name won't get dragged through the mud. So, fingers crossed."

They looked at one another for a few heartbeats, the air crackling with tension. Keaton always made her feel like she was on the back foot, one little toe away from making a misstep and trouble within her reach.

It was wrong. Exactly *not* what she wanted.

Then why did it feel so damn good?

"So," she said, clearing her throat. "How's, uh...work going?"

"Same old, same old," he said. In the slight pause, insects chirruped and the trees rustled overhead, alive with nocturnal activity. "My boss wants me to crush this small company so our client can swoop in and make a killing."

"What do you mean?"

He told her the story of the deal he was working on, how he was trying to get Thomas to take a fairer approach and how his research assistant had been roped into digging up some dirt to leverage. And how it was the same thing they'd done dozens of times before.

"All so they can reduce the price for his client to buy their company?" August asked, aghast. "That's terrible!"

"That's Wall Street," he said with a sigh. "This kind of stuff happens *all* the time. Shorting stocks, sneaky share buyouts, insider trading. You name it."

"But this is people's livelihoods, and for what? Money? Greed?" For a second she didn't recognize the man walking next to her. Her vision swam and she saw her father's face, instead of his. That desire for *more, more, more* no matter the cost. No matter what had to be sacrificed. "And you support it?"

"I don't support it, no. But...I've tried convincing them to do it another way and Thomas won't listen to anyone. I keep a close eye on what the researcher comes up with, and I have definitely 'misplaced' things before that felt too out of line, but still...it's a dog-eat-dog world out there, August. That's the nature of business."

She blinked. "I can't believe you just said that."

"Why not? I have my own goals. Everything I make goes toward helping my family, so it's not like I'm blowing my pay on yachts and Rolexes and shit."

"That does *not* make it any better." She shook her head. "I admire that you're so unselfish with what you earn and that you want to take care of your family, but do you think it's okay to do it at the cost of destroying other people's lives?"

They'd reached the cabin, and the automatic light flicked on, illuminating the welcome mat and door. But neither one of them made a move to go inside. Overhead, a moth fluttered around the light, bumping against the glass. Drawn to something that would destroy it, if the glass weren't there to protect the moth's delicate wings.

"If the CEO keeps running the company the way he is, it'll go broke anyway." It sounded a whole lot like he knew Thomas was going to get his way, and that he was trying to justify his role in the destruction of the little guy.

"Please," she scoffed. "Are you really drinking the Wall Street Kool-Aid, Kea? You're smarter than that."

His jaw ticked. "Do you think any of these corporate assholes would have helped me when I was young and fresh out of juvie? No. In fact, I went for an interview at a company this CEO's second-in-charge was previously running when I was in college, looking for an intern position. I got an interview, but when they did the background check, the guy called me up to tell me they wouldn't hire criminals."

"I'm sorry that happened to you and I know it was probably a huge blow at the time, but that doesn't excuse helping your boss wrench the guy's company out of his control against his will."

Keaton was a good man, but he could be so blinkered at times. Just because he did good things with the money he earned, didn't excuse the kind of work he did.

"How do you think Leah would feel, knowing her house was paid for with a bonus you got for lining the pockets of the rich and greedy?"

"That's low," he said, his voice gravelly. "The only thing I've ever wanted was for my family to be safe and secure."

"What about other people's families? Don't they deserve that, too?"

He looked down at his hands. She could see the guilt in his eyes. Argumentative as he might be, he *knew* that his work skated the boundaries of ethics. And yes, maybe he tried to influence things from the inside, but he still toed the company line when his boss demanded it.

"What am I supposed to do?" He raked a hand through his hair. "I don't want to be part of this, but—"

"Then quit!" she said, her voice raising. Keaton was telling her these things for a reason, because he knew it was wrong and he needed to hear someone say it.

"I can't just quit."

"Why not?" She tossed her hands in the air. "You're set for

life. You don't need more money for crying out loud. Leah is fine, your mom is fine. You can find another job, and even if it takes a year or two, so what? Do you think it's better to stay in a job that makes you justify doing terrible things or get out before it poisons you?"

"It's not poisoning me."

"If you think this stuff is okay, then it is absolutely poisoning you." She could hear the panic in her voice. Keaton *couldn't* end up like her parents—money hungry, with no care for anyone but themselves. She couldn't bear it. "You need to quit."

"Thomas..." Keaton shook his head. "He really helped me when I needed it. He helped me start my career and protected me from people like Asher Benson. After Ellery died, he was there for me. He's..."

She could hear the pain and conflict in his voice.

"I never had a proper father." He swallowed. "I never had someone to look up to, someone who would give me advice and actually give a shit about where I ended up in life. My stepdad thought I was worthless from day one. My real dad..."

August didn't know much about Keaton's biological father, only that he'd taken off while Keaton and Leah were young. She suspected there were substance abuse issues, based on a few cryptic things Keaton had said over the years, but she'd never wanted to pry since it was clearly a painful topic.

"My real dad told me when I was five years old that he wished I'd never been born."

August had a sharp intake of breath. "I'm so sorry."

"Thomas is the only man who ever stood by me." He looked down. "Doesn't that count for something? My job is... Some days it's all I have."

The words took the wind out of her sails and dropped the temperature in her blood. He wasn't looking at her. Instead, he'd reached for his room key and held it over the lock. It clicked and he pushed the door open, going inside. She followed him, letting the door shut quietly behind them. Keaton wandered to the window with his arms folded over his chest, like he was trying to shield himself from the world.

"How can you say that?" she said. "You have *plenty*."

He didn't reply.

"Is that all you think life is worth? Working to get more financial security for your mom and sister?" They'd never spoken about this before. In fact, she'd wager that they'd never spoken about *anything* so deep before. "Or is it something else?"

"I promised Ellery I'd get to the top," he said quietly. "I'd get there because it's what she wanted us to do, together. And since she can't, I feel like it's my responsibility to fulfill that dream. When I get my name on the wall, then I know I'll have reached the top."

"Mmm. And you climbed a mountain you don't even like." She nodded. "Smart."

When he turned, she'd expected him to look angry. Or defensive. Or prepared to argue his side. Instead, all she saw was defeat in his green eyes. It made her want to pull him into her arms and kiss him until that sad, bleak look went away.

"You deserve to do something that fulfills you, Keaton," she said softly. "I know you're not a person who wants to hurt people. But you *are* hurting people, doing this work. At least, doing it in the way your boss wants to do it."

"I know."

Silence settled over them like a blanket and the cabin suddenly felt extremely still and quiet. The end of the day was coming and it felt symbolic, somehow. Tomorrow was the last day of the competition and then they were due to head back to Manhattan.

Back to being single.

Back to pretending they weren't hot for one another.

Back to their lives with big gaping holes in them.

"What are we doing?" she asked.

She waited for Keaton to give some quippy, meaningless diversion of a response.

We're talking.

We're having casual sex.

We're taking part in a dog talent competition.

But instead, he simply said, "I don't know."

Against every sensible thought in her head, she went to him. The need to comfort him—and herself—overwhelmed her knowledge that doing so would be danger. They were pouring gasoline on a fire and hoping they wouldn't get burned. It was a losing game. A mistake waiting to happen.

But she did it anyway.

She went to him and wrapped her arms around his waist, pressing her face to his chest. Since she had no idea what she should say, she said nothing. Keaton's palms found her cheeks and he lifted her face up toward his. His green eyes were swimming with emotion—regret, sorrow, hunger. It was an intoxicating combination.

And she couldn't even think about resisting when he lowered his head toward hers, coaxing her lips open. He kissed her slow and deep, and it was like being lowered into a warm bath. Her body glowed. Her heart swelled. Her hands itched to be skin to skin.

She knew one thing for sure—there would be no resisting Keaton tonight.

★ ★ ★

He swept her hair to one side and kissed the tender spot on the side of her neck. The resulting sigh almost took his breath away. "I feel like I disappointed you."

"I should be saying sorry." She melted against him. "Your job is your business. I know you do everything in your power to take care of your family. It's admirable."

He wrapped his arms around her, simply holding her. Cradling her…or maybe he was leaning on her. It was so hard to tell and he wasn't sure what that was supposed to feel like, because he'd never leaned on anyone, ever.

"But at what cost? You're right." He sighed into her hair. "For a long time I thought it didn't matter if *I* wasn't paying the price. I have to protect my patch, my people. Damn anyone else."

She said nothing, but he knew what she thought. August was categorically *not* the type of person to take that mindset. She believed that everyone mattered and that a person's actions should bring good to the world, not just to the people closest to you.

"Do you think I'm a terrible person?" The question slipped out raw and jagged, like a piece of rock that had dislodged itself from a slowly crumbling cliff face. That's how he felt—like something that had stood strong for as long as it could and was now giving up the fight.

He couldn't resist her anymore. He couldn't ignore the doubts about his work. He couldn't…keep being numb.

"Of course not." Her hands reached up to clutch his arms, which were interlocked around her waist. Warmth seeped into him, like goodness transferring from her body to his. "You love your family with a ferocity that…"

"That?"

"I wish I knew what that was like, to be loved so wholly."

I can love you wholly.

The thought should have scared him. It should have fucking terrified him. Because he was never supposed to put himself through this again. But it dawned on Keaton that these feelings were...familiar. They weren't the shock of a new discovery. They weren't the jolt of a realization.

They just...were.

Because he'd loved August a long time ago, when he was a disillusioned kid and she was the girl who wrote him long letters in girlie handwriting about everything that was going on back home. She was the girl who'd helped plan his "welcome home" party when he finally made it out, because his mother was struggling to do it herself. She was the young woman who'd attended his wife's funeral with tears in her eyes and her arm wrapped solidly around his sister's shoulders.

And now she was the woman who dropped everything to be here, to put up with his bullshit and peel down his walls brick by brick.

Of course he loved her. While he'd been married to someone else that love had transitioned to a platonic type of love, where he viewed her as one of his family. One of his small inner circle. But now, all these years later, he understood that the fire hadn't been put out. It had simply been waiting for oxygen.

"I..." The words clogged the back of his throat. But he couldn't find the strength to say it out loud. Because admitting to himself that he loved her was one thing, but acting on it was an entirely different prospect. "You deserve someone who's going to give you the world."

"No." She turned, fire in her eyes and her face shining

with sincerity. "I can get the world myself, Keaton. But I want someone who's going to stand with me when I do."

"That's the hottest thing you've ever said."

The sincerity turned to smoldering heat as she planted her hands against his chest and gave him a little shove so he stumbled back and landed on the bed. Looking up, he drank in the sight of her standing strong and majestic before him. August was the strongest person he'd ever known—nothing held her back. No matter how many knocks she received, she got back on her feet and dug her heels in for the next round.

She stepped toward him, hazel eyes dark with intent as she lowered herself to straddle him. Keaton's hands automatically went to her thighs and he smoothed them up and down, his mind already starting to go foggy with lust. She had awoken an insatiable appetite in him, where before he thought he'd be happy to starve the rest of his life.

She circled her hips, giving him the barest hint of contact. It was enough to fully ignite him—turning his resolutions to ash.

"You like ambition, huh," she said with a wicked smile.

"I like a woman who doesn't hesitate to reach out and grab what's rightfully hers."

"Like this..." She reached down, brushing her palm along the hard length of him. He let out a soft moan and tugged her face to his, capturing her mouth in a searing kiss. "Are you rightfully mine tonight?"

The end was coming. Neither one of them believed this would last the second they headed back to Manhattan, and that was proof. Because here, in the middle of nowhere, they could pretend. But back home, with memories embedded in the walls, she would be competing with an army of ghosts.

"Yes." The word hissed out of him.

"I want to make the most of this," she said, guiding his hands to her breasts, encouraging his greedy fingers to take, take, take. "I…this has been incredible."

"You're incredible," he whispered. More words hovered on his tongue, things he *shouldn't* ever say again. Words like *more* and *forever.* Words like *I need you.*

"You're fucking incomparable."

Her lips found his and she pushed him against the bed, taking charge. He rolled his hips up against her. She was so hot, with her breasts pressed against his chest and her hair tickling his skin.

"One more night?" she asked, looking deep into his eyes.

"The *whole* night." He brushed her hair back and glided his thumb over her cheek. August nodded, bringing her mouth back down to his and kissing him like the air in her lungs depended on it.

He peeled the T-shirt from her body, up and over her head. Underneath, she wore a white lacy bra that served up her ample bust on a sexy, frilly platter. When he popped the button on her jeans and saw she had the matching bottoms on, he groaned.

She climbed off him and pushed the denim down over her hips.

"Turn around, I want to see you from every angle."

The white lace contrasted with her fiery red hair and freckle-dusted skin. Her thighs rubbed together as she turned, and her hips swayed, giving him everything he wanted. Then she divested herself of the lace and stood before him, naked. God, she was beautiful—inside and out.

When she came back down to the bed, he yanked her to him, tucking her back against him and wrapping his arms tightly around her.

"You make me feel safe," she whispered.

What was he supposed to make of that? It was a trap. A rocky, crumbling edge luring him to emotional ruin. His baggage was a fortress keeping them apart, his fear a gaping wound that refused to heal.

There was too much history.

"August…"

"Let's not talk." She pressed a finger to his lips and turned in his arms, shimmying down his body until her hands found the button of his fly and pushed it open. He was hard as granite. "Let's *do* instead."

She drew his zipper down and palmed him through his boxer briefs. When her hand connected with his warm flesh, his mind blanked. And as she lowered her head, her hair tickling his stomach and his fingers threading through the curling strands, he forced himself to focus on the physical.

When you go home, you'll go back to ignoring how you feel. It's what's best for you both.

"August." He moaned her name.

She took him deep, using her hands as well as her mouth, and for now, he could only submit. Because walking away from her—from this wonderful, kindhearted go-getter of a woman—would be torture.

He'd never forget this time. This connection.

But was it salt or a balm on his scars? He wasn't sure.

All he knew was that she deserved so much more, and because he loved her, he wouldn't stand in the way of her reaching for the kind of relationship she wanted.

20

Keaton was expecting to wake with the warmth and comfort of a woman's body cradling his—at least, that's how they'd left things last night. After making love with August, they'd showered together again and had another round against the slick tiles. Sated and satisfied, they'd then crawled into bed, quietly holding one another and wondering what morning would bring.

Molly had decided to join them at that point, not wanting to be left out, and the three of them had felt like a family for a brief moment. It was a fantasy, one that had burrowed into his mind overnight, fueling him with dreams of what might be if only he could take the plunge. If only he could open himself up to the risk of loving someone again. Of letting August in.

But now he was in bed alone.

Stretching his arms above his head, he arched his back, loosening his muscles and enjoying the delicious ache deep in his body from a hot and sweaty night of deep kisses and tangled limbs. Outside, the weather looked confused. Gloomy gray clouds clustered in the sky to the west, while the east shone brightly with an azure backdrop. The day wasn't quite sure what direction it would take as yet.

He got out of bed and spotted a flash of bright pink—a sticky note stuck to the bathroom door: *I've taken Miss Molly for a walk because she was whiny. I'll meet you at breakfast.*

Heading into the bathroom, Keaton took his time showering, hoping that August would turn up before he left. He didn't like the idea of hanging out in the dining hall without her. But even with a lazy shower and time to dress and brush his teeth, she still hadn't returned.

He hunted around for his room key and headed outside. The air was crisply cool, with a thickness that told him rain was imminent. The gray clouds had multiplied in the time that he'd been getting ready, blotting out the sun and blue sky. He felt a fine mist on his skin as he walked to the breakfast hall, holding his hand up in a wave as someone greeted him with a friendly *hello.*

Keaton had found himself really enjoying being out of the Wall Street concrete jungle these past few days, surrounded by trees and nature rather than glass and steel. It was a surprise, since he'd never considered himself the "outdoorsy" type, and he'd been wondering if perhaps a property upstate might be a good idea. Somewhere to get away on the weekend if work was bothering him. Maybe Molly and Leah could come for a visit, even.

But today the walk didn't relax him. In fact, a hard knot of anxiety was tightening in his gut. Something was wrong.

You're being dramatic, he told himself. *You're always looking for the thing that could go wrong.*

August and Molly would be happily munching away on some breakfast in the hall. He could practically see it—her red hair flopping down in her face as she tore off the end of a croissant to feed to the eager dog.

But as he approached the hall, the tightening in his stomach didn't go away. He practically burst through the doors to the hall, his eyes sweeping across the room. It was a much smaller setup now, on the last day of competition, since a good number of contestants had already gone home.

And he couldn't see a single redhead.

But he did spot Scout, who was sitting with her and Isla's husbands at one of the tables. He approached and they all smiled.

"Have you seen August and Molly by chance?" He tried to keep the stress out of his voice, but judging by how Scout furrowed her brow he probably hadn't done the best job of it.

"Not this morning." She shook her head, her blond ponytail swishing back and forth. "Is everything okay?"

He raked a hand through his hair. "I'm sure it is. They just went out for a walk and she should be back by now."

"I'm sure Molly just found something interesting to sniff," Lane said with an easy smile. "But if you want someone to help look for them, I'll give you a hand."

Keaton was almost taken aback by how willing Lane was to jump in with assistance. It made him feel silly for asking—the girls were probably taking their time and enjoying themselves. He was worrying for nothing.

"I'm sure you're right," Keaton said with an awkward laugh. "Molly likes to get her nose on everything when she goes out for a walk. It's probably nothing."

"Why don't you join us," Theo suggested, gesturing to an empty spot at their table. "Then if they don't turn up by the time we've finished breakfast, we can have a look around together."

They were likely humoring him.

This was a side effect of losing his wife—he always assumed the worst outcome. If Leah had a stumble, he thought she'd broken a bone. If his mom was in a bad mood, he thought her mental health issues had returned. If it was spitting outside, he thought a blackout storm was coming.

But even knowing all that, he couldn't shake the feeling that something was wrong.

"Where the heck *are* we?" August looked around at what she was sure was the same cluster of trees that she'd been staring at not ten minutes earlier. It had felt like they were going the right way back to the main hall, but then Molly had decided it would be fun to follow a butterfly and suddenly they couldn't find the path anymore.

Now Molly was back on the leash, so August didn't lose track of her again.

"I swear, I thought we were going the right way..." She chewed on the inside of her cheek, trying to ignore the flutter of nerves in her stomach.

Molly whined.

"It's okay," August said. "We're not lost. We're simply... directionally challenged."

Molly snorted, throwing August an unamused expression that said, *Speak for yourself, human. I'm amazing. You're the one who can't tell your left from your right.*

August pulled her phone out of her pocket to see if they could use the GPS function, but there was no service at all out on the hiking trail. The little service icon blinked uselessly and then disappeared as it tried and failed to connect. Huffing, she shoved the phone back into her pocket.

A splatter of raindrops came down through the trees, misting August's face and hair. That was *not* a good sign. The leisurely walk through the hiking trail had taken them a good thirty minutes, and then they'd spent the last fifteen or so trying to find their way back after Molly's detour.

Had they gotten closer or farther away from the cabins? She had no idea.

The rain started to come down more steadily and August wiped at her eyes with the back of her free hand. "It's okay, everything is going to be okay."

Molly looked at her as if to say, *Press X to doubt, human. I don't believe you for a minute.*

A crack of thunder shattered the quiet, sending small animals skittering into the brush not far from where they stood. Molly yelped and hunkered down low to the ground. *Uh-oh.* Molly *hated* thunder.

"Stay calm, girl. It's okay," August said in her most soothing voice, but the husky was growing quickly agitated. Her voice reached a high-pitched whine, followed by a sharp bark.

Make it stop! I hate the sky noises.

Another grumble of thunder rippled through the sky, and August tried to lead Molly in what she hoped was the right direction, but the dog refused to budge. Her ears were flattened right back against her head and her eyes darted around. No amount of tugging on the leash would move her.

"Come on, girl. Don't do this now. Please." August tugged but the husky was planted low to the ground, trembling. "Shit."

She might have to carry Molly. It wouldn't be an easy feat, since the dog weighed close to forty-five pounds, but it might be the only option. August crouched low and attempted to scoop Molly up, but the dog snapped at her and skittered backward suddenly, causing August to lurch forward and lose her balance. She fell, her hands hitting the dirt and sending shocks up her arms from the impact.

Molly yanked on the leash and it slipped right out of August's hand. "No, Molly!"

She scrambled to her feet and made a lunge for the leash, missing it only by a fraction of an inch. At that exact moment, a giant flash of lightning lit up the sky and then the clouds opened up. Rain poured down, hard and fast, obscuring her sight momentarily.

August stepped forward, bracing herself against the weather, just in time to see where Molly had run.

"Stop right now!" She jogged after the dog, her sneakers sliding on slick stones. "Don't panic. Panic is a pointless emotion that will not solve anything. You are a calm blue ocean. A cool cucumber. An unruffled feather. An…unwrinkled chocolate bar wrapper."

Was that even a thing?

Unfortunately, the pep talk did little to tame the drumming of her heart as she followed Molly deeper into the trees.

The rain beat down, drumming against the top of her head and soaking her hair and clothing through. She had to find Molly and *then* she had to figure out how the heck they'd get back to the campground in one piece.

One problem at a time.

"Molly! Come here, girl!"

She stumbled past another cluster of trees and realized they were going in a different direction than before. Was it the right one? She had no idea. Grabbing onto a low tree branch, she moved carefully past a clump of raised roots. The ground was becoming muddy, fast. Gingerly, she stepped into what looked like a small clearing.

But August's heartbeat halted when she realized they were standing at a lookout. There was a drop over the edge and what looked to be scrapes or marks in the muddy ground.

"Oh my God…"

As carefully as she could, August approached the edge and peered over. Molly! The dog was on a ledge about two feet below. Thankfully it wasn't a sheer drop. But it *was*, however, an awkward angle, and August didn't have much to grab onto.

The dog looked up, holding one paw in the air as if wanting to shake. At first August thought she might have injured her paw, but on closer inspection it appeared she'd gotten some tree sap on herself. The sticky amber goo had made her fur all stuck together in clumps.

On the long list of things Molly hated was anything sticky.

"Hang on, girl. I'm coming."

August got down on the ground, anchoring herself by grabbing a sturdy tree root. There was no way she could try to climb down there to get to Molly, because one wrong move and she'd slide over. Mud squelched against August's stomach as she wriggled to the edge, keeping hold of the tree root. Maybe if she could grab Molly's leash, she could try to guide her back up the incline.

But as she tried to reach down, she realized that her arms weren't long enough. Her hands dangled uselessly above the dog's head, fingers waving.

"Come here, girl. Get a little closer and I'll help you up."

Molly looked at her paw indignantly, and then up at August as if to say, *Get this gross shit off me right now!*

"Oh, Molly," August groaned. "Can you not be a drama queen for, like, *one* second? It's just sap!"

The dog didn't budge.

Looking back over her shoulder, August wondered if she should try to go back for help. But she had no idea which way to go, and what if the rain came harder and Molly slipped off the edge of the ledge she'd landed on.

You can't leave her.

Drama queen or not, the dog was her responsibility.

"You've got to work with me here, Molly," she said, huffing as she tried to reach again. "Help a sister out!"

Straining, August tried to grab her again, but it was no use. She couldn't reach the dog. How did it all get out of control so quickly? One minute they were having a nice walk in the woods and the next…

"You can't lose your cool," August said to herself. "The second you start acting like the dog, this is all over."

"August! August!" Faint voices cut through the storm, and August's heart pounded in her chest. "August, can you hear us?"

"I'm here!" she yelled into the wind. "Hello?"

A few seconds later she saw Keaton tear through the dense green trees, eyes wild and body soaked to the bone. He rushed forward, mud splattering the bottoms of his jeans, his hands reaching for her.

"It's Molly," she said, pointing. "She slipped onto a ledge and now she has sap on her paw and she's throwing a tantrum."

It sounded ridiculous to even say it out loud, but here she was. August had a feeling she would *never* live this down.

Remember that time where you got lost in the woods and everybody you know and respect had to come and save you.

Ugh! She hated being the damsel in distress. It was so *not* her style.

Keaton looked over the edge, swearing when he caught

sight of the dog. Molly whined pitifully, still holding up her sticky paw.

"Goddamn dramatic husky," he muttered.

Behind them, Lane and Theo rushed over.

"I've got to get down there." Keaton looked back at the two other men, who were ready to protest. But Keaton was already on his knees. "Hold my feet."

Theo shook his head. "This is dangerous. You can't—"

"Just do it." Keaton wasn't waiting.

He wriggled to the edge of the lookout, and Lane and Theo got down low to hold on to him. August grabbed the waistband of Keaton's jeans, and kept hold of the tree root. With three of them holding him in place, he should be okay.

She held her breath, praying that he could reach the dog.

Please, please, please…

"Got her! Pull me back."

August, Lane and Theo all worked against the slippery mud to bring a dirty and bedraggled Keaton and Molly back up to solid ground. The husky clung to Keaton like he was her life raft. When he set her to the ground, she yelped.

"Did she hurt herself?" Lane asked, worried.

"It's a sticky paw. Tree sap." August pressed a hand to her chest as she knelt, her fear abating as she wrapped her arms around the dog, not caring that she was going to have wet dog smell clinging to her the whole way back. She grabbed the end of the leash and wrapped it around her hand twice. "Thank goodness you're safe. Your mom would have *killed* me!"

"Let's get you back." Keaton helped August to her feet and held her tight against his side. His head lowered to hers as they walked as quickly as was safe on the slippery ground. "You scared the shit out of me."

"Sorry." She looked up at him, brows furrowed.

"I'm just glad you're both safe. That's all that matters."

For some reason, his words made a heavy sensation settle in the pit of her stomach. Whatever warm, happy bubble they'd created last night was now well and truly shattered.

21

An hour later, August and Molly had both been released from medical supervision. Thankfully, there were no serious injuries. Molly had been saved from the evil tree sap with the use of some olive oil, a wide-tooth comb and a very patient vet. Otherwise, Molly thankfully appeared to be fine. And other than needing a cup of hot tea and a blanket, August was also unharmed.

They had been gone long enough that they'd missed the final activity for the morning. But August was sure Isla would let them do the activity late, if they asked.

August took a hot shower to get the chill out of her bones and changed into a fresh outfit. She had every intention of walking Molly back over to the main building so they could retake their place in the competition.

But as she came out of the bathroom, she found Keaton crouched on the floor next to the bed.

"What are you doing?" she asked.

His bag was open on the bed, clothes folded neatly inside. He was leaving. Her chest clenched hard—the pain so sharp and unexpected that it stole her breath. It was over. He was leaving, and he wasn't even going to say goodbye.

"Work called," Keaton said, folding up one last item and pulling the zip closed. His eyes didn't meet hers. "I have to get back."

"But..." August shook her head. "Molly could still win."

She knew in her heart of hearts that it was a very slim chance—Molly was curled up in her doggy bed, snuggling with her stuffed lobster, watching them both with keen eyes and looking like she wasn't about to budge for anything.

It was like she knew there was a storm brewing—a metaphorical one, this time.

"Molly is in no state to keep going," he said, gesturing to where she lay. "Every time the thunder cracks outside she whimpers like she's been hit. She's terrified."

That was the truth.

"Were you going to say goodbye?" August asked.

As much as she knew that they could only exist in this bubble for a limited period of time, she'd started the day hoping that maybe they would dawdle home after the competition. Linger in the perfect storm—no pun intended—of chemistry and knowing, indulging in one another for as long as possible before they let go.

But Keaton seemed eager to cut and run...and that was on her.

Why did you have to go and prove that humans are such fragile creatures, huh? You reinforced every one of his fears.

"I thought it might be easier if I left quietly," he replied. "I don't want to…"

"Be stuck with a stage-four clinger," she finished, trying to make light of it even though her heart felt like it was being pulled apart.

Keaton walked over to her, close but not touching. In this light, the angles of his face looked sharper and more devastating than ever, his cheekbones ready to slice her heart in two.

"Thanks for saving my ass, by the way," she said, not able to meet his eyes. "I have no idea how I would have gotten out of it if you didn't come for me."

"Technically I saved Molly, not you." He managed a smile, which somehow made her feel worse. "That big bad glop of tree sap was no match for me."

But his attempt at a joke didn't make her feel any better.

"I shouldn't have gone for that walk…" She shook her head.

"Augie," he said softly. "It was an accident. Don't beat yourself up."

"But that's why you're leaving." She looked up at him, her heart already aching at the loss she knew was coming. "Isn't it? Because I proved you're right to be scared about things going wrong."

"I… I don't want to make this more painful than I have already," he said, scrubbing a hand over his face.

"I'm not some wounded teenage girl," she replied, toying with the hem of her T-shirt. "I'm not going to make a mixtape and face plant into a bucket of ice cream because you've dumped me. I know what this is."

"It's interesting that you assume I'm talking about *your* pain. Maybe I was talking about myself."

August frowned. "What do you mean?"

"It might shock you, but I don't fuck around and… I've…"

He let out a breath, as if he were trying to gather himself. "I crossed that line with you because it was *you*. Not because it was sex. When I thought you and Molly had gone missing..."

Something inside her softened. The raw edge to Keaton's voice lanced right through her, and since he wasn't one to be open about his feelings, she knew this would be hard for him. "I'm sorry I did that to you."

"It was bound to happen eventually. But it's not your fault."

She swallowed. "People always make mistakes."

"Yes, but I can't expect someone to walk on eggshells around me and not live their life because something bad might happen." He sighed. "I would never want to trap someone with the fear I have. It would be cruel."

"What if that someone was willing to work through the fear with you? What if they didn't see it as cruel, but instead understood your position?" She hated the desperation in her voice. "What if they thought it was perfectly reasonable that you were scared and they wanted to help you?"

The life and light went out of his eyes. "I can't do that to you, August."

Don't say goodbye. Don't give up.

August's brain spun, trying to figure out how to voice what she wanted without making things worse. It was like walking along a crumbling cliff's edge—one wrong step and she'd go tumbling over, breaking away a piece of him that could never be replaced.

Eventually, she settled on the simple truth. "I like you, Keaton. A lot."

"I like you, too."

"Not to the same extent, I don't think." She bit down on her lip. "Because when I say like, I mean..."

Love.

Something flickered in his eyes—fear. He was afraid of how

strongly she might feel and she could see it written all over his face. The reaction was like another lash over her heart. Which sealed her truth: no matter how much she loved a person, she could never allow herself to be in a position where she wasn't loved the same amount in return. She couldn't be with a man who locked his feelings away.

Feeling unloved and unworthy had been the single most painful aspect of her childhood. She wanted to love and be loved in return.

"I mean..." The words were heavy on her tongue. It felt pointless to say it out loud, because she knew she was staring down the barrel of the end. But what did she have to lose? It was already ending. At least if she made her voice heard, she could walk away knowing she'd left nothing on the table. "I love you."

No shock registered on his face. He knew. He'd always known.

"I loved you that night you tried to kiss me, but I was young and nervous and it felt so important that I just... I froze. I wasn't ready." She let out a breath.

"I thought you wanted a practical partner with all your checklists and shared goals and your perfect compatible hobbies and topics of conversation." For a moment, the teasing Keaton was back. "You wanted a perfect-on-paper relationship."

Not anymore.

Because she knew that focusing on those things made it easier to hide from what she really wanted—*him.* The man who was her worst possible match because his ideal life looked nothing like hers, a man who was capable of great love and yet refused to allow himself to get close to people. A man who let fear guide his decisions.

A man who wouldn't even let people into his home.

He was a worse match for her than any bad viral Tinder date. Worse, because he had the capacity to hurt her.

Why did it have to be him, of all people? But there was no denying the intuition that fanned to life in her gut. She loved Keaton with all her heart…and he would never allow himself to love her back.

"Why are you going back, Keaton?" she asked. "Because of work?"

"Yeah." He nodded. "I have to."

I'm calling bullshit on that.

"No, you don't. You *choose* to." She looked deep into his eyes, her heart begging him to listen. To see that there was more that life could offer him. To believe in himself. "I can't stand to see you waste your life at a place like that, doing a job you don't even like, working for a man who wants to change who you are. Who wants to change what's good about you."

Keaton looked away, shaking his head, barriers firmly in place around his heart. She would never reach him.

Because he was a man who didn't want to be reached.

Part of him had been hoping for a quick getaway before August finished her shower, because it would have been easier that way. Easier for him, because he wouldn't have to face her judgment and her love.

The fact was, when he'd seen August on the ground before he called her name, he'd thought the worst. The very, very worst. For a split second, he was convinced she was dead. It made his last day with Ellery play on a loop in his head. All that pain, the helplessness, the regrets.

The fear.

Love.

He felt the gravity of it. The weight. It was a pressure on

his chest, making it hard to breathe. Because he could see this image ten, twenty, thirty years into the future. He could see them together—happy, complete. But he could also see the pain, the suffering, the loss. The aching blackness that consumed every part of his day, holding him back from living.

How could he possibly risk going through it all again?

"Kea? Did you hear me?"

"I'm not wasting my life, August." He sighed. "I'm trying to fulfill Ellery's dream because I promised her I would."

"Did you know what Wall Street was *really* like, back then?" she asked. "When you were fresh out of college and working at the bottom of the ladder."

"No," he admitted.

"Did Ellery know?" she prodded.

"I don't think so."

His wife had been the high-achieving, ambitious type from the day he met her, but would she have climbed over others to get to the top? Would she have caused whatever collateral damage was required for her to reach her goal?

No.

He'd never thought about it before, but the answer was there.

"If she was still alive, do you think she would be happy with the kind of work you were doing?" August's voice was soft. She wasn't frustrated with him. She wasn't yelling. Instead, she was trying to get him to look at things from another angle…one he hadn't considered before.

"If she was still alive, I'd be very happy to ask her that question. But the fact is, she's dead and she's not coming back." He gritted the words out, grief welling anew, bright and glossy like blood rushing to the surface of a cut. "Just like you could have been this morning."

She winced and he felt like a bastard.

"I'm not trying to poke at a raw spot," she said. "I promise."

Out of the corner of his eye, he saw Molly watching them. She was lying on the very end of the bed, head resting over her paws and her eyes wide and alert. For once, not a peep came out of the usually vocal, dramatic dog.

"Then what *are* you trying to do?" he asked—though the question felt aimed at himself as much as August.

"I'm trying to show you that promises are…"

"Made to be broken?"

"No, of course not. But promises are made to be revisited. They're made to be evaluated and updated," she said. "And I know you can't have her input into that process, which is a great tragedy. But *you* can do those things. *You* can ask yourself if you think she would have wanted you to make such a promise with the information you have now."

She wouldn't have.

"I can hear the answer in your lack of response," August said. She came over to him but didn't touch him, almost like she was approaching a wounded animal with caution.

Everything was too close to the surface right now—anger, fear, desire, regret. After spending the last ten years doing his best to pack that all down as far as it could go, the feelings had sprung back up like a jack-in-the-box and it was too much.

"I know I'm saying some things that are pretty hard to hear," she said.

"But you say them anyway."

A white T-shirt covered August's top half, shaping and hugging her curves. The effect was tantalizing and that only made him angrier at himself.

You should have gotten out of here on the first night. You're weak around her.

"When you care about someone, you say the hard things. You have the difficult conversations. Because a moment of anger is worth it to know that you tried to help." She bit down on her lip. "You've twisted the promise you made your wife so you can justify the stasis in your life. Would she really want you to work in a job that makes you go against your ethics just for the sake of money that you don't actually need anymore? Your mom and Leah are set for life."

"You should worry about yourself, August. About *your* life." He raked a hand through his hair. "I'm releasing you of any obligation you have to care about me, okay? I'm not your family. I'm not your boyfriend. I'm nothing to you."

Her eyes welled but there was no sadness in her face, only fiery anger. "You're *not* nothing to me, Keaton. And if you think I only care out of a sense of obligation, then I guess you don't know me very well after all."

"Maybe that's your problem," he said. "Since we're being honest. Maybe you care too much."

Her mouth popped open and she pressed a palm to her cheek as if he'd slapped her. "How do I care too much?"

"You spend all your time helping other people and getting involved in their problems to the point that you've neglected your own needs. I don't buy for a second that the reason you're single is because there are no good men out there who match your desires."

"And what do you think the real reason is?" She folded her arms across her chest.

"Because you're hanging on to the past."

"I went to a freaking matchmaker, okay? Those things are expensive. I'm *trying* to have the life I want."

"And you really think someone else can tell you who your perfect match is? That a computer can spit out some code and know better than you?" He made a sound of disbelief. "You don't trust your own instincts."

"Why would I? They constantly lead me to the wrong people."

Oof.

But, in fairness, he totally deserved that jab.

"Have you tried going out with friends to a bar and just talking to people?" he asked. When she didn't respond, he knew he'd hit a nerve. "No, because you're a workaholic like me. You want to be efficient, because you don't want to waste time getting out and meeting people organically."

Her gaze swept over him, hurt brimming and lip quivering slightly. He'd landed a blow and he hated himself for it.

She nodded slowly, taking a step away from him. "You'd better get going, then. Don't want to get stuck in rush hour."

At that moment Molly got out of her bed and padded over to them, disappointment radiating from her like toxic fumes. Her head swung from him to August and back again, her markings making it look like her face was set into a deep frown.

You are ridiculous humans, both of you.

He had to agree. But that was human nature, wasn't it? They were prideful, egotistical creatures who would do anything for self-preservation, often to their own detriment.

"Are you taking Molly or leaving her behind?" August asked. "Since it looks like the competition is over for us, I guess she doesn't need to stay. I can get a ride back with Scout and Lane, or Isla and Theo. There's plenty of room."

"Maybe we should let her decide," he said, knowing full well she would choose August. After all, he and Molly barely tolerated one another's presence and that was a step *up* from how it had been ever since Leah brought her home.

They both crouched and extended their hands out toward the dog. She sniffed the air, put one paw forward and hesitated. Then, to his shock, she trotted over to Keaton, tail swishing and tongue darting out to swipe at his hand.

"You saved her, Keaton. She won't forget that anytime soon." August smiled, but the expression was heavy and sad. "I knew you could win her trust. Great job."

A lump formed in the back of his throat as he ruffled the dog's fur. There were no words left to say. It felt like he'd been wrung dry, squeezed out and was now a damp thing swaying in the wind.

He had nothing left to give.

"I'm going to head over and watch the final part of the contest," she said, tears making her voice wobbly. "Have a safe drive back, okay?"

She threw a sweatshirt over her T-shirt and stuffed her feet into her sneakers. Then she was gone. The sound of the door closing behind her felt like a book being snapped shut. Whatever he shared with August, it was now officially over.

22

Despite August's somber mood, the final day of the competition was a fun affair. After they got down to the last five animals—which didn't include Molly, on account of her early departure—Isla presented a multitude of awards to the participants, including Biggest Personality for Molly, which August would pass on to Leah when she got home.

When the final winner was announced—the adorable Hungarian sheepdog named Swish, who looked like a giant mop head—there were cheers and commiserations in the audience. The camera crew went around the room, getting final words from contestants and following the Paws in the City team for a little longer, until everyone bundled off to the main hall to get coffee and sweets before packing up to hit the road.

The fun was over.

August left Isla and Scout to wrap things up and say goodbye to everyone, not wanting to intrude on what would likely still be a very busy day for her friends. Once people had cleared out, she'd find them to help pack everything up for the trip home. Scout had said she could catch a ride with her and Lane, and that they had plenty of space.

August found a quiet spot to sit and reflect, a cup of coffee warming her hands.

It was over between her and Keaton.

Most of her hadn't expected anything different—he was, if nothing else, a man of stasis. And August had proved that his fears about losing people around him weren't unfounded. But even without this morning's dramas, it probably would have ended the same way. Why did she think that a few nights of hot sex and some meaningful conversation would be anything more than a temporary diversion for him?

But part of her *had* thought that. There had been a little tiny, hopeful, rose-colored glasses part of her heart that wondered if she laid it all on the line, then maybe…

Maybe he felt the same way she did.

Isla headed over with a wave, pulling August out of her thoughts.

"Hey!" she said, sympathy pulling her brows into a frown. "How are you doing?"

"More embarrassed than anything else," August admitted. "But the only thing bruised is my ego, thankfully."

In more ways than one.

"I'm so glad you're okay." Isla shook her head. "That storm came out of nowhere!"

"Let's not talk about it anymore." August waved a hand. "You guys did a phenomenal job with this whole thing. Truly."

"Thanks." Isla plopped down into the empty seat next to her and let out a sigh. "I'm going to sleep for a week."

"You deserve it."

A minute of silence passed and August got the feeling her friend was building up to something.

"I wanted to have a chat about Molly and your friend Leah," Isla said eventually. She seemed a little nervous, twisting her hands in front of her.

"You don't have to explain why Molly didn't win, Isla. She didn't even finish the competition, so I knew she couldn't possibly be in the running. Besides, you chose the right contestant—Swish was fantastic! I know she'll make a great client and I would *never* expect favoritism. You know I hate that stuff."

Isla nodded and let out a breath, her shoulders dropping. "Good."

"Did you really think I'd be upset?" she asked.

"No, of course not. But you seem…a little off."

"It's nothing to do with this, trust me." She looked down.

"Well, I can guess what it *might* be about. But before I start asking questions, I wanted to run an idea by you." She smiled. "I've been thinking about starting a mentorship for a while, as a way to give back to upcoming social media creators. And while Molly wasn't able to finish the competition, I think she has *loads* of potential, and your friend Leah is already in the social space, right?"

"That's right. She runs a YouTube channel."

"Do you think she would be interested in some ongoing mentoring? I'd love to have her into the Paws in the City office so we can talk about her plans for her channel and blog, and what other platforms she might want to expand to. Doesn't even have to be pet social media, because I've got plenty of experience in other spaces, too."

"You would do that for her?" It felt like August's heart might burst from the kind gesture.

"Absolutely. I had a quick chat with her on Zoom after the workshop and she's super bright and motivated. I love working with people like that and I loved hearing her story of how she wants to help educate people about MS and provide inspiration and support to other women in her situation. If I can help her grow her platform, then I'd like to do it."

Emotion welled up inside August—probably because she was already feeling so raw—and she threw her arms around Isla. "Thank you."

"Oh my goodness, it's totally my pleasure." Isla squeezed her back. "This business can be quite cutthroat and competitive. But I really want to be a force for positivity, and I feel like Leah wants the same. We'd make a great team."

"I agree."

"You want to tell me what else is going on? It didn't escape me that a certain BFF's hunky big brother isn't here anymore."

"He had to get back for work." She avoided Isla's inquisitive gaze.

"Right." She nodded. "That's all?"

"Uh-huh." August looked studiously at the ground.

"The floor is really interesting, is it?"

Smiling sheepishly, August looked at her friend, who'd raised a pointed eyebrow. "Is it okay to say I don't want to talk about this, either?"

"Of course. If you change your mind, you know where to find me." She smiled and reached out to pat August on the shoulder. "And I've been there, feeling miserable and not sure what to do or how to make it right."

August's instinct should have been to say that Keaton was the one who had to make it right. But was the blame *entirely* on his shoulders? She'd poked and prodded and then wondered why he'd pulled away. She firmly believed that if you wanted to change someone to make them lovable, then that wasn't love at all.

But hadn't she tried to do that to him?

"Thanks, Isla," she said, trying to force a smile. But it felt watery and weak. "I just need some time."

"I understand. Scout and I are here whenever you need us, okay? We'll be round in a flash with ice cream and booze the second you need it."

It helped knowing she had such wonderful, supportive friends around her. Female friendships that were the antithesis of the competitive, backstabbing types so often falsely portrayed in movies and television. *True* friends. In that part of her life, she was overwhelmed with love.

But Keaton had left a hole behind, whether she wanted him to or not.

And finding a man who made her feel even an ounce of what he did would be a very tall order indeed.

By the time Keaton made it back to Manhattan, he felt like a shell. Riding up the elevator to his apartment, he caught a glimpse of himself in the mirrored paneling of the elevator's carriage. He looked…numb. Hollow.

He knew this face.

It was the same face he'd worn home from Ellery's funeral, where the gravity of things hadn't yet settled like boulders on his back. He couldn't think. Couldn't feel.

"She's not dead, stop overreacting," he said to himself.

Molly looked up at him, brow furrowed. For once, there wasn't a hint of disdain or judgment in her expression. He couldn't hear the snarky voice he'd made up for her in his head any longer. Nor did he feel like she was this larger-than-life diva, a source of amusement and full of sharp wit and personality. She was back to being a simple dog, again.

Molly nudged his hand, her tongue darting out to swipe at his fingertips, and he absently rewarded her with a soft ruffle of her fur.

Why didn't he stop by Leah's place on the way back to drop her off? He'd been on autopilot, desperate to get home. Back to his space, back to his life, back to comforting nothingness. The past few days with August had been like sensory overload—all the things he'd promised himself he wouldn't feel again had come rushing to the surface, like an unexpected wave, ready to suck him under and fill his nose and mouth and lungs with suffocating salt water.

He didn't want to love her, still. He didn't want to know that she loved him. That their history wasn't neatly filed away in either of their minds, archived for record only.

Why?

There were times when he wondered if he would change the past, given the chance. If he would have left his house to go out for a walk instead of hanging around and being introduced to Ellery. If he would've taken August's rebuff for what it was—nerves, rather than rejection. But every time he thought about it, he couldn't imagine his life without the blissful year he'd spent with his wife.

Even if it broke him.

Even if it made him cling to fear like a life raft.

Even if it froze him in place, turning him into a stone gargoyle.

The elevator doors slid open and Molly walked ahead like she owned the place, but every few steps her head swung back to check on him. "I'm still here," he said.

But he wasn't. Not really.

He was deep inside himself, shell hardening over his body and making him numb again. As he walked to the door, Molly slowed so she could walk beside him—an equal rather than the leader. He had his overnight bag slung over one shoulder and his keys dangling in his hand, punctuating each slow step with a jingle.

He unlocked the door and let them inside. Molly stepped cautiously into his space, sniffing and exploring. It occurred to Keaton that aside from his mother and sister, Molly was the first guest he'd allowed into his home since Ellery died. Dumping his bag on the ground, he pulled his phone out of his pocket and half expected to see messages lighting up his screen—at least from his sister berating him once August had told her what'd happened.

But there was nothing. Not a single message or missed call. It felt like a warning—what his life would become if he kept pushing people away.

Molly trotted over to the window and pushed her wet nose against the glass, making a little smudge along with the ring of fog caused by her breath. She made a snorting sound, tail wagging. Then she looked back to Keaton with her mouth hanging open, happy.

"Yeah, it's a pretty good view." He walked over to her. "I don't take enough time to appreciate it."

Molly's wagging tail thumped against his knee, leaving behind a sprinkling of white fur. For once, he didn't mind. Her presence was a comfort—because it made the silent phone and quiet rooms feel a little less lonely.

"What do you think? Would you want to come and hang out with me sometime?" He looked down at her, reaching to run his fingers through her fur, and her tail wagged harder. "I'll take that as a yes."

They stared out at the sparkling city together, and for the first time in a long time, Keaton found himself wondering about the lives taking place in the specks of light—who the people were and what they did and if they were happy. Was anyone happy?

"I don't know if I'm doing the right thing or making the biggest mistake of my life," he said, looking down at the dog. "I like August a hell of a lot. She's funny and smart and beautiful and positive and motivated and...did I mention she's beautiful? Not just in looks, but...more than that."

She was beautiful in her soul.

There was a goodness that frightened him, because it felt like she was the sun and he was a shadow. Like deep down they were opposing forces. Like one of them would have to overtake the other if it were going to work.

He headed to the couch and flopped down. As if sensing he needed comfort, Molly came over to him and jumped up onto the couch, throwing her paws over his thigh and plopping her head down, ice-blue eyes tilted up. Her tail continued to wag, sweeping over the throw cushion on the other side of the couch and leaving hairs everywhere.

"Thanks for being here," he said. "I understand why my sister keeps you around now."

"Wrow wrow wrow," Molly replied, as if to say, *Now I know why she keeps you around, too.*

"What should I do?" he asked, smoothing his thumb between the dog's eyes like he'd seen August do. But Molly didn't respond. She let out a big sigh and lay heavier on him, pressing down into his leg as her eyes drifted shut. It had been a big day.

There was no answer—not from Molly, not from inside his own head. Not from anywhere.

As Molly drifted off to sleep, the apartment was silent once again. For the last ten years, he'd craved his silence at the end of each workday because it felt like peace. Like escape. But now it reminded him of his time in juvie, in the deep, deep hours of the morning where time seemed to stand still and the oppressive quiet was like a terrifying, endless purgatory.

He'd dreamed of being successful in those moments—of getting out and starting over and making something of himself. Yet in many ways, he'd simply circled around to who he was back then.

A tender heart fearful of all the mistakes he'd made, utterly alone and without anyone to blame but himself.

23

The following evening, after work, Keaton drove Molly back home. Thankfully, Molly seemed in good spirits and had taken the opportunity to nap all day after a busy weekend of performing tricks and being around people, and, therefore, she hadn't destroyed his apartment, as he'd feared.

The closer they got to Leah's house, the noisier and more excited Molly got in the back seat of the car Keaton had borrowed to get them to and from the competition. He'd return the vehicle tomorrow—but part of him wondered if he should buy one. It would be fun to get out of the city more often, maybe take Leah and Molly with him. They could do trips upstate to the wineries or even a longer road trip. Possibly up to Quebec or Ontario.

Since when do you want to drive and take trips?

He scratched his head. The whole day he'd been having

these strange, uncharacteristic thoughts—like that he should buy a car, or get a dog of his own, or take up a hobby…any hobby.

That he should quit his job.

Ignoring the weird shit going on in his head, he kept his focus on the road ahead of him. Eventually he pulled up in front of Leah's house and found a good spot to park. Molly almost leaped out of the back seat when he opened the door, practically vibrating with excitement.

"Yes, we're almost there. Leah is going to be so happy to see you."

He walked Molly up to the front door, which was already open, and Leah stood there, arms extended. Molly yanked so hard on her leash that Keaton gave up and let it go so the husky could fling herself into her mom's arms, tail wagging and fur flying everywhere. Leah giggled and embraced the dog, cooing at her while Molly tried to lick her face.

"My girl, it's so good to have you home!" Leah squeezed her eyes shut.

Leah's boyfriend, Will, stood behind her, watching on with soft eyes. "We missed you, Molly girl."

Leah looked up at her boyfriend with total adoration. "We sure did."

"Hi, Keaton." Will raised a hand, looking a little nervous like he always did whenever Keaton showed up.

They'd met a handful of times and, like always, he'd taken his time to figure out whether he liked the guy Leah had chosen to date. The jury had still been out, but Will was proving he was ready to be by Leah's side whenever she needed him, like he had done these past few days. And, in truth, Keaton's wariness of Will had nothing to do with the younger guy, and everything to do with his own baggage.

His fears that Leah would one day be heartbroken like he was. That Leah would fall madly in love and not need him anymore. That if it were to happen…Keaton would have no purpose or meaning in life.

"Hi, Will." He nodded, though he couldn't find it in him to smile.

Will glanced at Leah as if to say, *I told you he doesn't like me.* Leah leaned in and whispered something in Will's ear and squeezed his arm.

"I should get home and make sure my roommate hasn't eaten everything in my cupboards," Will said with a laugh. He leaned in to kiss Leah on the forehead and give Molly a scratch, then he was gone.

"Want to come in?" Leah asked Keaton. "We've got left-overs from dinner last night if you're hungry."

"That sounds great."

The three of them headed inside and set about making drinks and heating up some of the fried rice and honey chicken that Leah and Will had ordered the previous evening. Keaton grabbed a seat at the table and was surprised when Molly sat on his feet.

"I never thought I would see the day," Leah said, laughing. "My big brother and my dog acting like best friends."

"I wouldn't go that far," Keaton said dryly. "We had our moments."

"I saw the pictures from the photo shoot." She laughed, her eyes sparkling. "I've asked August to send me the lot and I'm going to get them printed and hang them on the wall in the living room."

"Did she tell you about the 'talent' portion, where Molly didn't execute a *single* command?" He cringed.

"No. Tell me everything!"

Fifteen minutes later Leah was laughing so hard tears rolled down her cheeks as Keaton regaled her with all the funny stories of Molly's antics and how they'd slowly become friends over the course of the long weekend.

He'd downplayed the scariness of finding Molly and August stranded during the storm, making out like it was a dramatic tale told for her amusement rather than something that had seriously scared the shit out of him.

The moment he thought he'd lost them both…

It had almost split him in two.

But he didn't want Leah thinking about that, so he skipped over the scary bits and focused on Molly's hatred of tree sap and how she'd clung to him like a baby and licked his face so hard he thought he'd have to scrub it for a week to get the doggy drool off.

"Oh my goodness." Leah's eyes squeezed shut and she brushed the tears from her cheeks. "Stop. My stomach is hurting."

"I'm sorry we couldn't win for you," he said, turning serious.

"Don't be ridiculous. I never thought she would win." She held up a hand. "And that has *nothing* to do with your talents or Molly's. I just know she can be a little difficult and honestly… I thought it would be fun. And anyway, August told me that the lady who runs Paws in the City wants to mentor me! Isn't that amazing?"

Leah's beaming smile was almost able to wipe all the darkness from his heart. Almost. "That *is* amazing. Sounds like a great opportunity."

"I hope it might be helpful for my YouTube channel and website, too. I've been planning a series on why pets are great for mental health when you have a chronic illness." She nodded. "I think it would help a lot of people."

He swallowed and looked down.

"What's wrong?" she asked.

"You're..." He shook his head. "I wish I was half as strong and kind as you are, Leah. You're going to change the world."

She blinked. "I don't know about that. But if my content can help even a few people, then that's pretty good, right?"

"Don't sell yourself short, you have big things in front of you."

"Something's different, Kea." She cocked her head. "I mean, I appreciate your faith in me but I don't like that you're acting as if you're not a strong and kind person."

He wasn't. He was fucking weak.

Not like his mom, who'd battled her way out of not one but two emotionally abusive relationships to find love with Harv.

Not like his sister, who lived vibrantly even when in pain.

Not like August, who wore her heart on her sleeve and always said the brave thing.

It was the women around him who were kind and strong, and if he had any sliver of those attributes at all, it was because they reflected onto him. Not because he'd found those qualities himself.

"I promise I'm not upset that you didn't win." She scooted her chair over to his and wrapped an arm around his shoulder.

"Are you sure?"

"Kea, listen to me. I know you're quite hung up on winning—you have been ever since we were kids. But always focusing on winning cuts out the *most* important bit—the journey to get there." She grinned. "Let me finish, before you tell me I'm talking mumbo jumbo, okay?"

"I wasn't going to say anything."

He totally was.

"If there's one thing I learned dealing with all this—" She

waved her hand around, gesturing to her body. "It's that if you only focus on big wins, then there are a lot of days that feel like failure. But they're *not* failure! Some days, winning looks like washing all the dishes myself and taking Molly for a short walk. Other days it looks like signing a sponsorship contract with a brand for my YouTube channel. One is small, the other is big…but they're both wins."

"That's true."

"And by always focusing on the destination—the 'what's next' part—you miss all the great stuff that happens along the way. Did Molly win? No. But I've now got a great opportunity to work with Isla and Paws in the City, and I learned a lot in that workshop," she said. "But if I was only focused on the end, then I might feel sad for no reason."

Wasn't that how Keaton had been living his life the last ten years? One promotion after the next, one deal after the next—yet the journey felt hollow. How could he enjoy the journey when he was walking the road alone? Wasn't the destination the only point?

And what *is your destination, huh? Your name on the wall of a place you've grown to hate, working for a man whose ideals you don't respect while compromising your ethics simply because staying the same is easier than changing?*

Oof.

"I see your point." He nodded, but it felt too painful to keep discussing the matter. "How are you feeling, anyway? Do you need me to do anything while I'm here?"

"Stop." She shook her head. "One, don't try to change the subject. And two, just because I had a flare-up doesn't mean I can't support you when you *clearly* need it."

"Who says I need it?" he grumbled.

"It's all over your face, misery guts." She poked him. "What's going on? You know I can be persistent. I'll just keep asking until you tell me."

"I don't like what my life has become." There, he said it. "I'm fucking lonely and sad and I hate it."

For a moment, Leah didn't say anything. She simply rested her head against his shoulder, her hand finding his. They sat there for a while, and he let her comfort him.

"Aren't you going to tell me I don't need to be lonely, because I'm not alone?" he said eventually.

"No."

He frowned. "Why not?"

"Because you get to decide how you feel. It's not for me to tell you that you're wrong."

He grunted. "That's very wise."

"Here's the thing—you're going in a direction you don't like. So why do you keep walking in that direction?" she asked.

He swallowed. "Change is scary."

"Regret is scarier. Because you can't do anything about it then. At least now you can course correct and find the right path. And if you make a mistake, you can change again. But once you reach the end, you don't get to turn around and do it over."

His sister's words bounced off the aching hollow cavern in his chest, scattering the ghosts inside him. She was right. Change *was* scary, but not changing was even scarier. Because where would he be in five years? Ten? Twenty?

Alone.

And that didn't sound as safe as it once did.

He didn't go home. Instead, he went straight to work, opening the office door at midnight with his all-hours pass, and went right up to his desk. Everyone was gone for the night. The lights were dim but they brightened when he passed the sensors at knee level.

He logged on to his desktop and accessed the company server, navigating through the shared folders that his team used to store and organize the data they collected for their clients' deals. He found the one for Waterline Press, where his researcher had added file after file with information about the company, their weak points, their debts, the things they could use to pressure them.

He deleted the lot.

It was a good thing Thomas was too arrogant to think Keaton would ever do something like this, which was why he had admin-level IT privileges. So when he deleted something, it was gone. Forever.

Then he sat down and typed out his resignation email.

Thomas,

I think we both knew this time would come, although I personally didn't see it happening quite so soon. But things have changed. I've changed.

I'm grateful you saw fit to take me under your wing, and I'm even more grateful for the support you've provided me over the years, especially after my wife passed away. I'll never forget that.

But having my name on the door won't make me happy now. Spending my days finding ways to screw the little guy won't make me happy. Staying tied to the past won't make me happy.

I've found a reason to choose a different path.

Therefore, I am tendering my resignation effective immediately. Thank you for being my boss and mentor, you have no idea how much I needed it. But ultimately, I've decided I am not cut out for Wall Street...and I couldn't be happier about it.

Keaton

By the time Thomas was back in the office tomorrow, Keaton's desk and shelves would be cleared out. He was never coming back here again.

24

One week later...

WALL STREET WHIZ GHOSTS FAIRCHILD & HILL IN SHOCK DEPARTURE.

THE FINANCE INDUSTRY'S SHARK POPULATION IS REDUCED BY ONE—SHOCK RESIGNATION FROM THE WALL STREET WHIZ KID.

SOURCE CLAIMS SAX BURNED A DEAL ON HIS WAY OUT THE DOOR—FAIRCHILD & HILL PREDICTED TO SUE.

The articles were *everywhere*. August stood in the middle of her client's kitchen, scrolling on her phone as New York media exploded with the news of Keaton's resignation from the firm where he'd worked for years. Apparently, it had happened sometime last week and they'd kept it hush-hush, but someone had finally leaked the news to the media. She hadn't realized just how much of a big deal he was in that world—because it was about as far from her world as you could get.

But he'd been touted as a future big player, a mover and shaker.

And the news reports claiming that he'd taken a bunch of information about the deal he was working on…

He hadn't taken it, she was sure of that. He'd destroyed it to save that small company.

August pulled up her text messages to fire one off to Leah.

AUGUST: Is Keaton okay?? His name is all over the news.

LEAH: I know!! I can't reach him. I'm going to give him an hour before I take Molly over and bust down his door.

AUGUST: Call if you need reinforcements. I can stop past after my next appointment.

LEAH: Aren't you having coffee with one of your potential matches?

AUGUST: Yes, but I can cancel.

LEAH: Don't cancel. But call me right after, okay? Don't worry about Keaton, I'll handle him.

She wasn't sure Keaton would want to see her, however. To say their last conversation had been painful was putting it lightly. And not painful because he didn't feel the same way as she did. Or because he was being a jerk. Or because he was surprised when she confessed that she loved him.

But because he felt something for her, too.

It only served to reinforce all her regrets about that night. He'd held the future out in the palm of his hand and she'd been too chickenshit to take it.

Now he was too afraid to try again and she'd lost her chance. Fear was the killer of their chances—her fear back then and his now. It made her want to scream and throw something at the wall. But there was no point. She *had* to keep going. She *had* to move on.

August was, if nothing else, motivated and resilient.

"August," her client called out as she poked her head into the kitchen. "You can come through now."

Sara was a Broadway star, retired and in her late fifties, and she walked with the grace and excellent posture of someone who'd trained in dance for decades. She wore a vibrant yellow shirt tucked into loose white pants, and her black hair was a halo of tightly coiled curls around her head. Her brown skin glowed and she wore her signature mahogany-brown lipstick. Even now, August was starstruck by getting to groom the pet of a legend like Sara, whom she'd seen in several shows over the years.

"How's Liza doing?" August asked as she followed Sara through the brownstone out to a large laundry, where there was an ample sink and bench with which to do her grooming.

"You can see for yourself." Sara bent to scoop up an adorable silky terrier whose coat already gleamed.

"You do such a good job taking care of her, I feel like I barely need to do anything when I come to see her." August reached out to stroke the dog's head. She was a friendly little thing, and her tail wagged with affection.

"A full brush out two to three times a week and a bath every month," Sara replied, with a proud smile. "We love our bath time together, don't we, Miss Liza?"

The dog's head pulled back at the mention of the word *bath* and August was quite sure that Liza did *not* enjoy it. But her owner took great care of her and the little dog was well trained and compliant, so she put up with the bathing.

"I'll leave you to your work, but if you need me, I'll be around," Sara said. "Just call out."

August took the dog from her client and popped her up onto the bench, securing her with a clip at the collar to prevent her from accidentally falling off. She started by spraying the dog's fur with a pet-safe detangling spray, because the silky terrier had such fine hair that it was at risk of breaking if brushed dry. Then she used a pin brush to start working out any of the tangles common to the breed.

As she worked, she praised the little dog, who stood patiently, moving this way and that as instructed.

"You're such a good girl," August cooed.

By the time she finished the grooming session, she'd run over by fifteen minutes because she'd stopped to check her phone half a dozen times. August *never* did that—she was always very aware of her clients' time being precious, as well as her own. But she was desperate for an update. Was Keaton okay? Had Leah gotten through to him? What if he'd taken off and she never saw him again?

You're being ridiculous.

But the irrational thought sat like a weight in her stomach. And it *continued* to sit in her stomach while she headed home to shower and change for her date, and while she hoofed it back up to the fancy little cafe where she was due to meet one of her matches, Kai.

Pausing outside the cafe's window, she checked her appearance. Her cheeks were flushed from rushing to make up the time she'd lost earlier, and her red hair was wild and frizzy. She hadn't even bothered to put any lipstick on, or change her earrings out from her usual practical gold ball studs to something fancier.

"Oh well, he can take me or leave me as I am," she muttered to herself, feeling more like she was walking into a doctor's appointment than a date.

Well, to be fair, it wasn't a date. Technically. Maxine had set her up with three "meet and greet" coffee sessions with the men that would apparently tick all her boxes.

☐ Intelligent, but with a good sense of humor.
☐ Driven to succeed, but also likes to have fun.
☐ No desire to have children.

But August couldn't seem to muster much enthusiasm. She'd been hoping all the way through her appointment that Leah would call on her for help, so she would have an excuse to cancel the not-date. But a deeply ingrained sense of responsibility had brought her here, even though she would rather be anywhere else.

That's not fair to this poor guy. You're wasting his time.

No matter how perfect on paper Kai might be, the truth boiled down to one simple fact: he wasn't Keaton.

None of them would be Keaton.

None of them *could* be Keaton.

They would never live up to the man who'd taken up residence in her heart, no matter how much she wanted to evict him. So what was the point in getting anyone's hopes up? Practical, it turned out, didn't trump passion no matter how much she wished that it did. It wasn't fair to Kai to put him through a date knowing she wasn't going to want to see him again. As someone who'd been ghosted and dumped before, she couldn't bring herself to do that to someone else.

So she texted Kai to say that she was very sorry, but they wouldn't be meeting today. Instead of feeling sad, it was like a weight had lifted from her shoulders. In her heart, she knew it was the right move.

But where to from here?

That was the million-dollar question. Because she was stuck between her desire for a solid, stable partnership and her feelings for a man who would never change.

He quit his job. Don't you think that's a sign of change?

She didn't know what to think anymore. As she walked away from the cafe, forcing herself not to drag her feet along the pavement, she got a text from Leah.

LEAH: I found Keaton. He's home and doing fine. Unemployed, obviously, but fine.

August let out a long, relieved breath. Frustrating as the situation was, she was glad he was okay and proud that he'd quit a job that so obviously didn't suit him anymore. He deserved the world, even if he didn't believe it.

AUGUST: Do you need me to come over?

Despite her head knowing better, her heart desperately wanted to see him. Ironic, since only a few weeks ago she'd openly complained to Keaton about how Leah not-so-subtly kept trying to put them in a room together.

Now she wanted it to happen.

LEAH: No, we're fine. I've taken Molly over and we're going to chill at his place. How did the date go?

AUGUST: It didn't. I think I'm done with this whole dating thing.

As soon as she typed the words into the text bar, she knew they were true. In her quest to find a perfectly practical partner, she'd simply circled right back around to the only man she'd ever truly wanted. Even working with a professional matchmaker hadn't helped.

Or rather, it might have if she'd wanted it to. But deep down, she knew that no matter how many dates she went on, there would always be the niggling voice in the back of her mind telling her that they would never live up to him.

How could they? She'd been in love with Keaton since she was thirteen years old. He'd seen her grow and blossom, and she'd seen him stumble and soar. No computer algorithm could ever beat that.

LEAH: Come over tomorrow night. I'll have wine ready.

But August knew wine wouldn't help. No amount of alcohol could drown the realization that she was destined to pine after the most unavailable man on earth, and that the best she could ever hope for was to be his friend.

25

The Christmas tree was standing, decorations twinkling like stars in the night sky. Atop the tree was an angel—a bit cliché, perhaps, but secretly Keaton loved a little tradition when it came to holiday decorating. Red and green, gold and silver, tinsel, baubles and a piece of velvet to cover the base of the tree.

The only thing that didn't match the festive picture inside the house was the blazing sunshine outside. And all the green on the trees. And the fact that people were walking past wearing shorts and T-shirts.

"This is a bad idea," he muttered to himself.

"It's *not* a bad idea." Leah stood in the doorway. She was feeling energetic today…which meant she was hovering around Keaton to make sure he didn't chicken out. "It's incredibly thoughtful and sweet and romantic."

Re-creating the night they almost kissed…what could possibly go wrong?

She might reject him a second time.

She might think he was doing some weird social experiment on her.

She might not even turn up.

Leah had invited August over via text yesterday. Then, like the crafty fox she was, she'd plied Keaton with wine and wrenched every last detail from him.

About quitting his job.

About the fact that Fairchild & Hill might try to sue him.

About realizing he still had feelings for August. Deep feelings.

"What if… What if she thinks I'm having some kind of grief episode?" He shook his head. "I have no idea what I'm doing. I have *zero* experience in grand gestures and I'm so good at screwing things up."

"You're not nearly as much of a screwup as you like to think, Kea." Leah came over and wrapped her arms around him. "And August loves you. I've known it for the longest time *and* I knew you felt the same about her. Did you think I was trying to get you two together because I was bored? No! But you're both as stubborn as each other and if I didn't give you a push, you'd waste your damn lives being too freaking scared to do a thing about it. I had to take matters into my own hands."

"It's deeply annoying when you're right," he grumbled.

"That must be frustrating. I'm right *all* the time." Leah grinned up at him.

"You wish, little sis."

His heart pounded as he looked around the room. It was different now than it had been all those years ago. The walls were a different color and the floor had been replaced and there was no more thumping around from neighbors upstairs. But the heart and soul of the place was the same. The love that was etched into every corner by his family—a family that had faced challenges and fought bravely as a team.

"I hope it doesn't come across like I'm trying to erase that night," he said, raking a hand through his hair. "I won't ever regret meeting Ellery and being married to her. That was an important part of my life."

But it was a part that had to be put where it belonged—in the past. He had to stop letting those painful days after his wife died dictate how he lived his life now. He had to stop being afraid of losing someone he loved again, because the fact was, he *had* lost August by pushing her away. It had become a self-fulfilling prophecy.

But at the same time, he didn't want to disrespect Ellery's memory or the love they shared.

"It's not a bad thing to move on," Leah said gently.

"Kind of goes against the whole 'one true love' thing, though."

"The one true love thing is bullshit, if you ask me." Leah shrugged. "Love is what you make of it in the moment. And loving August now doesn't mean that you never loved Ellery. She would want you to move on and be happy, Kea. That's the kind of person she was. It would make her weep to see you wasting your life away."

Keaton found his eyes prickling for a moment, but he blinked the emotion away. He'd spent long enough oscillating between being miserable and numb. It was time to start living again.

"Thanks for helping me see past my own shit," he said.

"That's what family is for. You do so much for me, the least I can do is show you when you're being a fool." Her eyes sparkled mischievously. "But seriously though, I want you to be happy. I want her to be happy. You're my favorite people in the whole wide world and you deserve each other in the best way possible."

He nodded, nerves creating a knot in his stomach. "I'm going to lay it all out there and if she says no—"

"She won't."

"*If* she says no," he repeated, "then I won't fall in a heap and go back to how I was. This is a turning point, and I hope she's there with me. But it's ultimately her choice, and if not, then… I still need to move forward."

"I'm proud of you, big brother." Leah squeezed him. Then she caught sight of a flash of red as August strolled up the street toward the house. "Time to hide!"

"I can't hide, I have to answer the door."

Leah whacked him. "Don't you know anything about a reveal, Kea? It has to be a surprise! Besides, she's got a key. She'll let herself in."

"Are you sure?" He looked toward the door.

"Trust me, okay? What's the point of putting up all this stuff if you're just going to open the door yourself?"

He wasn't sure he agreed, but Leah knew her best friend and, for once in his life, he was going to listen to what she said. He just had to hope that he could show August how much he cared. How much he'd *always* cared…

And that he wanted to take the other path with her.

August walked toward Leah's house, a shopping bag swinging on one arm. Her friend had said she would supply the wine, but August was sure that it would take more than a bottle of red to drown her feelings tonight. So she'd picked up some of her favorite egg custard tarts from the Portuguese bakery around the corner, along with a tub of ice cream, a bag of Chicago mix popcorn and some tequila.

And by "some" tequila, she meant two whole bottles.

The house appeared quiet as she approached, and when she knocked on the door, no sounds came from inside. Frowning, she waited a moment and knocked again. Maybe Leah had taken a nap. She tried not to worry as she fished her key out and unlocked the door, stepping inside and closing it behind her.

It was perfectly still and quiet. Not even the familiar click of canine toenails over floorboards.

Out of the corner of her eye, August caught lights flashing in the living room. Turning, she almost dropped her bag of groceries from the shock of seeing a fully decorated Christmas tree right in the corner of the room, near the fireplace.

"What the heck…?" She put the bag of groceries down on the floor and toed off her shoes. Then she headed toward the twinkling lights.

Was this some weird Christmas in June event? Was that even a thing? Wasn't it supposed to be Christmas in *July*?

"Hi, August." Keaton's voice startled her so much that she immediately brought her hands up in a faux martial arts stance.

What the heck did you think was going to happen? That you would karate chop an intruder who broke in to decorate a Christmas tree?

"I'm so confused right now." She lowered her arms.

Keaton stood in the archway that separated the living room from a small dining area. He leaned against the wall, looking every bit his usual delectable self, in dark denim jeans and a black V-neck T-shirt.

"I, uh…" He came forward. "I wanted to talk to you and

when I went to Leah for advice, she told me to go big or go home."

August's mouth twitched. "That sounds like something she'd say."

"It all made sense in my head, but now that we're in the moment..." He glanced at the Christmas tree. "I'm going to say what I planned to say, okay? It's probably going to sound ridiculous but we're here now and I'm already making a fool of myself, anyway, so why not go all the way?"

August's tummy fluttered. It felt like something big was coming—something important. And she didn't trust herself to speak, so she simply nodded.

"I don't know if I ever told you how much it meant that you wrote me while I was in juvie," he started. "Those were some of the darkest days of my whole life and I believed I didn't deserve for a single person to remember who I was. I expected everyone to abandon me, because it felt like that's what I was owed. But you didn't. You kept me in touch with the world and life back here. I know you came around a lot to keep Leah company because my mom was struggling with her mental health and with her marriage falling apart, and then with Leah's diagnosis."

August nodded. "You guys are my second family."

"Some days I'm pretty sure your letters were the only thing that kept me going. That kept me believing I could get out of there and make a change for myself. That I could be the man Mom and Leah needed me to be." He raked a hand through his hair. "Then when I went off to college, I missed your letters."

"I thought you'd be too busy to worry about writing back to a silly high school girl," she replied, looking down at her feet.

"There's nothing silly about you, August—not then and not now. I thought about you all the time, looking forward to summer break because I knew you'd be hanging around the house and I could see you."

"You never made a move," she said, shaking her head.

"Two years felt like a huge gap even though you were more mature than anyone my age. I didn't want to be one of those creepy college guys leering after young high school girls. So I waited..." He let out a breath. "I waited until after I'd graduated and you'd gotten a little older, and when I came home for Christmas, it felt right."

The words struck her in the chest. He'd been biding his time, waiting for the right moment to be with her, and she'd blown it.

"Keaton wants to talk to you," Leah said, pointing to the front door. "Outside."

"Why?" August tried to play it cool, but inside her body was a riot of color and excitement, like the rainbow flickering lights she'd strung on her tree the week earlier.

Leah shrugged and winked. "I don't know. Maybe he wants to kiss you."

Most sisters would hate the idea of their brother making out with their best friend, but not Leah. She'd thought they should get married ever since she was thirteen, because she wanted August to officially be part of their family and that seemed easier than trying to get her mom to file for adoption.

"He doesn't want to kiss me," August scoffed.

"Just go." Leah shoved her toward the door and August was so nervous she thought she might puke. That would not make a good impression.

"Fine," she huffed, pretending to be annoyed rather than excited.

Inside, the house was noisy and warm and fun, with Leah and

Keaton's extended family gathering around and some of their mother's friends dropping by, too. But outside, the world felt still and quiet. Snow drifted down in fat, fluffy flakes and caught in her hair and on the outer layer of her velvet dress.

Keaton was waiting for her, fire in his smile and devilish temptation in his eyes. "Good," he said, his voice liquid smooth. "You came."

Passion bubbled up inside her like champagne and it was the best feeling in the world.

"I never knew you felt that way about me," she said. "It took me by surprise."

"I know. And it's important that you know I didn't run off with Ellery that night because I was angry at you for rejecting me or anything like that. It wasn't… I wasn't trying to make you jealous."

"I know." She nodded. "That's not the kind of person you are. I know you loved her very much."

"You pulled away and I respected that." He nodded. "It obviously wasn't the reaction I'd hoped for, but… I was never going to push you to do anything you didn't want to."

I should have said yes. I wanted *to say yes.*

"That night was like a *Sliding Doors* moment," he continued. Then he chuckled. "Leah made me watch that damn movie a dozen times."

"She really loves that one."

"That night could have gone two ways and lately I've been wondering what lay down the other path. The path with you."

Her heart hammered and her hands grew clammy. "What do you mean?"

"If we'd kissed that night and I'd stayed with you out in the snow, what might have happened? Where might we be now?" He shook his head. "I guess it's easy to romanticize it, but spending time with you in the cabin made me wonder if there *was* something down that path. Something special."

"I think there was." Tears pricked her eyes and she tried to blink them away, but they dampened her lashes. "I think there was something really special down that path."

"Was?" he said, taking another step forward. "Or is?"

"I don't know." It was the only honest answer she could give. "Because we can't unwind the past, Keaton. We can't go back to that night and change things."

"I don't want to change things. Regret is something I've lived with for a very long time and I've decided that it needs to go. I can't regret fucking up when I was an angry, disillusioned kid. I can't regret waiting to tell you how I felt. I can't regret working myself into the ground to bury my grief."

"You did what you needed to do to survive."

"Yeah, I did." He nodded. "But surviving isn't enough for me anymore. I want to *live*, August. I want to wake up in the morning and not be on autopilot. I want to feel the things I used to feel—satisfaction, anticipation, desire, excitement, playfulness. Things I've forgotten."

"You deserve those things," she said, meaning it with every cell in her body. "You deserve a full life that makes you happy."

"And I'm ready for it now." He sucked in a breath. "I just hope I'm not too late."

He'd wanted to show August how he really felt. But being so vulnerable was way more than laying himself on the line. It was throwing himself on the line, tearing his heart out and asking her to take a swing at it.

It was terrifying. Exhilarating. Real.

He couldn't remember the last time such emotions had coursed through him and it was like drinking coffee for the first time—he was energized in a way that was foreign and new. She might say no. She would *probably* say no after him taking so damn long to figure his shit out.

But he'd taken a step out of his comfort zone and that meant something. It meant he could take another step, and then another, and keep going until he'd left that dark, stagnant place behind him entirely.

"Too late for what?" she asked. Her hands were interlaced in front of her, red hair tumbling down around her shoulders. Hazel eyes stared at him, glimmering.

Could she forgive him for being so stubborn? So slow to adapt and change? So slow to heal?

"For you," he said simply. "I want to go back to that night and see what's down the other path. I want to act on this gripping, relentless chemistry we have and finally make it work for us, instead of against us. I want *you*, August. I always have."

She looked up at him, pale skin flushed pink against her plain T-shirt. Even dressed in the most basic of clothes, she glowed. She was vibrantly alive. Engaged. Emotional.

And he loved all those things about her because for so long she was his opposite. But he wanted to meet her in that place now—a place of hope and love and striving. A place where life was more than trying to make every day feel the same.

"Keaton, I..." She shook her head. "I don't know what to say."

He held his breath.

"I..." She let out a breath. "I canceled my account with the matchmaking company."

"You did?"

"Yeah." She nodded. "Because they sent me another match and he's everything I'd asked for."

His stomach sank like a stone. She'd found someone else.

The last day they were at the cabin together, she'd tried to reach him. Tried to connect with him.

And he'd pushed her away.

History was repeating itself, but this time in reverse. Maybe they were destined to never make the leap into being together. Their timing was all wrong. Always.

"I'm happy for you," he said, the words sour in his mouth. "That's great."

"No, it's not great. It's *terrible*!" She threw her hands in the air, tears shining anew. "Because I didn't even want to meet him. He has a great job, loves animals, has plans for a bright future. He was *so* good-looking. And what do you think happened, huh?"

"What happened?" he asked, the sinking feeling turning to churning waves in his gut.

"The whole time I was walking to the place where we were supposed to meet I was thinking *oh yeah, he seems great and all…but he's not Keaton*." She jabbed him in the chest, her voice rising. "Because no man, no matter how amazing, will ever compare to you in my head."

She sounded angry. At her wit's end.

"I'm sorry?"

"Is that a question or an actual apology?" She folded her arms across her chest. "You know what, it doesn't matter. It's not your fault I've been infatuated with you from the moment my hormones kicked in. That's *my* fault. Because I'm incapable of making good choices when it comes to men. I keep searching and trying to find someone that makes me feel the way you do but it's fucking pointless, Keaton. It's pointless."

He stood there, wide-eyed and unsure exactly how to take the outburst. On one hand, he was thrilled to hear she still had feelings for him. But on the other hand, she didn't seem happy about those feelings.

Don't screw this up now. You were making good progress. But this could all blow up in your face at any moment.

"Uhh..."

"And now you invite me here and you put up this beautiful tree and you say all these amazing things." She was sniffling now, the tears dropping down onto her face. "When I had just decided that I was going to be a spinster! I was going to make peace with being single forever and I was going to adopt some dogs and save for a nice house and make some other single lady friends and learn how to crochet and be happy. Alone."

"You can still learn how to crochet," he offered.

She laughed through her tears, the sound filled with humor and raw emotion.

"And we can get a dog," he added. "I like dogs now. But... and I understand that maybe this isn't the time to put in requests. Can we please not get a husky?"

She swiped at her tears with the back of her hand. "Stop it, Keaton."

This wasn't going very well. "Stop what?"

"Being so sweet and perfect and—"

"I am *not* perfect."

"Yeah, you are. Perfect for me." She pressed a hand to his chest. "Because it turns out that perfect for me isn't about ticking any boxes on a matchmaking list. It's not practical at all. In fact, it's decidedly emotional and illogical and I'm not sure I like it."

"Then what *is* perfect for you?" He closed his hand over hers.

"Someone who knows me, inside and out. Someone who has a strong sense of family and the resilience to keep turning things around. Someone who's willing to make a complete ass of themselves by trying to convince a dramatic husky to behave while you take a bunch of photos just to make your sister happy."

"The couple who makes an ass of themselves together, stays together?" he offered with a hopeful smile.

She smiled. "You're not too late, Keaton. Not at all. Because it wouldn't have mattered if I was eighty-five and sitting in a rocking chair. I would still want you."

"I'm glad I didn't wait that long," he whispered, lowering his forehead to hers. "I've already wasted too many years."

"It's not a waste." She cupped his face. "You needed that time to get to this place. To be ready."

"I *am* ready, August. Ready to be with you. Ready to give you everything I have to give." He swallowed. "Ready for forever."

At that moment, Molly walked into the room just like he and Leah had planned. Oh boy. This was going to be the make-or-break moment. Could he pull it off? Would Molly execute the things they'd practiced? Would August say yes?

Molly trotted happily over to Keaton, a red ribbon tied around her neck with a small velvet pouch dangling from it. Her tail swished back and forth, and her tongue lolled out of her mouth. In his head, he begged the dog to be on his side.

"Molly, sit," he said, and the dog plopped her butt on the ground. "Good girl."

"What…?" August shook her head. "What on earth?"

"Shake." Keaton held out his hand and Molly obediently placed her paw in his palm. "Now, drop."

When he pointed to the ground, she lowered to her belly, allowing the little velvet bag to rest on the floor. He reached down and ruffled the fur on her head, giving her a hearty scratch behind the ear.

"Great job," he whispered. "You are still the most excellent girl. Now, sit."

She got back to her feet and looked at August as if to say, *See! We're friends now.*

"I'm so proud of you both," she said, clapping her hands together. "What a good team."

Keaton reached forward to untie the velvet bag from around Molly's neck. This next bit wasn't something he'd rehearsed, however, since every time he even thought about it, he clammed up with nerves.

He opened the bag and produced a key.

August's eyes widened. "What is that?"

"It's for my apartment." He let out a breath. "I want to share my space with you, August. I want to wake up and see you in my bed or in the kitchen or the shower. I want to come home and know there's love waiting for me."

She pressed a hand over her mouth, her eyes welling up again. *This* was the most important shared goal of all—a house filled with love.

"I want those things, too."

"Although *I* might be the one waiting at home for *you*, at least for a while, since I don't have a job anymore." He shot her a crooked smile. "Maybe I could cook dinner?"

She wrinkled her nose. "Or perhaps we could order in?"

Nobody deserved Keaton's cooking.

He laughed, and the sound was rich and warm. "I love your blunt honesty."

"And I love how strong you are." Her eyes welled again. "Keaton, it's… I'm so touched."

"I love you, August. I *have* loved you since before I truly knew what the word meant."

"I have loved you for that long, too, Keaton." She rose onto her tiptoes and wrapped her arms around his neck, pressing her lips to his. "Knowing we want the same things…it means the world to me. I'm sorry I didn't kiss you that night."

"Well, if you stop being sorry for the past, then so will I."

"Deal." A smile blossomed on her face and her eyes fluttered shut as he lowered his head to hers, lips clashing in a searching kiss. He held her tight, because in that moment it felt like he was a balloon about to float away and she was the thing tethering him to earth.

"Arwoooooooooo!" Molly tossed her head back and howled, as if serenading the couple.

That's when Leah poked her head around the corner of the living room door, a huge grin on her face. "Can I come in now?"

"You've been listening this whole time?" Keaton groaned. "I told you to go upstairs."

"I was never going to do that."

She came over and wrapped her big brother and best friend in a tight group hug. Then Molly nudged her way in, not wanting to be left out of the action. Beside the four of them, Christmas lights twinkled.

"We're going to make Christmas in June a thing," Keaton joked.

"I'm so happy!" Leah declared. "I have been trying to get you two together for *ages* and you've both been so stubborn. This is wonderful."

"Not anymore." August laughed. "The only stubborn one left is Molly."

"Woof!"

They all laughed as the dog chimed in, happy to have the crown for "most stubborn" firmly atop her furry head. Keaton looked down dotingly at his little sister, the woman he loved, and the dog who'd stolen his heart. *This* was what life was all about—love, family, connection.

And he'd never shy away from those things ever again.

EPILOGUE

Christmas that year...the real Christmas

The best thing about August's day was coming home. Because no longer was she greeted by an empty couch and an empty bed and creaking, quiet rooms. Now, when she came home, it was like stepping into a pair of open arms.

Sometimes literally.

Sometimes, when she returned home, she was attacked by a four-pound puppy with gold fur and a tongue that seemed to be everywhere all at once.

"Oh my goodness, you're a little floofy tornado!" August dropped her bags and bent down to scoop up the puppy, whom they'd had for three weeks and had *finally* settled on a name for.

Noelle.

Christmas-themed, of course, because it felt like an important moment in their relationship. And now it was their first *actual* Christmas together, it felt like August's life had finally come together the way she wanted it to. Nothing was missing.

Her business was booming.

Her friendships were strong.

Her love for Keaton had blossomed.

Of course, her parents were still annoying whenever they took swipes at her career or did their "keeping up with the Joneses" bullshit that they liked to do. But she'd made peace with the fact that it wasn't her job to change them. She and Keaton visited them every so often, and he really tried to be friendly and connect with them, which she appreciated.

Would she ever be super close with her parents? Probably not. In their eyes, she would never quite be what they'd wanted her to be. But she was perfectly okay with that, because in *her* eyes, she was everything she should be.

Besides, family was the people you chose to surround yourself with…like all of those who were due to arrive in the next two hours for a festive Christmas Eve *eve* dinner. Isla and Theo, Scout and Lane and their adorable baby girl, Leah and Will—her people.

"I'm home!" she sang out, and she snuggled Noelle. "You're going to be well-behaved tonight, aren't you? Molly is coming over."

To say that Molly wasn't exactly a fan of Noelle was slightly understating things, but the husky did her best to be tolerant and made it clear when she'd had enough. Noelle, of course, *adored* Molly and wanted to play with her every second they were together. August had hopes they'd become good friends in the future, once Noelle's puppy ways calmed down a bit.

"Kea?" she called out again as she put the puppy down.

Since the day Keaton had declared his love at Leah's house,

it felt like everything had changed. August had moved into his apartment and sold her place, and they were on the hunt for a house in Brooklyn, which would be closer to his family. Now that he didn't need to commute into Manhattan every day—and August's clients were all over the place, anyway—the thought of having a house with a backyard filled August's heart with possibilities.

They could have a grooming station in the house for some clients to come to her, plus a spare bedroom for any friends who wanted to stay and *plenty* of space for Noelle to run around. They'd already planned to get another dog, since Keaton had now decided that he was, indeed, a dog person.

In fact, since he'd been gloriously unemployed, it was his job to take Noelle out for walks each day, and he'd taught her all kinds of tricks, like jumping through a hoop and playing dead and balancing a dog treat on her nose. Watching him find joy in things outside work was like watching a flower bloom, and he was, for the first time, trying to figure out what he wanted to do with his life…for the sake of enjoyment, rather than money.

The fact was, he'd made more than they could possibly need in a lifetime, and August's business easily covered the basics. He'd dabbled with the idea of consulting to small businesses who were facing hostile takeover attempts, to help educate them on how to defend themselves and make sure their businesses weren't vulnerable. But for now, he was simply living and enjoying all the things he'd forgone the past decade.

And mercifully, Fairchild & Hill had decided not to sue. Keaton had been very quiet on the whole thing, but she suspected that he had enough dirt on his old boss to keep them from lashing out at him. One lost deal was nothing compared to all the things they'd done in the past—things Keaton knew all the dirty, intricate details of.

Life was grand.

"I'm in the bathroom," Keaton called out.

Frowning, August shook her head. She couldn't hear the fan going, which seemed to be the only thing they ever argued about—a silly, real-relationship thing like leaving empty toilet rolls on the holder or not filling up ice cube trays after they were emptied.

"Kea," she whined. "We've got guests here in an hour. Don't tell me you're fogging up the bathroom again!"

Sure enough, the bathroom looked like a sauna. The mirror was totally fogged and she would have to wipe it down before their guests arrived. But it was hard to be mad at the man when he'd just stepped out of the shower. A white towel was slung low on his waist, showing off his fit body to perfection. His dark hair was glossy and damp, his skin dotted with beads of moisture.

Her eyes traveled down to where the towel was knotted at a very enticing spot. "Is that just excess towel fabric, or are you happy to see me?"

He snorted. "You're so cheesy."

He pulled her in for a hug and she squealed, because he was getting her all wet. But as he wedged her between his hard body and the bathroom vanity, steam swirling around them and encasing them in their own private, sexy bubble… all was forgiven.

"I love you," she said, tipping her face up to his.

"And *I* love *you*," he said, lowering his lips to hers.

The kiss was searing and exploratory, and even though it felt like they knew one another inside and out, there was always something new to discover. Learning Keaton had become one of the great joys in her life, because now he was open to letting her know all parts of him.

"Are you going to be ready by the time everyone arrives?" she asked, pulling back. "I need to shower and get ready, but we have to set the table and give the wine time to air and—"

"Shh." He silenced her with another kiss. "Everything will be fine."

"But the charcuterie board—"

"Augie, I promise that if we're still setting up the charcuterie board when our friends arrive, they won't be mad." There was a mischievous twinkle in his eye. "Besides, I need to borrow you for a bit."

"No, you don't! I have to get ready." Keaton *loved* to try and tempt her back to bed when she needed to get things done, and he always managed to succeed. She never could find the willpower to resist him.

"Don't worry, I'll save that for after everyone's gone." He kissed down her neck, making her melt against him. "But I have something for you."

Okay, now her curiosity was well and truly piqued.

Keaton pulled on his underwear, a pair of jeans and a T-shirt, and August let herself ogle him the whole time. The man was *fine*, in every sense of the word.

"Follow me." He took her hand and led her back out to the main room, right over to the Christmas tree.

"We're not supposed to open gifts yet," she said, her eyes scanning the pretty foil-wrapped boxes decorated with ribbon sitting under the tree. They were all labeled and ready to be transported to Keaton's mom's place on Christmas Day.

"This is a special one, just for you and me." He reached for a small velvet box. It wasn't wrapped like all the others. When had he put it there? Surely, she would have noticed.

Her breath stilled. "What is going on right now?"

"Just open it."

When she opened the box, a gasp caught in the back of her throat. Nestled on a plump navy velvet cushion was a simple silver band with a heart in the middle.

"Okay, I'll admit that the design is a little cheesy," he said. "But my taste hadn't quite matured in my early twenties. All I knew was that girls were supposed to like hearts."

August's breath hitched. "It's beautiful."

"I was planning to give it to you that Christmas Eve, but I got ahead of myself and tried to kiss you first. It was in my coat pocket the whole time." He rocked on his heels. "Obviously I was a bit too embarrassed to give it to you after you… ah, well you know. And then when I met Ellery, I wasn't sure what to do with it. There was no way I could give it to someone else, because that felt wrong. But taking it back to the store didn't feel right, either."

"So you kept it?"

"I put it in the back of my sock drawer and forgot about it. I could never force myself to get rid of it."

"It's so pretty," she said.

"I know hearts are a little tacky and maybe it looks juvenile—"

"No, it's sweet."

"I held on to this for over ten years because there was part of me that couldn't give up on the idea that one day you might wear it." He took the box from her hand and pulled the ring out. "I'll be honest, part of me wondered if I should go out and get something fancier, like with gold instead of silver, or something. But I saved up for this when I was a broke college student and…it feels honest."

Before she could say anything else, he lowered down onto one knee.

"August, I know we took the long way to get here. But you've been in my heart as long as I can remember," he said. "I want to make it official. I'll take you out to pick a proper ring that's exactly your style, but I couldn't wait a moment longer to ask you if you'd be my wife."

The tears she'd been holding back spilled over, splashing onto her cheeks as she nodded. "Yes, Keaton. A thousand times yes."

"This is a placeholder, okay?" He slipped the ring onto her finger and a wave of relief washed through him that it fit, since he'd bought it so many years ago. "But it felt right to finally bring it out of hiding."

"It feels more than right. It's perfect." She tugged him to his feet and threw her arms around his neck. "Deep down, I knew we'd get to this place. We were meant to be, even if our brains took a while to catch up to our hearts."

"I love you, Augie," he murmured against her lips.

"I love you, too, Kea."

His hands traveled across her hips and around, seeking out all the places where she loved to be touched. This time she didn't even bother trying to resist. With Keaton's lips on her skin and his arms wrapped around her, and the future laid out like a canvas in front of them, the life they could create together seemed brighter than ever.

★★★★★

ACKNOWLEDGMENTS

Writing the Paws in the City series has been a wonderful experience during a difficult few years. It has been a blessing to be able to pour my hope for better days into a project that whisked me away from my troubles. I sincerely hope it does the same for every reader who picks it up.

As always, my first and most heartfelt thanks to my incredible husband, Justin. I could not be more grateful to have someone as supportive and invested as you in my life. Thank you for all the brainstorming sessions, for wiping away the tears and holding my hand as I tried to figure it all out. I love you.

Thank you to my dear friend Becca Syme. I love knowing we can jump on Zoom and talk for hours about the weirdest things. Input and Learner friends are the best. Thank you to the Supper Club ladies—Shiloh, Myrna, Madura, Jannette and Tammy. Our dinners out and trips away are a highlight in my life. Never forget "stone the flaming crows."

Huge thank you to my incredible editor, Dana Grimaldi, and the entire team at Harlequin for helping me bring this idea to life. It's been a dream working with everyone here, especially in the Toronto office. Thank you for your guidance, support, and for all the fun we had brainstorming the titles for this series.

And thank you to my family for always having a recommendation for a new book or an interesting podcast or a documentary that had you gripped. This collective curiosity is the reason I've always wanted to write. Love you all so much.